Richard A. Andrews

THE NEW ORDER

iUniverse, Inc.
Bloomington

The New Order

iUniverse books may be ordered through booksellers or by contacting:

iUniverse
1663 Liberty Drive
Bloomington, IN 47403
www.iuniverse.com
1-800-Authors (1-800-288-4677)

Because of the dynamic nature of the Internet, any web addresses or links contained in this book may have changed since publication and may no longer be valid. The views expressed in this work are solely those of the author and do not necessarily reflect the views of the publisher, and the publisher hereby disclaims any responsibility for them.

Any people depicted in stock imagery provided by Thinkstock are models, and such images are being used for illustrative purposes only.

Certain stock imagery © Thinkstock.

ISBN: 978-1-4620-2490-2 (sc)
ISBN: 978-1-4620-2488-9 (e)
ISBN: 978-1-4620-2489-6 (dj)

Library of Congress Control Number: 2011908503

Printed in the United States of America

iUniverse rev. date: 9/12/2011

PROLOGUE

Have you ever felt that you were powerless to change your fate, or anyone else's? If so, you are pretty much an average human being. Most people feel powerless to change their lives, let alone have some real power like the power to change the fate of the world in general.

But what if you were offered the chance to have some real world-changing power? I don't mean a little power, such as the ability to be a big frog in your present little frog pond, but the ultimate power, the power to control the world. Would the chance to have that type of power interest you?

Most people would think about an offer of such power for a while, and then they would turn it down. Why? Because they could not handle the heavy authority over their fellow human beings. The vast majority of people would be right in turning down this power. The average person would simply not measure up to the task. Most people would not know what they were doing in such a position. Others would look forward to exercising said power. Such people are very goal oriented. They are people of vision. These people are not afraid of making mistakes and, as the saying goes, crashing and burning. Would you be one of the few who would say yes to such an offer?

The second question is this: would you be willing to pay the price for such power? History is littered with men and women who acquired great power, and they all paid a heavy price either in getting it or just keeping it. Some historical figures, such as Cyrus the Great of the Persian Empire and Jesus Christ, acquired great power and influence without much effort, but they both had trouble keeping it. Other rulers, such as Stalin, Hitler, and the great khans of the Mongol Empire, butchered millions of innocent people to get and keep such great power. History books have even given some of these butchers the title of *great*, such as Alexander the Great.

When the idea of having such great power pops into the head of the average person, he or she at first only thinks about what he or she can do with it. The person will not think about the cost of acquiring the power. Climbing the ladder of success, which is sometimes called *paying your dues,* is the part of the dream that is to be avoided by the average daydreamer.

If these daydreamers considered the cost of gaining great power, almost all of them would drop the subject. The subject of payment would certainly put a damper on any good daydream.

If you were one of the few who would pay a heavy price, how much would you be willing to pay? Would you be willing to disown all your friends and your family? Would you be willing to kill millions, or even billions, of people in order to get and keep such authority? Could you be a heartless bastard to get what you want?

The people who would still say yes to such an offer are usually very self-centered. They believe in themselves, and they usually have some sort of vision of what they want to achieve. Are such people blinded by their vision? It would not matter to the writers of history books. In the end, the only thing that would matter is if they succeeded. History books are written by the dominant culture or the victor in battle.

Let me introduce myself. I am Major General William Andrews

of the Federal Security Agency. About eight years ago, I was offered the chance to join a select group of people who were on the verge of controlling the whole world. We insiders call our organization "The Order." The general public refers to us as "The New World Order." We are a shadow governmental organization that is controlled by the big banking corporations of the world. These powerful banking houses control the new currency of the world, the world dollar. As the old saying goes, *He who owns the gold rules.* The gold is now the world dollar, and my organization controls it.

The Order rules from the shadows. It controls events and decisions. We say what is going to be a government's policy and what will happen in the world or in a nation's economy. National leaders are just servants to the Order. We, the Order, are the real rulers of the world. But officially, we do not exist. If something goes wrong, the Order does not take the blame. It is a perfect situation for us. We get the benefits, and any problems that may arise will be blamed on others.

If the people of the world actually knew the truth, that we rather than their leaders really run the world, they would be furious. The Order would probably not survive such a change in public reality.

But things in the Order are not all benefits and no problems. The Order has had its problems, as some successful organizations do. On the eve of our success in gaining financial control of the world's monetary system, the Order split into two opposing sides. One side I call the Moderates, which is the side I support. Our opponents I call the Fascist Element.

Both sides agree on the overall goals of the Order, such as the end to the threat of nuclear war and wars in general and economic stability for world markets. But the two sides have different methods of achieving said goals.

The Moderates want to rule from the shadows and give the people of our world the image that they and their leaders actually run their countries and lives. We believe that the stopping of wars can be accomplished without a harsh fascist-style rule and the people of our world will be able to overcome problems, such as feeding, housing, and educating the world's population with the use of future development in science and basic teamwork among nations. The Moderates in general just want to leave people and their lives alone as much as possible.

The Fascist Element wants a more open and harsh rule over the people of the world. They also want to greatly cut down the population of our planet. In short, they are in favor of mass murder as the solution to our world's population problems. That last point is the reason that I joined the Order. My life is now devoted to stopping the Fascists from achieving the power they need to set their depopulation program into action.

In my efforts to fight the Fascist Element and their allies, I have committed what average people would consider horrible crimes. I had to pay my dues to get into the position of power that I now have—heavy dues, the type of dues that could rip a man's soul apart.

Was it worth it? I will let you be the judge of that.

Contents

Contents

CHAPTER 1: BIRTH OF THE ORDER

How did this situation develop? How did a few thousand very wealthy and powerful people gain basic control over the whole world? It all has to do with one of the seven deadly sins that are mentioned in the Christian Bible. The sin I am talking about is *greed.*

Greed is the cause of the present situation that the world is in—the greed for money. Money is not just something nice to have, something to buy things with. Money is power. The people who run the Order know this, and, to gain basic control of our world, they first gained control of its money supply.

Remember the old historical sayings *He who holds the purse strings rules* and *He who holds the gold rules.*

Both sayings mean the same thing. Whoever controls the money supply is in control of the economy, the political system, and the culture of any nation that allows private interests to control its money supply.

Baron Rothschild of England said it best: "Give me control of a nation's money supply and I care not who makes the laws."

As an example of what the baron was talking about, the following quote by him should explain his line of reasoning: "I care not what puppet is placed on the throne of England to rule the

Empire. The man that controls Britain's money supply controls the British Empire. And I control the money supply."

Who are the people who run The New World Order? They are the big banking corporations of the world. They are the people who control the economies of whole nations, cause a nation to go to war, topple governments, cause revolutions, and, yes, even decide if millions of people live or die. The bankers are the legendary power behind the throne, and now they have achieved their age-old dream to control the whole world.

How did this happen? Why did the people of the world allow such a situation to develop? Well, let's just say, to be kind, that the people were too busy running their own lives to really pay attention. Too busy watching football games and specials on their big-screen TVs, or just trying to feed their families, to notice that their freedom was slipping away. Economics is a subject that few well-educated people really understand; common people do not even try.

So, when the people who are the current powers behind the throne decided to use their influences to create massive new trading blocs with trade agreements like NAFTA and GATT and multinational currencies like the euro, the average person paid very little attention. It looked like a good idea: we could sell more stuff and get richer.

When the powers of the future order caused the economic depression of 2008 to 2015, the common people started to pay attention. The people wanted their governments to do something, and they did. The result was even more control in the hands of The New World Order. The deep depression of 2030 to 2036 caused a worldwide panic. The result was a new world economy and a call for a world currency, promoted by the elite of The New World Order. The currency change gave the big banking interests more controls on society and the common people. How could the people have known? Average people don't understand economics and how the money system works.

The end result of the whole process was the establishment of a world currency in 2040: the world dollar. This major accomplishment put the big financial interests of the world in firm control of almost all governments.

Baron Rothschild knew in the nineteenth century how all of this would come about when he said the following:

> The powers of financial capitalism had another far-reaching aim, nothing less than to create a world system of financial control in private hands able to dominate the political system of each country and economy of the world as a whole. This system was to be controlled in a feudalism fashion by the central banks of the world acting in concert, by secret agreements arrived at in frequent meetings and conferences. The apex of the systems was to be the Bank of International Settlements in Basel, Switzerland, a private bank owned and controlled by the world's central banks, which were themselves private corporations. Each central bank ... sought to dominate its government by its ability to control Treasury loans, to manipulate foreign exchanges, to influence the level of economic activity in the country, and to influence cooperative politicians by subsequent economic rewards in the business world.

First, the bankers got control of the currencies of major countries, like the establishment of the US Federal Reserve in 1913, a privately owned banking system. Then the profits from such control were used to buy up control of a nation's businesses, giving the bankers control of that nation's economy, its political system, and its media.

Second, the world regional trade agreements became world trade agreements. These trading blocs established their own currencies. Europe created the euro; North America created the amero.

Third, in 2040, the currencies of the world became the world dollar, which was controlled by the bankers. The bankers did what no figure in history had ever come close to doing: they had the power to rule the world. Corporate fascism had conquered the world.

Chapter 2:   My Life

After graduating with honors from Harvard University, I returned home to my aunt and uncle's house near Boston. I have lived with my aunt and uncle since my parents were killed in a plane crash when I was twelve years old. My father was from a wealthy Irish American family, and my mother was of French and Saudi Arabian decent. My mother was a princess of the House of Saud, the ruling family of Saudi Arabia. My mother was a Muslim, and my father was a Christian. I was exposed to both religions, but I was raised a Catholic, my father's religion. Yes, it is a very odd pedigree, but it comes with a very big trust fund and great family connections.

How did I, a son of a wealthy East Coast, blue-blood family, a person who is related to the king of Saudi Arabia, who was educated in the best schools, end up as an officer in the Order? I would like to believe that I am in control of my own life, but that assumption would be grossly wrong. To face the reality of my life up to the present, I would have to admit that I lost any control that I had when I was just a teenager. Every step of my education and career up to the present has been decided by other people. The doors that have opened for me were not always of my choice. Most of my life decisions seemed to have been made by people who were just shadow figures that I never met, but I feel that these figures are controlling my fate. My education, summer jobs, and even my roommates at school were the decisions of other people. No, this wasn't just *being a boy and a teenager* stuff. With my special psychic talents, I could sense the hands of powerful people guiding my life course. After I progressed through different college prep schools and then Harvard, the feeling of being controlled in some way only got worse. No, I'm not a little nuts. This is the reality that I live with on a day-to-day basis.

I made my last really independent decision when I had just turned twenty-two, just after I had graduated from Harvard University. I decided to visit my grandfather in Saudi Arabia. My grandfather is my mother's father, and he is a prince. He is a member of the House of Saud, the royal family of Saudi Arabia. I am one-fourth Saudi Arabian, but I am not a Muslim, a fact that somewhat bothers my grandfather.

My grandfather is a senior prince of the House of Saud. He is a governor of a piece of territory called a governorate, which is located in western Saudi Arabia on the Red Sea. This area does not look like the desert image people have of Saudi Arabia. It is mostly a fertile, green area that even has marshland. From the time I was a little boy, I have always looked forward to visiting my grandfather and going fishing with him.

After graduating from Harvard and being accepted to graduate school at Stanford, with help from my shadow protectors, I'm sure, I decided to visit my grandfather. I flew from New York City to Cairo, Egypt. The long flight gave some welcome time to review my life up to present. I was a young man who had just graduated from Harvard University. I had a great mind, a straight-A average in school, and a healthy body. I was also, very good looking. I had a multimillion-dollar trust fund, and I was psychic. Oh, that last part? Only my grandfather and a few close friends knew about it. I found out early in life that I could predict the course of events months in advance, such as elections, horse races, stock and commodity movements, and even what people will do.

The one talent I have always kept to myself is my ability to read a person. I know if a person is lying or not. I can tell what he or she is really thinking. This part of my talents that I learned at a very young age—ten years old—really freaks people out. It is hard to keep friends when they know they cannot keep any secrets around me. Knowledge of my talents began to open doors for me in life. The doors were controlled by very powerful people who began to guide my life from behind the scenes. I know that they were there, but the *who* and *why* part of it was always hard for me determine. I couldn't really read them. They were always too far away for me to read. They were like shadows in the distance.

My grandfather had sent his private jet to pick me up in Cairo. It was only a short flight to western Saudi Arabia. As I departed the plane, I saw my grandfather waiting for me on the tarmac. As I approached him, he lifted his arms to embrace me.

"Welcome, my little desert warrior," he said.

I looked at my grandfather and smiled. "It is good to see you again, Grandfather."

With our greetings over, my grandfather led me to his waiting limousine, and we departed for his seaside villa.

As befitting a prince of the royal House of Saud, my grandfather's villa is more like a small palace. It has over two hundred rooms, fifteen bedrooms, fifteen bathrooms, a movie theater, a gym, a bowling alley, a billiards room, and two swimming pools. My grandfather jokingly calls it his *country shack*. His main home is a palace in the Saudi capital of Riyadh.

The sight of the marble hallways of my grandfather's villa bought back old memories of my childhood, like the time I was ten years and I ran naked through it. The servants and guards did not know what to do; my grandfather was not at home at the time, so I stayed naked for the whole day. My grandfather just laughed when he was told of my little prank.

He told me, "William, if you want to be nude in my house, it is all right."

This reply startled me. Saudis are usually very uptight about nudity. This took the fun out of something against the rules, so I got dressed and acted like a good little boy.

But I was twenty-two years old, and I didn't think like a ten-year-old boy anymore. So I just settled into my suite, and I took a nap in the nude for two hours to shake off the jet lag I had developed from my flight. When I awoke, I got out of bed and walked over to the chair where I had left my clothes. In front of me stood several large dressing mirrors. I just had to take a look at myself, naked in the mirrors, and make an evaluation of myself. This inspection was very physical in nature.

I was definitely not a ten-year-old boy anymore. I had developed a man's body. I started to make mental notes. I was good looking, and not just in my opinion. I had dark red hair, stood six feet two, and weighed 195 pounds. I had a very muscular, gym-toned body, a nine-inch cock, and very little body hair. I turned around to view my nice rounded ass and strong muscular back. I smiled. I had turned into a young man—most would say *a hot number.* The ten-year-old boy was gone. But I must confess that I did get a small urge to run around the villa once again naked. If I had, I am sure this time the servants would have paid a lot more attention to me than when I was just ten years old.

After I got dressed in my Western-style clothes—jeans, a short-sleeved knit shirt, and running shoes—I headed downstairs to talk to my grandfather. On the way, two very good-looking teenage boys, who were some of the villa servants, looked at me and smiled. I smiled back. Well, at least some of the staff didn't think I was one of those American devils.

My grandfather was in his office, in what Westerners would call a *guesthouse*, behind the villa. As I walked in, I could see that my grandfather was not alone. Several of his sons—my uncles—were with him, and a few cousins were present.

"Sit down, William, and join us."

"Yes, Grandfather." I knew this was not going to be all that pleasant a visit, because some of my uncles were not really fond of me. I was that infidel American boy.

"William, we are discussing the administration of justice in my state."

I nodded.

"The subject of this meeting is the execution of a murderer," he said. "It is traditional for each male member of my family to do his duty and administer justice."

At this moment, I got a tight feeling in my waist. Uncle Omar, who frankly did not like me, said, "William, I have recommended you for this family duty." He smiled.

He was, I believe, very surprised when I said, "For our family honor, I accept this duty."

My grandfather looked a little startled at my reply. "Then the matter is settled. William will execute the criminal."

After everybody except me and my grandfather had left the room, my grandfather turned to me and looked straight into my eyes. "William, are you sure you can carry out such a duty?"

"Yes, Grandfather, you have taught me to handle a sword, and you know how strong I am. You don't have to worry. The criminal is as good as dead."

Did I realize what I had agreed to? No. I had really stepped in it this time. But the deal was made, and now I had to muster up the courage to carry it out.

My grandfather looked a little relieved, but it seemed he still had some concerns.

"William, the execution is in three days. I will send my chief executioner to you tomorrow to give instruction on how to use a sword to cut off a man's head."

"Yes, Grandfather, that would be helpful."

His name was Abdul Jamil. He was a big man, several inches taller than me. He had a weather-beaten, pockmarked, leathery face and a short black beard. When he walked into my bedroom, a sense of tension filled the air. I knew right away that no one in his right mind would mess with his guy.

"Your grandfather, my master, Prince Abdula has instructed me to teach you how to execute a man with the sword."

I just nodded in agreement. I couldn't think of what to say to such a brutal-looking man.

"Come with me, young man. I will teach you to be a man."

This tall desert warrior led me out the front door of the villa to a spot about a quarter of a mile into an area that was very wooded. Several swords were leaning against a tree. The warrior told me to pick one of the swords, which I quickly did. A ten-foot log, about the thickness of a man's neck, had been placed on several—what Westerners call–sawhorses.

"Boy, cutting off a man's head is about the same feeling as cutting through this log. You will master this. Then you will be ready. You will only have to summon the courage to do your duty."

The warrior then told me to put my foot on one end of the log to hold it in place as he demonstrated his method. The warrior's sword cut through the log without any real trouble.

When it was my turn, the warrior took my place holding down the end of the log with his foot. I followed the example of my teacher. I focused on the log, raised the sword over my head, and with one hard thrust downward I cut six inches of the end of the log straight off.

The warrior looked impressed. I smiled. But he did not let me pass the test until I had cut ten sections of log off. The first five times I had to hit a red line that the warrior had drawn. I hit the mark each time. The last four attempts were more difficult. The warrior drew his line and then proceeded to move the log around, as if the man to be executed could not sit still. I was told this is a common problem for men about to be beheaded. I passed this last test. Now all I had to do was summon up the courage.

The execution was to be held in a public square of a small local village. My grandfather gave me his best sword for my first public duty. He also assigned to me two experienced aides. The first thing I asked the aides to do was set up a meeting with the condemned man.

The man was being held in a house just outside the village. I walked in with my aides wearing Arab robes. My aides mentioned that I wished to talk to and inspect their prisoner. Both guards stepped aside.

I asked the man his name. My grandfather insisted that I learn Arabic at an early age. The man's name was Abdul Karim. He said he was twenty years of age. He acted very nervous. His body mildly shook at times.

I told him to remain calm for my inspection. I examined his neck. It was not muscular. I was relieved. This man's neck should be easy to cut through.

The rest of my duty went off without a problem. I wore traditional Arab robes, a headdress, and sunglasses. This was so that I would not advertise the fact that I was not a native of Saudi Arabia. My grandfather thought It best that I not attract too much attention to the fact that I was an American.

The prisoner was brought to the execution site. He knelt down in front of me, bowed his head, and with one fast, strong thrust downward with my sword, the job was done.

The man's headless body remained in a kneeling position in front of me. The assembled crowd of local people seemed pleased. My big test was over. My grandfather seemed very pleased with me. My Uncle Omar looked uncommitted. I got the feeling that he was not through testing me quite yet.

I learned something important that day about myself. When I needed to be, I could be a heartless SOB. Such a talent, I was to find out, would come in handy in my future career with the Order.

When my grandfather, relatives, and I got back to the villa, the two cute servant boys who had smiled at me earlier were at the front door and smiling as we entered. There was just something about those to teenage boys that seemed to be connected to my stay at the villa.

Before I went up to my room, I stopped by the house manager's office and talked to an old friend, Farras. He is my grandfather's house manager and chief butler. I asked him about the two servant boys, who seemed so fascinated by me.

"Oh, you mean Sabar and Muhammad. They are both nineteen years old, and they are not servants. They are your grandfather's house and pleasure slaves. Their job is to do housework, serve meals, clean up after meals, and basically please anyone your grandfather assigns them to."

This was the first time that I even suspected that my grandfather owned slaves. I know that slavery was not forbidden in the Muslim holy book, the Koran. Some Muslim scholars say that the Koran encourages slavery, and other scholars say this is forbidden. In 1962, Saudi Arabia outlawed slavery. But this law was not followed by many Saudis, which I now knew included my grandfather.

Farras looked at me and smiled. "Should I prepare the boys and send them up to your room, William? They are very well-trained and talented in pleasing a man."

I knew that my friend Karras knew one of my little secrets: I was bisexual. Having been dumped by my college-bound girlfriend only two months ago and being so horned up, it was starting to hurt.

I said, "Yes, send them up in about half an hour."

Farras smiled. "I will prepare the boys. You will be very pleased. I assure you."

"Oh, Farras."

"Yes, sir, what is it?"

"I am going to take a quick shower. Have the boys stripped naked and on their knees in my room in thirty minutes."

"Yes, William, it will be done."

It seemed my real reward for performing my family duty was going to be fucking two sex slaves. I just hoped that they performed as well as advertised. I was really horny.

When I finished my shower, the slaves were, as promised, kneeling naked on my bedroom carpet. I walked over to stand naked in front of them, and I gave them their first order.

"Boys, stand up."

"Yes, sir!" they both shouted.

They stood up, and, as they caught sight of my naked body, their eyes got really big. They smiled. They both stood several inches shorter than myself. They had what would be called swimmer's build. From the neck down, their bodies looked permanently shaved. They were completely smooth. They had beautiful, lightly tanned skin, and they both had about eight inches of cock hanging between their legs. Just looking over my naked body caused their cocks to get throbbing hard in less than a minute. It seemed that they thought I was really hot.

Both boys were smiling and looked eager to get started. As

they stood in front of me, I sat down in high-backed chair and ordered them to get to work. "Boys, get on your knees in front of me and lick my feet and suck my toes."

They looked at each other and then broadly smiled before they dropped to their knees. Each one grabbed one of my feet and went to work.

God, it felt soooo ... gooooood. These two had a good trainer.

After ten minutes of having these slaves massage my feet with their wet, warm tongues, I stood up and gave them an order. "Now, boys, lick my balls."

"Yes, sir!" each shouted.

I started to lightly stroke my big cock as the boys' moist tongues massaged my nuts.

I grabbed one of the boys by the hair on the back of his head and shoved my big cock down his throat. He gagged a little before he started to deep throat my cock. I ordered the other boy to rim my ass.

Both performed extremely well. In only a few minutes, I blew my load down the throat of the first boy. When I was finished shooting a two-month backload of cum down his eager throat, I turned around to give the other boy his reward. I picked him up, grabbed the hair on the back of his head, and led him over to lie face down on my bed. It was time to fuck one of these slaves, and, in just one minute, I was greased up and sliding deep into the boy's ass as his upper body bucked up about a foot and he let out a loud moan. It took me about thirty minutes of good, hard fucking before I shot my second load. This boy was good. His ass felt just like a tight, warm, moist pussy, and he really liked being royally fucked, long and hard.

After taking a shower with the boys and having them soap

down and wash my whole body, we dried off and slept for two hours, naked, on my bed.

When we awoke, I slapped the second boy hard on his cute bare ass, greased my cock again, and rode his ass for almost an hour before I was finally spent. Both slaves were really great sex. The boys then gave me a very professional, full-body massage before we showered again. I had never had two people massage my body at the same time. Man, it was a great experience!

After we showered again and got dressed, I told both the boys I was very pleased with their performance. They smiled, and they both kissed me on my cheeks. As Farras had said, both slaves were very good at what they were trained to do.

Just before dinner, I was able to talk to Farras about his two pleasure slaves. I told him that they performed well and that he should reward them. I also asked him how it was that both slaves were such great sex.

"William, it is all about their selection and training. The slave dealer in Riyadh selects only the best boys. He trains them intensely in mind and body to be total slaves. They are taught to be eager to please and serve their masters. During their training, they are required to sit on a cock stool for several hours a day. This is a wooden stool with an upright, rubber dildo in the center. The dildo is greased with a special solution. The end result is that the slave's ass will become more like a woman's pussy."

This was more than I wanted to know. But it did explain why both boys were such great fucks.

After having dinner with my grandfather, I was told that Uncle Omar was not done fucking with me. Since I was now an experienced executioner, he had arranged a bigger challenge for me: the execution, by sword, of nine hardened criminals. He, of course, believed that I could not handle such men.

My grandfather thought that I should just turn down the duty since I had performed my required civil duty. But my withdrawal from this event would just enable my uncle to keep messing with me again and again in the future. This was a chance to end my small war with my Uncle Omar. As with the first duty, Uncle Omar expected me to wimp out. He was in for another surprise.

I asked my grandfather for the help of the same two aides that I had at the first execution. He agreed.

The execution was to be held in another small village, this one thirty miles from my grandfather's villa. My aides and I arrived the night before. I wanted to talk to the men who I was assigned to execute.

After entering the dirt-floor building where they were being held, I found out my Uncle Omar had really set me up. After I walked in with my two aides, I attempted to speak to them. They would have none of it. The prisoners were sitting on the ground with their legs and hands in iron shackles, but this fact did not stop them from causing me trouble. They made loud noises, insulted me, and in general did not cooperate. My aides wanted to kick their asses, but I stopped them. I doubted that such an approach would make these hardened criminals listen to me and follow my orders the day of their executions. I needed a new angle to work.

I ordered my aides to turn around, and we walked out of the building as a landslide of insults *("Boos teezi, ila jaheem ma'ik, kol kharrak.")* from the prisoners followed us. Translated into English, they said, "Kiss my ass, go to hell, and eat shit."

I took my aides down the road. I needed some time to think. How in the hell would I get these men to follow my orders and not make a circus out of the next day's scheduled executions? Suddenly, I got an idea. I would use an angle that in the criminal world usually works quite well. I would use fear.

I conferred with my aides. Then I sent them to get the supplies that I needed to make the plan work: six three-inch, six-foot-long fence posts, a can of grease, and a sledgehammer. It took my aides about an hour to locate what I needed. We walked back to the building where the prisoners were being held.

The prisoners laughed at and insulted us as we entered the building. As they continued their defiance of my authority, I ordered my aides to sharpen one of the fence posts at one end and to use the sledgehammer to pound the fence post into the ground about two and one half feet. As my aides performed their duty, the room started to get quiet. What we were up to was the question on their minds.

When the fence post was ready, I took my sword and quickly sharpened the top end of the post. One of my aides greased the top of the sharpened fence post. The room was very quiet.

We were ready for the main event of the evening. I ordered my aides to grab the most vocal of the prisoners. My two aides grabbed a prisoner, tied his hands and feet together, and stripped him of his clothes. The prisoner kicked and cursed the whole time.

When the man was ready, I ordered my aides to gag him and mount him on the fence post. In just a few minutes, the greased fence post was sliding up his ass and his body was violently shaking in total agony.

In Arabic I said, "Now listen up. Each of you will follow my orders tomorrow and cause no problems. You will go to your deaths like men. If you don't, you will not die quickly by the sword. You will die like this man."

I did not wait for a reply. I didn't need one. The agony of watching their friend die in agony all night long would say all that needed to be said.

Early the next day the villagers and people from miles around came to see the executions of these hated men. The time of execution arrived without incident. The eight remaining criminals all died like men.

As the last man's name was read, I walked back into the prisoner building. The prisoner that I had ordered impaled on a fence post was still alive. The post was starting to cut through his front torso, just below his rib cage. His eyes had a glazed-over look, and his body was still mildly shaking. He was, after twelve hours on the pole, still alive. With one quick sideways blow with my sword, I beheaded the man. I brought his head out to the execution site and threw it on the ground with the others. The last criminal was dead, and the execution was over.

After cleaning up and having a good meal, I was in the mood to get laid again. I spent the next two hours power-fucking the two pleasure slaves. After we showered, I relaxed, naked in bed, on my back, with one naked slave boy on each side of me.

At that moment, I started to think what it would be like if, after I got home, I ran into my ex-girlfriend and she said, "How are you doing, William?"

And I said, "Well, Babe, I have been fucking two guys, and, to be frank, they are better fucks than you were."

Yes, I know it would be a stupid thing to say, but it would not be the first stupid thing that I have said to a woman. I slept very peacefully with the naked slave boys that night.

The next night my grandfather summoned me to his office. Several of my uncles were present, including my Uncle Omar. My grandfather and uncles all expressed their amazement with my performance the previous day. To my surprise, my son-of-a-bitch Uncle Omar even had a kind word to add.

"Well, nephew, you are beginning to impress me. I underestimated your abilities."

I just said, "Thank you, Uncle."

With that, I believed the war with my uncle was at an end. But I sensed his interest in me had just taken a new turn.

After my uncles had left, my grandfather wanted to talk to me.

"William, I know that my son Omar has been difficult for you to deal with. But it would be best for you to find a way to work with him. Omar has become a very important and powerful man these last few years. He can be a lot of help to you in the future. Just remember one thing. Omar can be a great help or a very cruel opponent. Which Omar would you like to deal with?"

Three days later, I was on my way back to the United States to get prepared for graduate school at Stanford. But my instincts were right. I was being watched. My future was about to be decided by someone else.

Chapter 3: The General

It was good to be home. My Aunt Mary's home near Boston had been my home since I was twelve years old. My parents had died in a plane crash, and my aunt took me in. I've always loved her home, and to me it will always be my real home.

My aunt's home is located in a mostly rural and expensive area. The area is dotted with large and in some cases historical estates. I really enjoyed my childhood living with my aunt in her large home surrounded by one hundred acres of private woodlands. My aunt is a very loving, well-educated, and worldly woman. Growing up with her as my substitute mother provided me with some very warm memories.

A week after I arrived back in the states, I got the phone call that was to change the course of my life. It was from my Uncle Roy. I call him the general. He is a retired army general.

My uncle simply said, "Will, I need to talk to you as soon as possible. It is extremely important."

I agreed, without asking any questions. The phone call startled me a little. My uncle was usually not so dramatic.

A limo arrived several hours later. The drive to Oak Manor, my uncle's estate, took about one hour.

My uncle greeted me as I got out of the car. "Will, it is good that you were able to make it on such short notice. We must talk."

I thought that he meant in his study over some glasses of brandy, but I was wrong.

"Let's take a walk in the garden. It is so beautiful this time of year."

I followed my uncle to the back of his mansion. He led me to bench in the back area and we sat down.

"Sorry, Will, for not inviting you in for brandy as we usually do. You see, my home may be bugged. They want you, Will."

Startled, I asked, "Who wants me and why?"

"The people who run The New World Order organization know about your psychic abilities, and they want you to work for them. They will be contacting you in the next week. Remember, *no* is not an answer. No means you are dead."

"Why would anyone want me dead?"

I stopped myself for a moment. Well, maybe Uncle Omar. The general said things had gotten to the point that one would have to take sides in the battle that would decide how the world would be governed.

"What do you mean, 'take sides,' Uncle?"

The general looked directly in my eyes. "Because of your abilities, you can tip the balance of power to one side or the other. You can figure out situations, find solutions, make projections about the future course of events. That type of talent in this war can determine the victor."

"What war are we talking about?"

"The war to determine which group will control the Order. The world government is here; it's a done deal. Now two main blocs within the leadership of the Order are starting to fight over the spoils. One group wants a form of velvet dictatorship over the people of the world. They want to rule from the background and basically leave the average person alone. The second group is more fascist in nature. They want firmer control. If they succeed in dominating the Order, many decisions will be made that will make the Nazis look like nice guys."

"What sort of fascist ideas?"

"The Fascist Element within the Order thinks in a very eighteenth- and nineteenth-century empire manner. They will exploit people and rape a nation's natural resources. Their ideas on population reduction are really scary. Ideas like starting a massive plague that will kill a third of the people in the world and sterilize most of the rest. The Fascists in the Order want to greatly reduce the population of the Earth."

"How many people would they allow to live?"

"The present game plan calls for four hundred million to a billion people."

"That means about nine billion people would be killed or sterilized."

"That is correct."

"Uncle, why would the Fascists want to kill billions of innocent people?"

"The Fascists believe that mankind cannot survive much longer with the burden of supporting such a large world population. In their opinion, our planet does not have the natural resources to support such large numbers without causing the collapse of civilization as we know it. Plus a small population will make the world easier to rule.

"The side that opposes the Fascists in the Order are called the Moderates, or some political scientists term them Neo-Fascists. They believe that it is a moral duty for us to find solutions to our world's population problems. In their opinion, the world population problem is solving itself. The world population seems to have peaked, and it will start to decline in a natural manner, making a mass killing of innocent people unnecessary."

I had heard people talk of such population reduction plans, but up to now thought it was only talk.

"Well, Uncle, which side's viewpoint do you support?" I smiled as I said this.

"The Neo-Facist side, of course."

My uncle now laughed a little. His humorous manner was starting to come back.

"And that would be?"

"The side that believes in controlling governments and events, but we also believe in leaving people alone as much as possible. This approach appeals to my basic conservative nature. Now listen carefully, Will."

My uncle looked directly into my eyes. "I want to recruit you to join me and what I will call the good guys. But I also want you to work with the Fascist side of this battle. In short, I want you to be a spy and a person who will rise to a high level of power. When the time comes, you will supply intelligence for our side, and, if needed, you will be in a position to put a stop to their bloody plans for the world. Do you accept my offer, Will?"

He was still giving me that serious look of his.

"Yes, sir, you can count on me. A few billion lives rest on your plan. I will be proud to join you. But I have one question. How do I get into the Fascist part of The New World Order?"

"Will, the bad guys have already decided to recruit you. They want you to work with them in establishing a corporate fascist rule over the whole world. Remember, they will be very polite when you meet them, but if you say no to their offer, they will kill you."

The last part got to me.

"Also, remember they know about your psychic abilities but not about your ability to read people's minds. Do not disclose that fact. If you do, you would have signed your own death warrant. These Fascist types would not trust a person who could read their thoughts. They have too many secrets."

"How did these Fascists find out about my abilities?"

"Some powerful member of the Order told them about you. He told them about your psychic abilities and your cold-blooded nature. He told them that you have no problem with killing people and that you would be a good recruit prospect. I don't know where they got such information."

I started to think, who? The answer came quickly. Uncle Omar could have done it, or whoever was watching over my life was another possibility.

"Uncle, how is it you know so much about the Order?"

He looked at me and smiled. "You already know the answer to that question, don't you, Will?" I nodded in agreement.

"Uncle, how long have you been a member of the Order?"

"Twenty years this June. But I work for the good guys. I have worked my way up to the top. I am a member of the governing board of the Order."

"Why did you get involved with the Order?"

My uncle was quiet for a moment before he answered my question.

"Well, Will, it was at first an opportunity to end the threat of nuclear war for good. Then I got to see it as a way to end the threat of war in general. A world government, under the right control, could work wonders to establish world peace."

"How is it, Uncle, that an army general wanted to stop warfare?"

"I know that the military's image is one of being pro-war in general, but it is a false image. Most career military people see war for what it is: mass murder. I've seen what war does to people, and I never saw anything good about it."

"Uncle, what is this about the Order being under the right control?"

"Yes, none of this UN 'every nation gets one vote' shit. All such a system would do is let the poor nations of the world rip off the wealth of the rich nations. I support the idea of an elite group of people—the highly educated, the rich, and the powerful—to control the world. It is not a perfect system by far, but it is a workable one. This system can deliver world peace and a stable world economy, if the right people run it. That, of course, does not include any hardcore Fascists.

"Will, when they arrange to meet you, just agree to join them. Tell them it would be a great career move to be part of this great change in world politics and economics."

"What will happen to me after I join them?"

"They will train you for two months at a secret camp in Texas. You learn their methods of operation. You will be schooled in very advanced technologies. Some of these technologies are not from this world. They were obtained from alien races through trade agreements."

That did not sound bad at all.

"Uncle, all of what you have told me sounds interesting, like something I would do for free. What is the catch? I know if I am dealing with Fascist personalities, there has to be a catch."

"Yes, Will, you read my mind as usual. There are catches. The first catch is that they will make a killer out of you. The program that you will be asked to join is mostly under the control of the Fascist Element of the Order. These people operate like the old Soviet KGB. The KGB believed that in order to train a reliable security force, they must first get their hands bloody. If security people have murdered innocent people, they will not turn against the organization. They would see the organization as standing between them and their victims' relatives and friends. Like all security personnel of dictatorships, they fear the wrath of their own people.

"The second catch is that you cannot tell them that you can read their minds or give them any reason to suspect that you can read minds. Fascist personalities do not like people with such a talent. Fascists have a lot of secrets to keep and a mind reader, like you, William, would be considered a threat to them. Do not make the mistake of telling them about your full abilities. If you do, they will have you executed."

I nodded in agreement. The whole idea shook me up a little. "Uncle, does this mean that I won't be going to grad school this September?"

"Yes, you will attend and graduate from Stanford on time. After your training, they will call on you to work on different assignments for them on a part-time basis. They won't completely trust you at first. They will need time to evaluate your progress and loyalty. But after you graduate, your ass belongs to them. There are two good points to your employment. You will have unlimited financial support. These people do not do anything on the cheap side. When you own the money supply, money is never a problem. Also, you will be untouchable by the local police departments. If the police in an area that you are operating in give you any trouble, you just have to show your badge, let them check you out, and they will not bother you again. You can even kill people and they will let you go."

I spent the next two days at my uncle's estate. We discussed, in the garden and on walks in the woods, everything about the Order that he thought would be of use to me.

The ride home was very lonely. I was not happy about this new turn of events. The subject on my mind was how long it would be before they contacted me.

Chapter 4: The Meeting

It did not take long for the Order to make contact. Three days after my talk with my uncle, two men in dark suits and sunglasses showed up at my aunt's home.

They simply asked me, "Are you Mr. William Andrews?"

I said, "Yes, what can I do for you?"

"Would you come with us, please? We have been sent to take you to a meeting with some very important people. I believe that you have been expecting us."

The two men led me out to a waiting car. The car, a four-door sedan, had tinted windows. As I got into the car, one of the men told me to put on a blindfold. He said it was for security reasons.

After driving for about a half hour, we stopped and the blindfold was removed as I was told to follow two of the men. As we got out of the car, I could see that we were in an underground parking garage. I was led over to an elevator. But to my surprise, the elevator started going down, rather than up—down quite a ways. I was going into some sort of underground complex. After the elevator had stopped and its doors opened, I was led to a big, oak-paneled conference room. I was told to sit down on one of the chairs that lined the walls of the room.

The twenty-minute wait had me feeling a little uptight. I knew that there had to be cameras in the room and that I was being watched. I tried my best to look very content and under control and definitely not scared. I figured a calm image was needed at this point.

Suddenly, a door opened and in walked three men and one woman dressed in expensive business suits. They were followed by the two security men who had picked me up earlier. Without saying a word, these people sat down on the opposite side of the big conference from me. The security men sat on chairs along the walls. They both started to stare at me.

The woman was the first to speak. "Mr. Andrews, please sit at the table. We members of this review panel will not be able to identify ourselves, for security reasons. I hope you understand."

I nodded in agreement. One of the security men got up and pulled out a conference table chair, which was just opposite the officials. A gray-haired man, who looked like he was in his early fifties, started to speak.

"Mr. Andrews, we are here to discuss a job offer that we believe will interest you. I am sure that your uncle has already discussed the matter with you. Am I correct in that assumption, Mr. Andrews?"

I looked directly at the man. "Yes, sir, that is correct."

I could read many of the panel members' thoughts at this point. They were starting to mentally evaluate me, both from what was in my file and from what they saw in front of them. So far, they had a favorable opinion of me.

I could not say the same about one of the security men who sat at my right. I read his thoughts. This man was eager to be given the order to kill me. He was prepared. He had a special rope in his pocket that was use to strangle people. My uncle was right. Either I said yes to the offer, or I was dead.

"Mr. Andrews, it is mentioned in your file that you are highly psychic and that you have no problem with killing people. Is this correct?"

"Yes, sir, both points are correct."

"Would you please describe what type of psychic talents you have?"

I remembered what my uncle had said: do not mention my ability to read minds.

"Well, sir, I can review paperwork on projects and determine if the project will work, or in some cases what changes need to be made in order to assure success. I can read stock charts, commodity charts, and earning charts of corporations and determine accurately their future prospects up to six months into the future. I can also project the winners of political contests, horse races, and athletic competitions. As for the killing thing, yes I have no problem with killing a person, if there is a good reason for killing said person."

The man asking the questions now looked firmly into my eyes. "Mr. Andrews, have you ever actually killed anyone?"

I was taken a little by surprise by the question. I sensed that they already knew the answer to their question, but they did not want to compromise their source. Their source, I was sure, was my Uncle Omar.

"Yes, I have. I executed ten condemned criminals by the sword during my last visit to see my grandfather in Saudi Arabia. It was a matter of family duty."

I turned to look at the security guard at my right. He seemed to be more nervous than he had been. It seemed I was not just the rich pretty boy that he thought I was.

One of the male panel members wanted more information about my being psychic.

"Mr. Andrews, a lot of people claim they have psychic abilities. Most of them, when properly tested, are judged to have no such talents. May I put you to the test here in this room, today?"

"Yes, sir, it would be no trouble to answer any questions that you may have."

The man then reached into his briefcase and pulled out several file folders.

"Now, Mr. Andrews, these files have information that I wish for you to read and evaluate. I want you to tell me things about some of these people that is not in their files. Do you accept this challenge?"

"Yes, sir, let's get started."

I was handed the first file folder. The names of the person in question had been erased. I quickly read through the two pages of information on the man it described.

I then said, "This man is a very powerful, wealthy man. He is also dead. I feel he has been dead for about three years."

The man who had given me the folder looked a little shocked. "Yes, Mr. Andrews, you are correct."

The second folder was about a woman. I read it and reviewed the content in my head. I had a slight smile on my face when I gave my answer. "This is a very important female. She is well educated; some would say she is brilliant. She is also sitting at this table."

I was right. It was the lone female on the panel. She smiled at me.

One of the three men now put the bar chart of a stock in front of me.

"Now, Mr. Andrews, this stock chart is a year old. Look it over and tell me what it has done during the last year." I scanned the chart and the information about the company. In about one minute, I answered, "The stock in question more than doubled in price during the last year."

I was then handed the current stock chart. "Right on the mark, Mr. Andrews, very impressive."

The last question that I was asked was a basic job interview question. "Mr. Andrews, why do you want to join the Order?"

"Because, after going over the subject with my uncle, a member of the Order, I have come to believe it is a great opportunity to make a lasting and constructive change in our world. The Order has the prospect of changing the world for the better by doing things like stopping the threat of global nuclear war and war in general. I would like to be a part of such a historic event as establishing a lasting, worldwide peace."

The one-on-one interview was suddenly over. The panel was pleased with my performance. But I believe that the panel had made up its decision before our meeting. They just wanted me to confirm that their decision was a valid one.

"Mr. Andrews, as your uncle has already mentioned, the organization we represent, which sometimes is called The New World Order or just the Order, is prepared to offer you a training position with our organization. This position will, at first, be part-time in nature. The job requires that you go through an intensive army-style basic training for two months this summer, starting this Monday. You will be required to graduate from Stanford with an MBA before you become a full-time employee. The job pays a high salary, and it comes with a very interesting expense account. Since your uncle, a member in good standing in our organization, has already discussed the job in detail with you, we feel that at this point we can ask if you accept our offer of employment and the duties and opportunities that come with it, or if you believe it is not for you. Which will it be, Mr. Andrews?"

I could tell by reading the minds of the people at the table that this was a very important decision for me. The security man to my right was slightly smiling, and he had put his hand in his pocket, the pocket that held the rope.

"Yes, sirs and madam, I would be glad to accept your offer. I am eager to start my training."

The panel looked pleased. The security man looked disappointed.

I shook hands with the members of the panel. One of them welcomed me to the Order and said that I would fill out the paperwork later. I was told to be ready at 8:00 a.m. Monday. A car would be sent to pick me up. I was not to pack any belongings; all I needed would be provided.

The drive back home was far less stressful. This time I was not blindfolded. I was going to be a card-carrying member of the Order, the people who control the world. I was also going to pay a price for such power. More of a price than I could have possibly comprehended at such a young age.

Chapter 5: Training Camp

The car that picked me up on Monday was a standard dark, four-door sedan. It was right on time. A man dressed in a business suit came to my door and introduced himself as Mr. Stevens. I was told to bring only the clothes that I was wearing and my wallet with a driver's license. I would not need anything else.

The drive to the airport took an hour. The two men in the car did not converse with me. I sat in the back by myself. The only form of entertainment I was allowed was my own ear device.

A private corporate jet was waiting near a hangar just off one of the main runways of the airport. Several other recruits were already onboard. The flight to Texas went faster than I expected. Talking to the other recruits and playing cards made the time fly.

The camp was in a densely wooded area. The car turned off the main highway and drove down a gravel road for about five miles before it stopped at a guard station. The driver showed his pass, spoke briefly to the guard, and then we were allowed to enter the camp.

I was taken to what I was told was the main administration building. A middle-aged woman greeted us politely and told us to follow her. I was led to small room with a view of the woods and a nearby lake.

She said, "Well, Mr. Andrews, it is time for you to fill out your paperwork."

This was a real downer of a way to start my New World Order employment.

After four hours of filling out mindless paperwork, I was escorted, along with several dozen other young men and six women, to what was called orientation. We were assembled in a barrack-like room and told to find a seat near the front.

As we all started to find a seat, I looked over the other new recruits. It seemed I was one of the youngest males in the audience. Most of the other guys and all of the women looked to be in their mid-twenties to early thirties. They were probably recent grad school graduates. Some of them looked at me and got a look of surprise on their faces. I could read their minds.

They thought, "What is this high school kid doing here?" I have always looked younger than I am. It has been a reoccurring problem in my life.

I could already see that since I was starting to be tagged with an image of being the kid in the group, I was going to have to prove my worth to these people as quickly as possible. I had joined the Order to lead, not to be a fucking kid.

Luckily for me, my physical talents were just as impressive as my psychic abilities. I have always been a natural athlete—a state wrestling champion in high school—and I have always been twice as strong as the average teenage boy. So strong that I could bench-press four hundred pounds at age fifteen and do twenty-five hundred push-ups at age sixteen. And this is not even mentioning my out-of-sight IQ. If these guys thought that I would let them tag me as a boy, they were in for a rude awakening.

Yes, I also have a big, inflated, ego. Yes, I believe that I am special. The world does not need any more average guys; it already has far too many. I intend to stand out in the crowd, not blend in. God did not give me all these talents just so I could be a member in good standing of the herd. Being an average guy is fucking boring. I would rather be in the spotlight with the powerful and famous people of the world. I wanted to achieve something important in my life. To do something important, you needed power. That would pretty much sum up why I was joining the Order rather just living out my life as a very pretty, educated, and rich trust-fund baby.

As the crowd settled into their seats, several uniformed men entered the room. They were high-ranking officers of the new Federal Security Administration. One held the rank of major general, and the other two were colonels.

One of the colonels, who we soon learned was Colonel Robert T. H. Williams, started to speak. "Gentlemen and ladies, we are here to give you an outline of the type of training that this facility offers and whether you people have the right stuff to make you a good Federal Security Officer."

The audience sat quietly.

"This facility is a top-secret installation. It does not exist. We do not exist. You are not here, and you never heard of such a place. Do you all understand?"

"Yes, sir!" we shouted unanimously.

"In the coming two months you will receive two types of training: basic military, such as physical fitness, weapons, and hand-to-hand combat training, and intelligence gathering for the killing of criminal and terrorist elements and the use of high technologies, some of which are really, let's say, out of this world, plus basic administration management.

"During the first part of your training in the coming four weeks, you can choose to leave at any time. If you chose to stay but are found to be unfit for service in the Federal Security Administration, you will be asked to leave. In both cases, you will receive your back pay and given transport home. Also, since you have all signed a contract to never discuss anything about you employment with the Federal Security Administration, a sum of thirty thousand dollars will be paid to you for your oath of silence.

"The second part of your training is a whole different ball of wax. Much of your training during the second part is top secret. If you are judged to be unfit at this stage, you will not be going home; you will be executed."

This announcement made several members of the audience very nervous. Several young men near my seat looked down and their bodies tensed up.

"From this moment 'til the end of the first part, any of you can choose to drop out of training and leave. But since the second half of your training is beyond top secret, the penalty for failure is death. Does anyone have any questions?"

Several hands went up. The colonel pointed at a young man sitting near me. "Yes, what is your question, sir?"

"Many of the people here are probably wondering, as I am, why the second part of the training program has such a harsh penalty for failure, sir?"

The crowd seemed to agree. They were intensely interested in hearing the answer.

The colonel continued. "If you had completed the second half, you would know why. But, of course, you are only starting your training. The technologies that you will be exposed to, and in many cases learn to use, are life- and world-changing. Word of their existence cannot, at this time, be allowed to become known to the general public. Have I answered your question?"

"Yes, sir, you have."

A few more questions were asked of a general nature, questions that were mostly about the upcoming month of training. Several of the recruits were strangely quiet, and some looked very uptight.

The women that had helped me fill out my employment paperwork now made an announcement. "New recruits, may I have your attention?"

The crowd stopped talking and turned to listen to the speaker.

"I am here to tell you who your roommates will be during the next two months. As I call your names, please come forward."

It seemed that we were to be housed two to a room in the dorm.

"Mr. Andrews and Mr. Holt."

As I came forward, I was introduced to my new roommate, Mr. Franklin J. Holt. It was not a good beginning.

He took one look at me and said, "Well, it looks like I am rooming with the kid."

I did not smile. Instead, I just stared into his eyes with a cold look on my face. He looked a little startled. Mr. Holt did not introduce himself to me as I expected. He looked a little frustrated. He asked to talk to the administrator in private. His request was declined. It seemed I was getting off to a cold start with my assigned roommate.

After having a fairly good dinner in the facility dining room, we were issued training clothes and personal items before we were escorted to our assigned rooms. The room looked more like a college dorm room than a military barrack.

My roommate immediately picked his bed and told me, "Kids sleep on that side of the room."

As he turned his back on me, a major error, I grabbed his arm and put a hammerlock on him, shoving him against the wall.

I said, "Now, Mr. Big Mouth, it is my turn to introduce myself. My name is William. You can call me Will. This kid stuff stops right now. Unless you want to learn how much I can really hurt a man."

The fact that he was hopelessly pinned against the wall and could not move, regardless of how much he tried, convinced him to develop better manners.

"Okay, I won't mess with you anymore."

"Now, I am going to release you. If you are dumb enough to try anything, I will be happy to send your sorry ass to the base hospital."

After I released my hold on him, I backed several feet away and waited.

"What are you, some sort of martial arts champ or something?"

"No, I was an all-state wrestling champion."

"Well, from now on, keep your hands off of me."

This seemed like a better arrangement than being called the kid, so I nodded in agreement. In a half-hearted manner, my roommate later introduced himself. He said, "By the way, since we are stuck with each other for the next two months, my name is Frank."

He offered his hand and I shook it while saying, "You can call me Will."

Frank was not the most warm-hearted person I have ever known.

At 5:30 a.m., the wake-up music started and was followed by an announcement instructing us on what we were supposed to wear that day: basic army clothes. All of the new recruits had been measured, and our rooms had been fully stocked with what we started to call our training clothes. After quickly dressing, the announcer ordered us to report to a field just outside our training dorm.

In military style, we were lined up in rows. I took a quick count of the recruits. We were eight recruits short of yesterday's total. I was relieved. I expected more to drop out. Putting their lives on the line in basic training, I guess, was more than some had expected. It was just my luck that I had talked to my uncle before I joined the Order, otherwise I may have been one of the dropouts. It wasn't just about the money and power angle for me. It was the chance to help shape the future course of the Order and save the lives of billions of people on our planet.

Our first assembly was followed by an hour-long exercise routine and then a five-mile run. Usually, a five-miler would not faze me in the least, but today the temperature was over one hundred degrees in the shade. By the time our unit got back to the dorms, we were all covered in sweat. We quickly stripped off our sweaty gym outfits and headed for the showers.

After getting wet and soaping down, I took a quick look at my competition in the nude. No one could match me in the athletic-body category. Most of the guys were in good shape, but only one seemed like he could possibly give me some competition. I was going to really stand out in this crowd. That was the way I liked it. I liked being the center of attention.

While I finished showering, I used my psychic abilities to figure out which way these dudes fucked. None hit me as bisexual. Two were gay, and the rest were straight. Most of the straight dudes were sexually uptight types. You don't have to be psychic to easily pick these guys out of a shower-room crowd. The uptight straights will always shower facing the walls, ass out. It's like they are afraid to look at other naked guys.

Potential future fucks, the types that turned me on: none. All these guys were either too ugly or just too uptight and unavailable. It was going to be a boring and horny two months.

The first week of training was heavy on the physical. Exercise was the name of the game. The people who were evaluating us wanted to see what shape we were, or weren't, in. Each day was harder than the previous. By the end of the week, only two recruits, my roommate Frank and myself, stood out from the crowd as the strongest and in the best shape.

I was the strongest recruit. I could bench-press a hundred pounds more than Frank. But my roommate could keep up with me in the endurance trails. It may sound self-centered of me, but I soon came to believe that there was something very strange about Frank. He just did not get as winded and sweaty as a normal person.

There was another thing that made me a little uptight about Frank. He was the first person that I had encountered that I could not read. I just couldn't seem to focus on his vibrations—his mind was something that I couldn't penetrate. He was a mystery to me, and it was starting to bug me. I just didn't know how to figure him. Was he a danger to me, or was he harmless?

The second week of training, our instructors cut back on the heavy physical training. Weapon training was added to the course. Our first training was with side arms. Since I had extensive experience with pistol shooting, it was like visiting an old friend. I was the unit's best shot by far.

Next were rifles or, to be more accurate, automatic weapons, such as the old-fashioned AK-47s and M-16s and more modern ones like the MR-105s. The 105s were out of sight. One person can destroy an average American house with one of those 105s. It was more fun than work to use one of these weapons. The bullets for a 105 do not just penetrate a body or a wall—they penetrate and then explode. One shot can cut a man in half and a full clip can destroy a good-sized building. For a gun lover like me, shooting 105s was great recreation.

The third presented some real challenges for most of the recruits. Getting real physical with some hardcore, streetwise criminals was more than some recruits could take. The training units lost another four people during this event.

Being a state wrestling champion, with martial arts training to boot, gave me a major edge in this type of fighting. The event was a chance to break up the stress of basic training and really enjoy myself for a few days.

We were to be paired up with a prisoner for several days of what our instructors called hand-to-hand combat. I was at first confused by this terminology. I assumed that this meant that we got to break the basic rules of wrestling and just fight dirty. My assumption turned out to be correct, and I could not have been more pleased. I was going to get a chance to really go all out on some dirt bag and really do some damage.

After our morning run, we were escorted to the camp gym. The floor was covered with wrestling mats. We were ordered to line up on one side of the gym and relax. The prisoners, dressed in bright yellow gym shorts, tank tops, and gym shoes, were assembled on the opposite side of the gym.

The prisoners were escorted by six big, brutal-looking security guards armed with nightsticks. Each had a very in-command look on his face. These guards gave me the impression that they were veterans who had seen it all. The prisoners seemed to know this, and none of them messed with the guards.

The contrast could not have been more complete. We, the recruits, were very clean cut and healthy looking. The prisoners were shorter than most of us and not in great shape. As for looks, forget it; ugly would have been a kind word to describe their appearance. The minute they assembled, they started to cop an attitude. This was basic gang banger crap.

One by one, our instructor paired us off. I got Carlos, a street hood and murderer. He stood about three inches shorter than me and was well built and muscular. I could see that he had several tattoos, most being prison, or banger, tats. He took one look at me and smiled. He thought that he had a real pretty pussy boy to play with. Someone he could really scare and take advantage of. He was in for a big surprise. His vision of his role in our relationship was about to be turned upside-down. It was going to be fun watching how he reacted to being my pussy boy.

Each recruit had been given a few days of instruction in wrestling and street fighting. It was, of course, not enough training to face such a challenge. As each recruit was called up to face the challenge, I sat on the mats on my side of the gym as my opponent sat on his side. He kept making facial and hand gestures that translated into, "You are my bitch." I just smiled and made some return gestures.

I puffed up my lips and kissed the air and followed by pointing at my dick, which I then stroked a few times. He got the message and flipped me the bird.

After our introductions were over, I knew that Carlos was going all out from the start to show me who was boss. I could read him like a book. That is a book written in simple language, with punctuation, spelling, and word-usage errors. He was in for a big surprise.

I was glad when my name was called. Up to now, the unit members were on the losing end of this competition.

I was right about Carlos. He came at me like a wild animal, running and leaping into the air with the intention of planting his feet into my chest. He missed, and I quickly had him in a very painful hammerlock face down on the mat. The instructors called the match for me. Carlos got up, pissed as hell.

As he walked back to his side of the gym, he turned around and said, "Tomorrow, white boy, I am going to hurt you really bad."

What Carlos said just made me smile. Today I was just fooling around with him. Tomorrow I would destroy his gangbanging ass.

Dinner in the dorm mess hall was something that I was looking forward to. The food was usually very good, and I was starving. The food was not the highlight of the night. I got to gloat a little at my rather boring, unsociable roommate. He had gone up against a really big gang banger. The match was a draw, but he paid a price. Frank was pretty banged up, and he was not in a good mood. I tried not to laugh or make any funny comments.

I slept well that night. The next day, I would finish off Carlos with ease. Well, that was the plan. But my instincts told me someone was messing with my image of an easy victory. My instincts are never wrong.

As the announcements on the intercom woke us up, I started to have a bad feeling about the upcoming matches. Something was not right. An unknown factor was at play, and I was the target. I always hated sensing that something was wrong and being unable to figure out what it was. The minds that I was able to read gave me no answer to the questions that I had. This whole situation did not give me time to plan a course of action. I would just have to do it on the fly.

After our morning run and the first meal of the day, the recruits assembled in the gym for the final day of competition: down and dirty street-style combat with the prisoners.

When my name was called, I was in for a little surprise. Instead of just Carlos, three names were called. Carlos was being allowed to bring two friends. One of them was the big guy that had mauled my roommate the day before. Yes, my instincts were right again. Someone was fucking with me.

Who? Said person or persons were always too far away for me to read them. The security cameras in the gym were on. This was a real setup.

I could just envision my shadow guardians saying, "This rich pretty boy is going to get his ass kicked."

Carlos looked very pleased. All three of these hoods were

smiling. They thought had me now. Overconfidence in fighting is a major weakness, but they did not think about that. As they walked toward me, I showed no fear. I just knew that in order to win this match, I had to move fast and strike hard. As the three hoods approached me, I suddenly faked a move to my left and then I quickly moved to the right, and with one fast kick I took out the big guy's right kneecap. As he dropped to the mat screaming in total agony, I grabbed his back with both of my hands and threw him at his fast-approaching teammates. That left just two homeboys to deal with.

For a few seconds, Carlos and his teammate had to deal with their friend falling on them. It was more than enough time for me to plant my right foot squarely in Carlos's face. He grabbed his face and fell to the mat.

His friend showed more spirit. He attacked me like an angry animal. He hit me in my right shoulder with a heavy punch just before he threw his right fist at my jaw. I made a fast move to the left, and, as his arm passed my face, I grabbed it. I twisted it hard and heard it snap. As he screamed in pain and his focus was broken, I saw an opportunity and took it. I kicked him hard in his nuts. He went down screaming.

At this point, the prisoners started to act like they were going to get involved. The camp guards moved to position themselves in front of the prisoners. They all calmed down.

As his two gangbanging friends lay on the gym floor twisting in acute pain, Carlos managed to get to his feet. He tried to grab me, and I took the opportunity to hit him as hard as I could in his gut. For a moment, Carlos grabbed his waist. It was long enough for me to finish him with a one-two-three punch combo to his jaw. He did not get up again, and the match was called for me.

As I started to walk off the mats, I turned, looked up at one of the gym's security cameras, and flipped the bird at whoever was watching the match. Fuck them and whoever thought up this event.

After walking off the wrestling mats, one of our instructors grabbed me by the shoulder and gave me a compliment.

Captain Lott smiled at me and said, "Impressive show, Mr. Andrews. Well-played, well-played."

It seemed that a game was in play. Yes, I was right; someone was fucking with me.

The remainder of the first month of training was mostly basic exercise and lectures about being organized and developing better self-management skills. But as I began the second and of course most dangerous month of our training, I still was concerned by the fact that I could not read my roommate. What was it about him? His body energy was different from that of anyone I had ever encountered. This fact kept festering in my head. There had to be a reason.

Chapter 6: Secrets Revealed

As we lined up on the first day of the second half of our training, I took another visual inventory of the recruits. Our training unit had suffered about a 40 percent loss of personnel. The hard physical training, and the fact that if you failed the second half of the course you would be dead, greatly thinned the ranks.

As for myself, I was confident that I would make the grade. But in the back of my mind, I had some doubts. The doubts did not concern my abilities. I knew that the Order needed my psychic talents, which I had already proved were on the up and up. No, the doubts were about the unknown factor involved in my training. I am referring to the people behind the curtain, so to speak. Who were they and what did they have planned for me? Were these people just testing me, as was the case with the match with Carlos and his two friends, or had they decided to play games with me before they killed me? Was I a threat to said persons and I had been set up for extermination, or was I being tested to see if I had what they wanted? After all, I was only twenty-two years old and not really experienced in the ways of powerful adults. I could only guess.

To my surprise, after our morning exercises and a five-mile run, we did not proceed to learning about some of the above super-secret stuff that we had been told about. Our first order of business was individual interviews and evaluations. The training unit commander, Captain Holt, said that it was only a routine procedure. This announcement did not keep me from scanning the minds of command personnel any time I got a chance. When your life is on the line, it is best not to trust anyone.

My personal interview was before three senior officers in a room in the unit dorm building. As I entered, I felt only good vibrations from the officers. I began to relax. Perhaps I was not going to be a pile of ashes by the end of the day. Captain Holt was the first to speak.

"Mr. Andrews, please sit down in the chair next to you."

I quickly sat down as ordered.

The officers briefly looked through some papers before speaking again.

"Mr. Andrews, we are very pleased at the progress that you have made in the first half of your training. You scored extremely high in all areas of performance. We have given you a good evaluation as you proceed to the second half of your training. We have no doubt that you will continue your high level of performance."

Than Captain Holt changed the subject. "Mr. Andrews, we would like to talk to you about another subject. This conversation will be completely off the record. You are not to discuss what is said. Do you understand?"

"Yes, sir, I will not discuss our conversation."

"Mr. Andrews, we would like you to evaluate your roommate, Mr. Alan J. Holt."

I paused for a moment to arrange my thoughts before answering. "My roommate has his good points and some bad points. He is physically fit and a good athlete. As a student, he is above average. His weak points are basically social in nature. He is one of the most boring people that I have ever had to deal with."

I knew that being boring would not disqualify my roommate from being a government employee. In fact, in most government agencies, he would fit right in. But it seemed this type of information was not what these officers were interested in obtaining.

"Mr. Andrews, we would like you to use your psychic abilities on him. We want you to evaluate him for us."

This was the moment of truth. "Well, that would present a problem, sir."

"What problem exactly do you mean?"

"You see, sir, I can read people, but I cannot read him. I have tried, but there is just something about his vibrations that are completely new to me. He is the only person that I have encountered that I have not been able to read."

The officers seemed startled.

I said, "I hope that I have answered your questions."

The officer in charge nodded in apparent agreement.

"The fact that a talented psychic like you, Mr. Andrews, cannot read Mr. Holt is the type of information that we are looking for. Thank you. This evaluation is now over. You should now report back to your training unit."

Nothing much happened in regard to my roommate the next few days. He stayed boring, and we went to lectures that concerned the structure, historical development, and future plans of The New World Order. Most of the information was old hat to me. My uncle, the general, had filled me in on such details before I got to this training camp.

The other recruits seemed impressed with the grand scope of the Order's plan for establishing a united world without war.

Not one of them seemed to know how outright fascist the whole plan was. That's not saying much for the influence of the American education system.

I just tried to look interested in what the speaker was saying. But I knew about the dark side of the Order and the intensifying civil war that was being waged behind the scenes for control of the Order and the world.

On the fourth day of the second part of our training, the routine was changed again. We were told that each of us would be given a complete physical exam. The exam was routine: the usual body inspections, blood tests, and X-rays. But then a new twist was added. We filed, one after the other, into the scanner room. We were there for a complete body scan. Someone wanted to know what made us tick, from our toes to the top of our heads.

I read the minds of as many doctors and nurses as I could. They did not know the whys involved in this procedure. Then I lucked out. A colonel entered the room to review the progress of the testing. Bingo! He knew why we were going through these complete body scans. What I had said about my roommate had set it off. They were looking for a way to detect them. "Them" was still a mystery. Who were "Them"? It was an unanswered question.

It was several days later, at the end of our unit lecture training, that I got a partial answer. At night, I read a colonel's mind while he was asleep. The commanders did not find what they were looking for, and they were going to meet the next day to decide what to do.

The next day, I was summoned to another meeting with the same officers that I had talked to in my evaluation. I was again asked to sit in a chair opposite the officers, who were sitting behind a table. As usual, Captain Holt was in charge.

"Mr. Andrews, the unit has a problem." I did not detect any sign of personal danger, but my mind started to get a little uptight anyway.

"It seems the security of this camp has been compromised. A possible spy has been identified. It is your roommate, Mr. Holt. I cannot go into details of why we have come to this conclusion. You do not have the security clearance that would allow me to discuss this matter any further with you."

I took a deep breath. Here it comes. "Mr. Andrews, you are hereby ordered to eliminate this threat to our security. You are ordered to kill Mr. Holt, your roommate, by the end of this day. How you will do it is your business. In your second-level training, you are required to kill one of the prisoners. But in this special situation, your roommate will count as your kill. Do you have any questions?"

"Yes, sir, one question and one request. The question is, what type of backup will I be getting for this assignment, and may I still be included in the killing-a-prisoner part of the course? I have a prisoner in mind that I have been looking forward to eliminating."

"As for your question, yes, you will have a backup crew to aide you in this assignment. Mr. Stewart, an expert on eliminating people who are a problem, will equip you with whatever equipment you decide that you need for this task. As for your request, yes, you may still kill your assigned prisoner, if you want to. I assume that the prisoner in question is named Carlos. Is this assumption correct, Mr. Andrews?"

"Yes, sir, I am looking forward to killing that scumbag. I see it as a public service."

"Then it is agreed. Mr. Stewart will be in contact with you shortly. Start thinking about what equipment you will need for the task. When the task in completed, Mr. Stewart and his crew will collect the remains. That is all. You may now return to your training unit."

"Yes sir."

As I walked back to my unit I kept thinking, *Kill my roommate, kill my roommate.* It was a totally unexpected assignment, but I found I had no trouble with it. I started to work on my list. Frank was as good as dead.

After quite a bit of thought, I completed my shopping list of the items that I would need to do the job. The list was simple: one set of handcuffs, a police nightstick, and a choker device. The choker device was a method to strangle people in a surefire and lazy manner. The device was a cord that slips around a victim's neck. On the back of the choker is a twist device that tightens the cord. The choker is equipped with a holder clasp that stops the cord from untwisting.

Mr. Stewart turned out to be a tall, powerfully built man in his late thirties. It was easy to believe that he had experience in killing people. My scan of his mind indicated he had once been a hit man for the CIA.

Mr. Stewart looked over my simple list of items and smiled. "Looks like you have a plan, Mr. Andrews. When do you plan to complete your assignment?"

"Tonight Mr. Stewart, in our dorm room."

Mr. Stewart at this point handed me a business card with his name, title, and phone number on it. "Call me when the job is done. I will collect the remains."

Everything went as planned. Mr. Stewart delivered the items on my list. How he got a choker so fast was a little confusing to me. I was ready to finish off Frank. This would be the first time that I had actually murdered another human being. Up to this point in my life, I had only executed condemned prisoners, which was a legal civil duty. This was a big line to cross. I was not sure how I would feel after completing this task.

The time and place were set in my mind: at 9:00 p.m. in our

dorm room, Frank would take his last breath. I knew Frank's evening routine by heart, what he did in preparing for bed and when his back would be turned. Hopefully, nothing happened to change his usual nighttime routine.

I hid the nightstick in my closet. The dorm room closets would be behind Frank as he got ready for bed. The cuffs and the choker I put under my mattress. Mentally getting ready to terminate Frank was all that was left.

I kept thinking about what my uncle, the general, had told me. "Will, you will have to get your hands bloody. In order to get in with the Fascist Element of the Order, you will have to earn their respect. They are a lot like the mob. You will have to be just as cruel as they have been. In the end, we may be able to stop their drive to control the Order and the world. Your actions could help in saving billions of lives."

Frank followed his nighttime routine perfectly, minute for minute. When he turned his back, I opened the closet, grabbed the nightstick, and laid him out cold on the dorm room carpet. In only two minutes, I had him cuffed and the choker around his neck.

I decided to say good-bye to him, which would show respect. "Good-bye, Frank. I never really liked you."

I twisted the choker, clipped the holder, and watched Frank flop around on the carpet like a fish on land. But I was in for a big surprise.

Yes, Frank died, but that was not the end. As Frank breathed his last breath and his body stopped moving, the unexpected happened. Frank's body started to glow. I mean, it was heating up. The light was so intense that the dorm room looked like someone had turned on a set of bright headlights. I did not know what to do. It happened so fast. I just covered my eyes with my hands. As suddenly as it happened, it was over. In just about forty-five seconds, Frank's body had been reduced to ashes. His clothes were still intact, but his body was gone. My mind panicked. How was I going to explain something like this to Mr. Stewart? He would think I was nuts.

Nuts or not, I had to phone Mr. Stewart. Either I was seeing things that were not real, or someone was not telling me something.

Mr. Stewart and two aides arrived in about ten minutes. The first thing Mr. Stewart said was, "Well, Mr. Andrews, you said something happened to the body?"

"Yes, come look."

I let Mr. Stewart and his aides into the room and showed them the ashes that had been my roommate. Mr. Stewart did not seem surprised. "Oh, not again. Well, Mr. Andrews, your roommate definitely was one of them."

I did not know who them was, but I was relieved that Mr. Stewart seemed to know what was going on.

"Don't worry about this, Mr. Andrews. The colonel will talk to you tomorrow. He will explain the situation more than I can."

With that, Mr. Stewart and his crew started to clean up what was left of my roommate. I felt a little sign of relief. It seemed I had not yet crossed the line. My roommate, it seemed, was not really a human being. What exactly he was, was an open question.

Early the next morning, just after unit assembly, I was ordered to report to the colonel's office. As I entered, I sensed that I was not in any danger. He looked up from his desk and told me to have a seat.

"Well, Mr. Andrews, you had quite an experience last night."

"Yes, sir, it was not what I had expected."

"Mr. Andrews, because of last night's events I have been authorized to up your security clearance to level five. Because of your unique talents and last night's events, you have been approved to be fast-tracked for promotions and top-level assignments. You must also not talk about last night's event with unauthorized personnel. At this camp, that means everyone but me and Mr. Stewart. Is that clear?"

"Yes, sir. May I speak, sir?"

"Yes, what is your question?"

"If I may ask, sir, what exactly happened last night?"

"You had an encounter with them. Them is the word we use to describe what seemed to be an alien threat to our security. Mr. Holt was not a human being. He was what could be termed a biological robot. This robot was sent here to spy on our operation and to become an undercover mole in our organization."

"My roommate was a robot. How is that possible?"

"Yes, a biological robot. We don't know how they make these robots, or how we can detect them, other than to kill one. Until we develop a way to detect and deal with them, we will have a security problem.

"So far, Mr. Andrews, you are our first line of defense. Your inability to read them is the only way we have of detecting them at present. That makes you a very valuable commodity."

"I will do all that I can to help out, sir."

"That's the spirit I want to see."

They need me. That would give me a clear path to get to the top of the Order.

"Sir, does this mean I am to be used to find them in the organization?"

"Yes and no. We want you to find one more of these creatures. We will put said person under strict surveillance. We can't use your talents to flush out all the spies that are in the organization. We believe that such a move would expose you to harm. These creatures and their handlers would figure out who is fingering them and that person, you, would be dead. We are looking for a possible electronic way to detect them before we move to arrest all of them. If you have any ideas of how this can be done, we will help you with any research that needs to be done."

"Thank you, sir. If I think of any angles that may work I will contact you."

"Anytime, Mr. Andrews, anytime."

On the way back to my unit, I smiled. I now had a higher security clearance and an inside track to the top. But all was not so rosy. When I started helping my uncle's project, there was only one enemy to worry about: the Fascists in the Order. Now there were two: the Fascists and them.

But my senses picked up something else during my conversation with the colonel. He was not telling me the whole truth. The colonel was part of the Fascist Element in the Order. These people had something going on, behind the scenes, concerning the things known as them. They did not want these creatures exposed. Why?

Two days later, I was allowed to look at the torture room that I was to use to dispose of Carlos. It was a gray, stone, cell-like room that measured about twelve feet by fifteen feet. It had a metal frame in the middle of it, with chains and shackles attached to it. A drain was placed just in front of the frame, which would make it easy to clean out the room. A heavy metal table, pushed up against the wall, was in front of the frame. A large mirror that covered half of the wall was behind the table.

At this moment, Mr. Stewart came into the room. "Mr. Andrews, that was quite a show in your dorm room last night. I wish that I could have been there. Anyway, I'm here to ask you to make up a list of the items that you will need to work on this Carlos dude. Could you get it to me sometime tomorrow?"

"Yes, Mr. Stewart, no problem. I'll start on it right away."

I followed Mr. Stewart out of the building and down to the dorm building. Making up the list would be easy. I had already reviewed the assignment several times. My list would be rather simple. I needed one ball of string, a six-inch sharp knife, a pair of pliers, a cat-o'-nine-tails whip, a second cat-o'-nine-tails whip with small nails on the tips, a ball gag, and a blow torch with a torch lighter. I then thought for a moment before I added two longneck beers in ice and a bottle opener.

I gave my simple list to Mr. Stewart early the next morning. The other recruits were making up their lists as well.

Mr. Stewart looked over my list and smiled. "Mr. Andrews, I see that you have planned a very interesting party."

"Yes, sir, it will be interesting for me, but not Carlos." I could sense Mr. Stewart knew exactly what I was planning. He was a veteran in such matters.

All the remaining recruits were being assigned prisoners to torture and kill. This was the big test of their abilities in the second half of our training. They were also working on their own lists. The only surprise in the preparations for this assignment was the fact that the remaining women in the unit, four in all, had chosen male prisoners to work on. There was a lot of anti-male feelings in the women recruits.

Alone with our lists, we were all told to write a short outline of how the prisoner was to be prepared. I wrote that Carlos should be stripped naked and shackled to the torture room steel frame, standing up spread-eagle.

As I entered the room, Carlos was hanging naked from the coiling, his arms and ankles securely chained to the floor and the ceiling. Carlos saw me and started to mouth off. This was not unexpected. He had no real class.

"What the fuck are you people planning? I want to see my lawyer. Hey, white boy, do you hear me?"

I paid no attention to Carlos. I went over to the table and inspected the equipment. Everything I had listed was on the table.

I turned around to inspect Carlos. He looked startled, maybe even a little scared.

"Hey, faggot, what are you looking at?"

He was uptight. I walked around and looked over his backside. All in all, Carlos was in good physical shape. He had a very well-defined, muscular body. He could have been a good athlete. His body had seven tattoos, mostly gang-related and religious symbols. Too bad this great body had such a small brain.

Just to piss him off, I started to physically inspect him. I ran my hand over his back and slapped his bare ass several times as hard as I could.

"Hey, faggot, you touch my ass again, and I will kill you."

So naturally I had to slap his ass real hard a few more times.

I didn't want to listen to Carlos mouth off anymore, so I picked up the ball gag, walked over to face Carlos eye to eye, and said, "Now, Carlos, open up."

He started to get ready to spit in my face, but I hit him in the jaw with a fast right hook. He was shaken up but not out. Before he could say anything, I grabbed his nuts and started to squeeze. He screamed really loud.

I repeated my order. "Open up, Carlos. If you don't open your mouth, I will crush your nuts."

After putting the ball gag on Carlos, I picked up the pair of pliers from the table. As I approached Carlos, he started to look a little scared. When I used the pliers to squeeze his nipples really hard, his whole body tensed up. I kept squeezing and twisting his nipples until they had almost ripped off.

When I stopped, they both looked more like hamburgers than

nipples. Blood was dripping down his chest. For the next twenty minutes or so, I yanked out strands of hair from his armpits, pubic area, legs, and ass. Small drops of blood started moving down his naked body from the areas that I had worked on. He looked relieved when I put my pliers back on the table.

Next, I picked up the cat-o'-nine-tails whip. The first hard blow was to his back and then multiple strikes to his bare ass, legs, waist, and chest. In the next fifteen minutes, his body twisted in pain. When I put down the whip, I began to visually inspect his body. His naked body had turned red from my whipping. Lash marks were visible on his ass, back, and chest. Satisfied with the results of my initial wipping, I now let Carlos relax for a few minutes while I sat on the table and drank a cold beer.

Carlos seemed relieved that I had stopped. Maybe he thought that I was through torturing him. What I really had planned would shock the hell out of him.

After Carlos seemed to be relaxed and breathing normal, I cut off two one-foot long sections of string. As I got down on my knees in front of him, he looked and started to shake. Did he know what I was up to?

I grabbed his nuts and pulled them down hard several times in an effort to stretch them. Carlos tried in vain to pull his balls out of my hand. I quickly used the first strand of string to tie several knots around the upper most part of his nut sack. Carlos's body began to violently squirm. Maybe he did know what I was up to. I tied the second section of string around his ball sack about a quarter inch lower. He was ready.

I got up, walked over to the metal table, and picked up the knife. When I turned around, Carlos saw the knife and panicked. His eyes fixed on the knife, and he acted like a wild animal that was trying to break free of its bonds. As I stood in front of Carlos, I grabbed his balls and yanked them toward me. Looking straight into his eyes, I smiled and then lowered the knife down to his balls.

"This is for all the pain that you have caused people."

A few seconds later, Carlos lost his nuts. When I held them up in front of his face, Carlos was crying. A look of acute agony twisted the muscles of his face. I dropped his nut sack on the floor and crushed them under my boot.

I walked over to the metal table and grabbed the second whip, the one with the nail tips. His eyes got really big and his body started to violently shake. The first blow to his back broke the skin. Blood started to run down his back. With each blow to his back, ass, legs, and chest, his body violently shook. When I finally put the whip down, his body was covered with blood.

The loss of too much blood would put a stop to my game, so I picked up the blowtorch. A blowtorch is a crude but effective way to close a wound. I didn't think Carlos had it in him after the pain that I had just put him through, but his body violently jerked and twisted in acute agony each time the fire from the torch touched his skin. When I finished closing his wounds, his body was a mass of welts, cuts, burns, and bruises. Carlos's eyes had a glazed, shell-shocked look to them.

It was time to finish him. But first I sat down on the table again and enjoyed drinking the last cold beer. If Carlos was still capable of thinking, he must have thought that I was one cold-hearted motherfucker. I just smiled. That was the exact image I was trying to give the people who were watching my performance on the security cameras.

As my uncle had said, "They won't really trust you unless they think that you are cold-hearted bastard."

Carlos acted as if he was barely alive. I lowered his body to a kneeling position and yanked his head back.

As I put my knife on the left side of his throat, I said, "Now Carlos, look at yourself in the mirror. I want you to see yourself die."

I pulled the knife across his neck. Blood gushed out of the wound.

After no more than a minute, Carlos closed his eyes and his body went limp. Carlos was dead. Justice was served, and I made a lot of points with the people who were watching me perform on the security cameras. They wanted to know how cruel I could be. Well, they now knew.

I left his body in a kneeling position. Mr. Stewart and his crew would pick up the remains and take them over to be cremated. By late tonight, Carlos would be a pile of ashes, and the world would not miss him.

Since my clothes and boots were covered in blood, I decided to use the showers that were part of the complex. The shower room was already in use. Several other recruits had finished their assignments and were using the showers when I walked in. My senses and eyes told me that many of these guys were seriously depressed. One recruit was sitting naked on the floor with the shower hitting him in the back. Several of these guys were definitely not happy campers. I did not try to talk to any of them. I quickly showered and left the room to towel off and put on fresh clothes.

In my dorm room, I tried to sleep, but I was still too physically tense. I just could not relax. This was the same tense feeling that I had gotten the many times before when I had to kill someone. I had the feeling, but exactly why was a mystery to me. I did not have any remorse about killing Carlos, so why the tense feeling?

The recruits in the shower room were another story. I had been told by my uncle that the first time that you have to kill a man is the hardest. The shower room scene sure proved that statement to be true. It took a while, but I was finally able to get some sleep.

The following day during assembly, I noticed that one male recruit was absent. It was the seriously depressed guy that I had last seen sitting naked on the floor of the shower room. Nobody in the unit ever saw him again.

It was now time to get involved with the technology part of our training. The idea of possibly seeing alien technology had us all in high spirits. We were all transported by buses to another installation about an hour's drive away from the training camp.

Chapter 7: High Technologies

We did not stop at some of the buildings on the site; we kept on driving until the buses stopped in the middle of nowhere, Texas. The only building on the site was an old, rundown barn.

The colonel was the first to speak on the intercom. "Listen up, recruits. You are going to witness the use of a powerful new explosive system. You may be using this device in your future assignments. Pay strict attention."

After exiting the buses, we were led into the open grasslands and told to assemble.

After we had lined up in rows, an instructor spoke. "Today you will witness the start of a new age in weapons."

He held up a small object that looked more like an ink pen than any weapon that I had ever seen.

"This little device is a flash device. When you set it off, it will vaporize anything within one hundred feet of it. I will now demonstrate what I mean."

The instructor started to walk into the open fields. After he was over a thousand feet from us, he did something to the device before he set it down on the ground in front of the old barn.

After the instructor had walked back to us recruits, he took out what looked like a cell phone. We quickly found out that it was a detonation control. The instructor pushed the button and a big fireball appeared at the spot where he had placed the flash device. Fireball would not be a good name for what we were watching. The ball of light was blue in color. As suddenly as it had appeared, it was gone.

The old barn was completely gone. It had been vaporized. No secondary fires had taken place, and there was no smoke of any kind.

All of us just stood there with an amazed look on our faces. Wow, this was like a sci-fi movie or video game.

We were ordered to advance and inspect the site. The little device had taken out the barn and left no evidence that anything had ever been there except a two-foot-deep hole in the ground. The pen-sized explosive device had vaporized the barn and two feet of soil! Impressive would be far too mild a word to describe what we had seen. If technology could alter the course of military history, I wanted to know more.

We were told later that the flash technology was the end result of several trade agreements that the Order and the US government had with alien civilizations. This was just the beginning of what we were to be shown.

After returning to camp, the colonel announced, "You recruits think today was fascinating. Tomorrow will blow your mind. You are going to see a real UFO."

I knew at that point that I would have trouble sleeping that night. The Order's secrets were starting to be revealed.

The next morning, after assembly, exercises, and the first meal of the day, we again boarded several buses. The trip took about an hour. We pulled into a US Air Force base. The buses stopped at a remote airplane hangar. It turned out that the airplane hangar was not our final stop. Several stories under the hangar was a complex of large rooms.

The recruits were shown into a conference room to hear several lectures on alien technology. I soon learned that I was not to be attending these lectures. As the unit was filing into the conference room, I felt a hand on my shoulder. It was an air force major.

"Are you Mr. Andrews?"

"Yes, that is my name."

"Come with me."

I hate these military-type situations. You don't know if you are being summoned to be given a medal or to be arrested. The major led me into a waiting room of what seemed to be an important person. I was right.

The major told me to sit down and added, "The general will talk to you shortly."

When I was told to come into the general's office, I was getting a little uptight. Did they find out something about me?

The general asked me politely to sit down. He wished to discuss a secret matter with me. I did not sense any personal danger. "Mr. Andrews, I have been informed that you can read people. Is that a correct assessment of your abilities?"

"Yes, sir. I have had a natural ability to, as you said, read people since I was a just a child."

Well, my uncle, another general, had been busy making my abilities known to important people.

"Good, Mr. Andrews. Since your security clearance is a level five, I may be able to use you in an experiment. But first, I want to test your abilities myself. I will tell you several things about my life, and you will then tell me what parts are true and what parts of my story are false."

"Yes, sir, I will do my best."

"To begin, I was born in Austin, Texas, in 1997. I later attended and graduated from the Air Force Academy in 2019. I was rated as fifth in my class. I attended and received an MBA from Harvard University. I am married and have five children, all boys. Now, Mr. Andrews, what parts are true and what parts are false?"

"What you have said is true, except for the part about having five children, all boys. It is a false statement. Am I right, sir?"

He smiled a little. "Yes, you are correct. I have three girls. Now, let's get down to business, Mr. Andrews. I want to test your abilities on some nonhumans."

Non-human. Did he mean space aliens?

He did mean what I thought he meant. "Mr. Andrews, we have several aliens visiting us at present. We have had a long-running technology exchange program with several alien races for the last nine decades. I would like you to interview three different aliens to see if you can read them as easily as you can read human beings. Such ability would be very helpful in our future relationships with these alien races. Do you think that you are up to the task?"

"Yes, sir, it would be a real challenge. When can we start?"

"We will have the interviews set up for tomorrow morning, after your unit departs to go back to camp. I expect the interviews, or test, will only take a few hours. We should know if your abilities can help our project or not by then. I will have a base car take you back to training camp."

"Yes, sir, I am looking forward to this assignment."

With the interview with the general over, I was escorted back to the conference room by the major.

As we walked down the hallway, the major informed me, "Mr. Andrews, your unit is just sitting down for the conference. You did not miss anything important."

He was right. I hadn't missed anything except the snacks that my fellow recruits had consumed. I was not to get anything to eat.

The lecture was conducted by an air force colonel. "Welcome, Federal Security recruits, to a top-secret lecture about America's involvement with alien civilizations. You are going to hear a lecture concerning the history of alien and American cooperation since 1947.

"In 1947, a UFO crashed in Roswell, New Mexico. The official viewpoint was that the incident involved a weather balloon. That was an official lie. It was a UFO. Not one UFO but two crashed in Roswell that night.

"Special teams recovered the crashed UFOs and two still living alien beings. One of the two died on site and the other lived for several years. The one that lived helped to set up communications and later physical contact with his civilization. Other alien races have since made contact, and the US government has ongoing technology trading programs and treaties with several of them.

"We have greatly benefited from these programs. We have gotten such inventions as fiber optics, microchips, night-vision equipment, and, of course, the ability to manufacture our UFOs. Many other items have come our way because of these programs and treaties, but because of your level of security clearance I cannot discuss them with you at this time. Let me just say that, as you advance up the security clearance ladder, you will be informed and you will be using much of the technology that we have acquired from alien civilizations.

"Now, do any of you have any questions on what I have just said?"

Several hands went up.

The colonel started to pick recruits to ask questions. "Yes, recruit, what is your question?"

"Sir, why were the American people not told of the existence of these alien civilizations?"

"Well, I have been told that the people who made such decisions did not think that the average person was ready for such information. They believed that such information would cause severe disruptions of the social order. Were they right? I do not know."

The colonel picked another recruit.

"Sir, will this information ever be released to the general public?"

"Someday, I believe, in the near future, the public will be informed."

The rest of the questions were, "At what level of security clearance will we be allowed to know such secrets?" and "What else will we be informed of today?" The answer to the second question was well received.

"Recruits, today you will be shown a real alien UFO. We got the craft in one of our exchange programs. Would you all please line up behind Captain Felton over by the door? He will escort you to underground hangar number 6."

The recruits eagerly lined up. I was one of the first in line. Being an old sci-fi fan, this was a dream come true.

We were led down a long hallway that had closed doors with numbers on each side. Finally, we stopped at a guarded door marked "Hangar 6." The captain stated our reason for wanting entry into the hangar, and the guards used a laptop computer to check out the request. Clearance was given, and we were allowed to enter the hangar.

We proceeded down a flight of stairs that must have dropped us down another two stories before we entered another hallway. This shorter hallway led us to another guarded door. Clearance was quickly obtained. When the door opened, we were all in for quite a sight.

The UFO was silver in color. It measured, I would say, about thirty feet wide and about ten feet tall. It was the traditional image of a UFO. An entry of some type was open and touching the floor. People in air force uniforms and white lab coats were working in the hangar.

The captain told us that we could walk around the UFO and touch it if we wanted. All of us quickly took advantage of this unique opportunity. The metal sides of the UFO did not feel like a metal such as steel. It actually felt a little flexible. This was a fact that was hard to believe. We all could feel a mild warm sensation when we touched the outside of the UFO. Every recruit, especially me, looked fascinated. This was the stuff that dreams are made of.

After inspecting the outside of the craft, we were allowed, two by two, to look at the inside. When my turn came, I eagerly entered the craft. Being six feet two in height, I had to bend down in order to get through the small door. This craft was not made for beings of my size. The inside was very simple in design. The pilot cabin was just bare metal walls, two small seats, a control-type panel, and a view screen. It was apparent from the start that the beings who piloted this spacecraft were not large creatures.

The captain confirmed what was already apparent to most of us. "Listen up, recruits. This craft is not a real spaceship. It is a scout craft. It is used for short missions. These types of space vehicles operate from a much larger mother ship. Do you have any questions about the craft?"

"Yes, sir. How is it fueled?"

"It is a simple craft that is powered by what we would call an anti-gravity engine."

"Sir, how fast can it go?"

"We have radar checks that have tracked these types of craft leaving our atmosphere at eighteen thousand miles per hour."

The questions went on for another half hour. The recruits were very impressed by the craft. I was very content. A dream that I had had since I was just a little kid had come true. I had seen a real alien spaceship.

The captain was not finished with the tour. We were shown spacecraft that had crashed and broken apart. The recruits were allowed to examine pieces of the wreckage that were like the legendary Roswell items. It was like heavy tin foil, but extremely durable. One of the recruits tried to hammer a nail through a piece of the foil-like material. He could not break the thin, metal foil. You could easily wad up the foil, and, when you let it loose, it would go back to its original shape.

A test with a blowtorch fared no better. The foil would not burn or scorch. This foil was almost indestructible. I say almost, because in the crash the metal had split up into numerous pieces. I kept thinking, *All this time the government and history books have told people that Roswell was just a weather balloon.*

The rest of the day included meetings with heads of research departments and of course a lot more questions. By the end of the day, we recruits knew more than the average American about UFOs. We knew more than even the UFO nut cases. Oh, sorry. After today, such people were, in my mind, no longer crazy.

The recruits and I spent the night in an aboveground military barrack. In the morning, the recruits boarded their buses and started back to training camp. I stayed behind as planned. My meetings with the aliens on the base were scheduled for early that day, right after I had something to eat.

The meetings were to be held in an underground conference room not far from the lecture hall our unit had used to listen to a colonel reveal some of the government's top secrets concerning

UFOs. I was led into the room by the same air force captain that had conducted the tour for us recruits.

After sitting down on one side of the conference room table, the captain informed me, "Mr. Andrews, what you are about to see may be a little disturbing at first, but you will quickly get used to the presence of aliens."

It was only a few minutes before a door opened and in walked a colonel and some civilians, followed by the first alien that I was supposed to review. He was about four feet in height. His skin color was gray and he had big, bug-like, dark eyes. This being the press had been calling a Gray. The humans and the Gray sat down on the other side of the table. The alien that we call a Gray looked like a little kid sitting in his chair. I started to pick up his vibrations right away. Now all I had to concentrate on was figuring out how to interpret what I was feeling.

I was introduced to the Gray by the people with him. I took them to be his handlers. He did not speak, but he did communicate with me. The Gray did not speak in our manner. He communicated with his thoughts. I was amazed that I could understand him clearly.

The captain spoke first. "Well, Mr. Andrews, I see that you have quickly picked up the alien's manner of speech. His name is Zee. He has been visiting us for about a year. He is here to help transfer technologies to us and help us to back-engineer their equipment. You may now ask him some questions."

I looked at the notes that I had written in preparation for the meeting. I was still a little excited about what I had just witnessed, but I got the nerve to speak.

"Zee, where are you from?"

The alien communicated that he was from a star system that is about fifteen light-years from Earth.

"Zee, are you here to help mankind?"

The word mankind did not seem to translate. I had to replace it with the word human. He answered yes.

I questioned the alien known as a Gray for a further thirty minutes, before the captain indicated that the conference was over.

After the alien and his handlers left the room, the captain turned to me. "Mr. Andrews, were you able to communicate with and read the alien?"

"Yes, sir, his vibrations were not unlike our vibrations."

"Well, Mr. Andrews, was he completely truthful with his answers?"

"Yes, sir, but he was in my opinion holding back information. He was only telling me what he was permitted to communicate."

I did not tell the captain that I was able to read his thoughts. That would be telling more than I should about myself.

I and captain now took a short break. We had a private snack and coffee in his office while the second interview was being prepared. The second interview was with an alien that he referred to as a Nordic. I did not know what he meant. But I was in for a shock.

We went back to the same conference room and took our usual seats. When the door opened, three men walked in. Each man was dressed in overalls. Two were wearing blue overalls and one, a good-looking, young, long-haired blond man, wore white overalls. They all sat down on the other side of the table. I kept looking at the door, expecting the alien being to arrive. But he was already here.

The captain laughed a little and finally told me that the alien being was sitting right across from me. He meant the long-haired, blond young man. The blond man just smiled at me. It seemed this sort of thing happened a lot to him.

The captain informed me that the alien's name was Caos. He was what we called a Nordic. The Nordics were human-like beings that looked almost identical to us. I started to talk to Caos verbally, and he spoke in a rustic form of English. As he spoke, I picked up on his vibrations, which were almost the same as a human being's. I used the term human being because I, at the time, did not know if this Earth-like being was really human.

My questioning of the Nordic man went well. He answered all of my questions in short and simple sentences. It was almost like he was answering questions from a lawyer in a courtroom. He was a lot more ready to talk to me than I was to talk to him. But, all in all, he was truthful and he did not seem to be withholding information.

The captain seemed pleased that the Nordic man was given a clear bill of health by me. The captain, I sensed, was seriously involved with this being.

The third and final interview was with a being that looked like a human reptile. He had skin and eyes like a lizard. His skin was green and black in color. Reading him was difficult at first. It took me fifteen minutes to adjust to his vibrations. This being scared me a little. He was not very truthful in his answers. My opinion was simple. This creature was dangerous to humans. Regardless of what the government thought of these creatures, they could not be fully trusted.

Reading this being's mind was frightening. I got some chilling images. This creature had a liking of human flesh. My skin started to crawl just talking to him. I got the feeling if I had run into this creature in the desert that he would try to kill and eat me.

I was glad when the interview was over and the reptile-like creature left the room. The captain did not seem to be surprised at my negative evaluation. I sensed that he had the same opinion. But the government wanted to work with these beings.

The next three hours were spent on writing an official evaluation of each being. I had no idea what the base commander intended to do with my report. It was filed, and I was out of there. This assignment was both a fascinating and nerve-racking experience. I had met real-life aliens. These beings from other worlds did not officially exist. People who say they have met space aliens are still considered to be nuts, or at least fakes. But they do exist, and our government has known this to be true for over eighty years.

The ride back to training camp was routine transportation. The driver did not converse with me, and I just sat in the back seat. I used this idle time to review what I had learned about aliens, UFOs, and the future plans of the Order.

The information was both personal and psychic in nature. My personal encounters with the crashed UFOs and the aliens were extremely interesting and informative. But my psychic information contradicted much of what I had been shown and told by the air force.

While I was talking to people who were high-level base staff, I was able to read people's thoughts. At night, while people slept, I employed a method that I had learned in the last few years. I called this method "subconscious talk." I first read about it from a story concerning an Italian officer in World War I. He had the ability, while asleep, to direct his subconscious mind to talk to the subconscious minds of enemy officers.

The Italian officer had a great record of bloodless victories. When asked, much later in life, how he had done it, he would say that he directed his subconscious mind to go talk to the subconscious minds of enemy officers. It seems the subconscious mind is a blabbermouth. It loves to talk, and it can't keep a secret.

The officer always knew what the enemy was going to do, and he was able to take advantage of such knowledge to not only win a victory, but to keep down the number of casualties on both sides.

It took me several years of practicing to train my mind to do what the Italian officer had done in World War I. I used my newfound talent the night before the alien interviews. My subconscious mind conversed with the subconscious minds of many of the high-ranking officers and officials of the base. What I found out went well beyond what I and the other recruits were told. The information went straight to the core of what the Fascist Element of the Order was planning to do. My uncle would be very interested to hear what I had to say.

Being able to gather intelligence like I do was highly exciting but also extremely stressful. If the people who ran the Order knew that I was able to do such things, I would be locked up, or killed. As long as they did not know of my full abilities and my real agenda, I was safe.

I arrived back at camp just before noon. The weather was hot and mucky. The temperature was over one hundred degrees Fahrenheit and the humidity was brutal. When I got out of the air-conditioned government sedan, I started to sweat like I was in a steam bath.

After changing into my training gear—typical army training fatigues—I walked over to the camp mess hall to join my training unit. By the time I entered the air-conditioned mess hall, I had numerous drops of sweat running down my face and neck and my armpits were soaking wet.

I was so hungry I could have eaten grass. After going through the food line, I spotted my new roommate, James. He waved and motioned for me to come join his table. The other recruits at James's table were eager to learn what had happened to me. They had not been told of the reason that I had been separated from them. They were, it seemed, a little startled to see me again. Their reactions were understandable. Up to now, whenever a recruit disappeared, it was bad news. Such recruits were not seen again and everyone thought the worst. That is, death.

After telling my new lunch mates the official lie, I talked to some officers about official business. But I started to pay more attention to the pain in my stomach. The recruits at my table seemed to accept my excuse to abstain from our tour group. Were they really that gullible? No, I could read their thoughts. They all seemed to know that the official truth was the truth, period. What really happened did not really matter to them. They just happened to see me again.

The unit's afternoon activities included a routine of basic exercises and weapons training. This was not the most mentally stimulating activity, but it did tend to reboot my mind back to the reality of basic training.

That night I was faced with a horny, young-stud problem. I knew that going two whole months without any sex would be rough for me. At Harvard University, I had not had a problem with finding sex partners. Being bisexual gave me more than double the chances of finding a sex partner anytime I got horny. I say more than double because of the simple fact that men are easier to nail than women. Harvard was full of horny young and, sometimes, extremely good-looking men and women. During my college days, I seldom had to sleep alone. I had majored in political science, but my dick had majored in pussy and ass. I and my big dick were very happy at Harvard.

Now I was faced with going without it for two whole months, and, after just one month, I was having problems. Even the sight of my new and very straight roommate's bare ass would make my dick hard. Whenever he took a shower or changed into new underwear, I tried not to look. But avoiding seeing James in the buff did not stop my thinking about how much I would like to nail his cute, hairless, bubble butt.

James was a sexually uptight, straight man. I knew, from reading his mind, that there was not chance in hell that I would ever be able to tap his ass. Such knowledge would explain why I never told James that I was bisexual. It would not serve any useful purpose.

It was just my luck that is, bad luck, that my unit was full of off-limits straight guys and gals, along with several gay males that were in the not-very-attractive category. It all added up to no sex for me.

The only bright spot in this sexually repressive picture was one young woman in the CO's office. Nancy's eyes lit up the first time I met them. It was the day I arrived at camp. She taught me how to fill out my paperwork. Since that initial encounter, she had been sending me signals each time I was lucky enough to run into her. The signals were clear. She wanted to jump my bones.

After reading Nancy's mind at night, I knew that this good-looking, young woman was mine for the taking. But there was a catch. I had to graduate from basic training before I could fuck her. It seemed I was not the first recruit that she lusted after and balled. But I would have to wait until I graduated in order to have her. It was the rules of the game. If I played by the rules, I would score. Knowing this to be a fact helped me to keep my mind off James's cute ass.

As promised, my training unit was shown more out-of-this-world technologies. On the day after we got back from the tour of the secret UFO facility, we were introduced to a mind-boggling technology. It was called "the knock-out device."

Again, we were loaded onto several buses and taken into what one recruit called "Nowhere, Texas." We were on the open, grassy plains again. It was hot again. The buses had no air conditioning, and we all started to sweat like pigs.

The buses stopped near a fenced-in herd of cattle. As I stepped off the bus, I looked around to see where we were. I could see nothing but rolling grassland as far as I could see. We were ordered to line up in formation. Nothing further was said. The whole unit just stood in formation and waited while our leaders unloaded some odd-looking equipment.

After standing in formation for about twenty minutes, we were ordered to gather around our training officers and listen. Our instructor, Major Klein, turned on the machine. It looked similar to a large computer, with some additions that I could not figure out.

The major turned the machine on. "Recruits, this is a high-tech weapon. It will be of great use in your work. This device can knock out a whole block. What I mean is knock out all the people and animals in that block. I have fixed the device on the herd of cattle that you see before you. There are over one hundred head of cattle in this herd. I want each of you to envision this herd of cattle as one hundred people that you wish to disable."

The major pushed a green button on the computer panel. Suddenly, all of the cattle fell over.

"In answer to your next question, no, they are not dead. The cattle have been put to sleep. They will be asleep for up to one full hour. That is more than enough time to deal with all of them in whatever manner that you may choose. The reality of what this machine could be used for seemed obvious to me. You could win a battle or even a war with this type of device."

In the following discussion of this technology, no mention was made of the source of this device. Just reading the major's mind gave me the answer. The Grays gave us this technology.

The next four days the recruits spent on basic training, mostly body conditioning and weapons training. Firing a 105 again was a blast. These weapons can really level the playing field in a military firefight. They are a great weapon. That is, if you are not on the receiving side.

How would a soldier defend himself against such awesome

firepower? We were taught to use an old time-tested method. "The ground is your friend."

That is the defense method used since the invention of gunpowder. Dig a foxhole, put in some earplugs, and pray. Only a direct hit on your foxhole will kill you. So, of course, we learned a little about digging foxholes.

The next technology that we were exposed to was not an alien device. It was technology developed in the US of A in the 1930s. It was based on the old Rife Generator. It was developed by a man named Royal Rife in the 1920s and 1930s as a means to conquer disease. We were told that his device was based on bio-frequencies. Each disease-causing pathogen has a color, or frequency. If you can discover the right frequency and overload it, the pathogen will die.

Rife, it seemed, cured twenty-eight diseases, including cancer. Was he awarded the Nobel Prize? Of course not. The medical establishment ran him out of business and suppressed his technology. It was all about money. Profits have decided what type of medicine has been provided to the American people for over one hundred years.

The machine that we were shown was not a typical Rife Generator. Most such devices did not work, or were of limited use. It seemed no one could really match the original machine that Rife used. The technology fell out of use.

The machine that we were going to use was based on a mistake that Rife had made in his San Diego, California, lab in the 1930s. It seemed that during a long period of changing channels on a frequency generator, there was a sudden high-energy pulse. Rife and his staff felt the pulse go through them. Rife did not know what to do. Did the pulse destroy anything in the lab? The lab equipment was checked out—no problems. What was wrong was that all of the pathogens in the lab were dead. It seemed that Rife did not follow up on this new method of killing disease pathogens.

Some people, financed by the Order, did experiments on high-energy pulsing of bio-frequency waves. They developed a simple method to kill any type of pathogen quickly, cheaply, and safely.

We were all eager to take up the offer to try the device. The recruits were all assembled in a large room. In the middle of the room was just a table on which was placed one of the new Rife devices. Major Klein simply pushed a button, and we all felt a pulse of energy go through us. No one in the room seemed to be hurt by the pulse. We were told that we could feel a little weak, or even sick. This was called the "die off." It was the effect caused by toxins that were released by dead pathogens in our systems.

I felt nothing, but some of the recruits started to look pale. They had to sit down. One man started to act sick to his stomach. While we were still assembled, Major Klein changed the channel on the machine and he again pushed the button. The pulse of energy again went through me. I now noticed that the recruits that were looking a little pale only a minute before seemed to improve. We were told to drink a lot of fresh water in order to wash the toxins out of our systems. It seemed the first pulse knocked out pathogens in our bodies and the second pulse neutralized the toxins that the die-off of pathogens had created. But by the time dinner rolled around, all the recruits were in good shape. It seemed some of us had a lot of unknown pathogens in our bodies. The pulse had no affect on me. I guess that means that I was in good shape, health-wise.

The major said, "This device will not be available to the general public at this time. It will be in the future. You, as members of the Order, will be able to use it anytime that you feel the need. These devices will be available to you at key administrative centers for the Order."

After a quick read of the major's vibrations, I had a different view of the subject. This device will be available to us, but not the public. It would interfere with the dark agenda of the Order.

The world-population-decrease plan of the Fascist Element in the Order came to mind. This device's main purpose was to safeguard the elements of the world population that the Order wanted to save. This dark plan was to be implemented in the next few decades. Its timing had not been fixed at this point.

The remaining weeks of our unit training were spent on lectures about the plans of The New World Order, some more new and alien technologies, and one more round of what I called "mortal combat to the death."

This last subject really got my blood boiling. The thought of killing another scumbag prisoner was starting to really turn me on. Was training camp for the Order changing me, or was it just bringing out the dark side of my personality?

While the idea of another kill on my record was a turn-on, there was still that feeling that I could not shake, the same feeling that I have had most of my life. Someone was watching me, and he or she had more control over my life than I did. Who were they? At this point, I still did not know. I had a lot of questions about who they were, but not any real answers. But I did know this: whoever they were, they were going to test me again. This kill-a-prisoner event was not what it seemed.

The next morning, one of the last few days of our training, was a typical hot summer day. The temperature was again in the low hundreds and sweating was the order of the day. After the first meal of the day was over, we were taken over to the gym one at a time. I was mentally ready for whatever they threw at me. Well, at least I was in a kill mood. But I soon found out my mental state would have to be radically adjusted to meet this day's challenge.

The gym was air-conditioned. It felt great to get out of the heat. I was dressed in a regular gym outfit, tennis shoes, gym socks, and sweat suit, most of which was soaking wet. Right after entering, I started to do some stretching exercises to get ready for what I considered to be a form of mortal combat. The only question on my mind was who I was expected to kill. My question was soon answered.

A couple of guards entered the gym from the opposite side. They were escorting what looked like a pretty fifteen-year-old-girl. She looked so innocent. As she noticed me, she smiled and her eyes sparkled. She acted like a teenage girl who was going to a school dance. She was dressed in gym shorts and a tight-fitting tank top. It was obvious when she walked over to the gym mat that she wasn't wearing a bra. Her firm breasts moved freely up and down. This young lady did not fit the image of a condemned prisoner. My instincts gave me a very different evaluation of this innocent little girl. She was, in fact, not a bit like the image that I was looking at. This girl was dangerous.

The rules of these encounters were simple. I was ordered to kill my opponent in any manner that I chose. My opponent was not allowed to kill me. The prisoners were told that if they killed a recruit, they would be executed. Were the prisoners told that I had permission to kill them? No, of course not. Yes, the rules were fixed in favor of the recruits.

I started to walk out on the mat. I smiled at her and she smiled back. When I got within a few feet of her, I took a fast flying leap at her and shoved my right foot into her forehead. She went down hard. Most fifteen-year-old girls would not get up from such a blow. They would either be out cold, or they would be crying a waterfall of tears. She did neither.

The girl quickly got up and said, "You fucking asshole. I am going to kill you." This was no innocent fifteen-year-old high school girl. This match was another setup.

The girl came at me like an angry animal. I deflected several hard blows from her arms and legs. This chick was deep into martial arts. When she threw her right leg at my waist, I moved fast to avoid contact. Where her leg missed me, I quickly took out her kneecap. She collapsed head first on the mat and let out a high-pitched scream.

I put my right knee square in her back, pinning her to the mat. It was all over in a few more seconds. I broke her neck and her body shook a few times, and then it went limp. This Barbie doll from hell was dead. Was this just another test of my abilities, or was this a set up designed to finish me off? It was a question that I could not answer.

As I walked off the mat, I did not show my usual contempt for the people watching the match from the security cameras. I did not flip them the bird. As I passed the officer in charge of the match, he smiled and said, "Very impressive, very impressive."

He also handed me a file. "Read this, recruit. It will help ease your mind."

The file concerned my late opponent. Her name was Jane Heller. She had committed several murders. Her real age was twenty-two, not fifteen. Ms. Heller was a martial arts black belt and she was considered to be very dangerous. The bitch was dead. That is the fact that made me feel better. Dead people cannot hurt anyone.

The graduation ceremony was held on the parade grounds. We were all dressed in dark gray dress uniforms. I was thankful that the uniforms were not black, as in Nazi SS. Well, at least the Fascists in the Order did not make that mistake. The uniform made us look more like regular county sheriff's deputies.

I counted the recruits as we lined up. I know others were doing the same. We were minus two. No one asked any questions. We knew they were dead. The reasons did not matter.

At the end of the graduation ceremony, we were each given our new ranks. Every recruit, except myself and one woman, was made a first lieutenant. I and that one woman, Helen Fall, were made captains. I was told I was on the fast track, but, until now, I had no real evidence that it was true.

The ceremony was over, and I turned my mind to more important matters. My dick really needed to be exercised. It had not seen any action in over ten weeks. Fortunately, fate came to my rescue. A brightly smiling Nancy handed me a note. It read, "Meet us at the Motel 6 at 4:00 p.m. today." I just smiled. This day was turning out to be a real winner.

Chapter 8: Nancy

Nancy was the first female member of the Order that I had met that really turned me on. She was a beautiful twenty-four-year-old, short-haired, blond dream. Her body looked so fine that she could have passed for a super model.

Nancy had a talent for quick communication with a man. All she had to do was flash her pretty eyes and move her moist lips as if she was throwing you a kiss and you were hers. Magnum sex appeal, I called it. She could melt your heart with just a simple look.

Nancy backed up her natural sex appeal with a great body, beautiful, flawless skin, and the most perfect set of knockers in the whole state of Texas. I could see that she was not wearing a bra. Her tits stood straight out without any support. Yes, I was later to find out that they were natural, a fact that made Nancy even more appealing to me.

I was not alone in my opinion. Most of the men, and probably a few chicks, in my unit lusted after Nancy. Now, after two months of lusting and no sex, Nancy was inviting me to a private talent show at a local motel. Just the thought of banging this hot chick had my johnson standing at attention most of the rest of the day.

After the graduation ceremony, I went back to my dorm room

to get ready for my encounter with Nancy at 4:00 p.m. After entering my room, I looked at the wall clock. It was 2:30 p.m. I had only an hour and a half to get ready and get to the motel.

After showering, shaving, brushing my teeth, and putting on some comfortable, casual clothes, I still had an hour to walk over to the local store, buy some wine, and get to the motel. It was an easy task since the store and the motel were right outside the camp's main gate.

When I got to the motel, fifteen minutes ahead of time, I asked the desk clerk which room Nancy Tillman was in. He told me room 15. Knocking on the door of room 15 made me feel like a teenage boy about to experience his first time. A good feeling? No. But I was so turned on that I was starting to think like a teenage boy. That is, with my little head and not my big head. I silently waited and hoped that tonight did not require any heavy thinking.

Nancy came to the door dressed in a light red bathrobe. She gave me a nice warm kiss. Nancy smelled like she had just taken a shower and used a lavender-scented soap. She took the bottle of wine that I had brought and put it on the dresser. Nancy then led me over to a comfortable chair with no arms and told me to please be seated. My eyes were all on her as she put on some soft music, just before she turned around and let her bathrobe drop to the floor. My eyes got bigger and I took a deep breath.

Nancy was one of those rare beauties that looked even more beautiful naked than she did with clothes on. Her body was flawless. She was perfectly proportioned, and to my amazement she was completely hairless from the neck down. Amazing is not the word I would use. Completely smooth-bodied women turn me on to no end. All I could think of was how great it would feel to lick, kiss, and eat every inch of her naked body.

Nancy noticed right away how turned on I was—my big cock

was making a pup tent out of my pants. She looked down at my pants and smiled. She said, "Well, let me help you with that."

Nancy kneeled down in front of me and started to unzip my pants. As fast as it took me to take a deep breath, she had my throbbing manhood in her right hand. She licked my cock up one side and down the other. It felt so good that I had to think about something else to keep from cumming. I wanted to enjoy the feel of her hot mouth and moist lips massaging my cock as long as I could. But after only a few minutes, I could not control myself anymore.

My body began to violently shake. "Oh, God, I'mmm goooing to cuuuuum!"

Nancy did not back off. Instead, she deep-throated my swelling cock as I shot stream after stream down her eager throat. She did not gag one bit. After I was spent, she started to slowly lick the last of my cum off the end of my cock. She seemed to like to drive me crazy.

"Now baby, let's get you out of these clothes."

I stood up and with her help I quickly stripped naked. I sat down again and motioned for her to sit on my lap. It was my turn at bat, and I started to please my lady by slowly kissing her on the lips, and then I worked my way around to nibble on her earlobes before kissing my way down her neck. I ran my fingers slowly down her spine until I was massaging the inner cheeks of her beautiful ass. Anytime she reacted well to what I was doing, I took note. Soon, she was shaking a little and moaning loudly.

Now I cupped both of her ass cheeks with my hands and I stood up. I gave her a deep, long kiss as I let my left hand drop down to her moist, warm pussy and I started to finger-fuck her, first one finger, then two, then three, and finally four. As Nancy started to moan and shake, I started to lick, and at times lightly bite, her nipples. She started to moan and got louder and louder, almost as if she was getting close to climaxing.

I guess cumming this way was not what she wanted. Nancy suddenly pulled my fingers out of her pussy, sat me down, and mounted my throbbing cock. The feel of her tight, moist, warm pussy swallowing my big cock soon had me moaning and shaking. She rode my cock for several minutes, until I just could not hold back any longer. When I shot off inside her, she started to violently shake and her moaning got louder until I had to hold on to her tightly as she climaxed. Her eyes rolled back in her head, her body tensed up for a minute, and then she grabbed the back of my head and she passionately kissed me as she started to rapidly ride my cock up and down.

After taking a shower together, we sat on the floor naked and drank several glasses of wine as we watched TV. Round two was over, but it was not to be the end. Rounds two, three, and, in the morning, four followed.

After I left in the morning, I had a big smile on my face, Nancy's e-mail address in my pocket, and the memory of licking, kissing, and eating every inch of a beautiful lady, not to mention all the fucking we did. I had just had one of the best days of my young life.

I still had a little unfinished business at the camp. I had to pack my belongings, check out at the administration building, and arrange transport back to my aunt's house. The first part, packing my belongings, went fast because I had not brought much personal stuff. The second part, checking out, was more time consuming. It took about an hour and a half to make sure that my personal paperwork was in order. Arranging transport was an easy task. Since I was one of the first to check out— many of the other cadets were nursing hangovers—I got a car out without any waiting.

The car was a Lincoln with the usual tinted windows. As my driver navigated the narrow country roads, I just rolled down the window and let the cool morning air massage my face. On the rest of the ride home, I had time to review my progress in the Order and figure out what my next move was going to be.

CHAPTER 9:   UNCLE

The first stop I made after moving back in to my aunt's home was to make plans to visit my uncle, the general. I needed to touch base with him and disclose what I had found out while going through federal police basic training. A quick phone call was all I needed to confirm an appointment with my uncle. My appointment this time was not to be at my uncle's estate but at his beach house in the Hamptons.

My uncle's place was in Southampton. The beach house was nothing special. It was a two-story, ranch-style structure with wraparound porches. It was probably built in the 1970s, and it looked unkempt, as if it needed some tender loving care. What made it extremely valuable was the fact that it had its own private beach. My uncle's beach house was a prime property. You would need twenty million world dollars or more to buy a slightly rundown place like this.

The general was standing in front of the house as I drove up. He was, it seemed, eager to see me. As I parked my car, he greeted me with a firm handshake and welcomed me to, as he called it, his cabin.

As we walked into his beach house, my uncle said, "Feel free to talk openly in my house, William. I just had the place tested for bugs, and the anti-bugging equipment is top-notch. No one will be eavesdropping on our conversations."

As we walked into the beach house, I could see a long-haired blond young man sitting in the living room. My uncle quickly introduced me to his friend Caos. Then it hit me. This man was the alien I had been introduced to at the air force base in Texas. What was he doing here?

After we all sat down, my uncle said, "I believe you have met my old friend Caos, William?"

"Yes, sir, we met in Texas during the second half of my training."

"Then I don't have to explain who Caos is. All that you need to know is that Caos and his people are on our side. Unfortunately, the Fascists have their alien allies as well. They are allied with the alien people that are referred to as the Lizards. Our side is allied with the Nordics and the Grays."

"Uncle, this is information that I was not given during training. Am I supposed to know such information?"

"Yes, William, it is okay. Your security level I had raised to level seven yesterday. You have been authorized to know. Now that the introductions are over, let's all put on some swimsuits, grab some beach towels and a few beers, and go down to beach."

I did not try to figure out why my uncle was so hip about going to the beach right after I had just gotten to his place. He had a reason.

I dumped my personal baggage in the bedroom that I always use when I visit my uncle at his cabin. After I stripped and put on a pair of blue swim trunks and threw a large beach towel over my shoulder, I walked out to the porch and followed my uncle and Caos down the wooden stairs that led to the beach. The walk to the beach chairs at the end of the beach only took a few minutes. The beach chairs, four of them, under an oversized beach umbrella, were located in a small cove surrounded by twenty-foot cliffs. As we each picked out a beach chair and sat down, my uncle started to speak.

"You are both probably wondering why we are meeting on the beach and not at a far more comfortable location, such as my living room. Well, the answer is security. It would be hard to listen in at this location. My friend Caos has never gone swimming in any large body of water like an ocean. Frankly, I don't even think that he can swim. This is going to be fun to watch. Caos hates to admit that he can't do everything that an Earthman can do."

My uncle now wanted some information on my training experience. "William, the first half of your training was basic shit, as I would term it. I wish to hear about the second half, to see if the Fascists are doing anything different."

"Well, not knowing what you know is a real handicap."

"Just start from the first day. I will tell you want if it is of interest to me."

The next two hours I went over in detail what I had experienced. The general only seemed to be interested in two parts of my story: the Rife generator that knocks out all diseases caused by pathogens and the killing of several of my fellow cadets for so-called security reasons.

"This Rife generator is a pulse device. We did not know about it, and you say that it will be made available to the members of the Order?"

"Yes, sir, that is what I was told."

"Well, let's hope they did not lie to you. I know of several members of the Order who really need the use of that device. The sooner the better, but what you said about the killing of your fellow cadets really pisses me off. The Order has the technology needed to erase several months of a person's memory. They did not need to kill those cadets. Their goal was just to install fear in the cadet ranks. I have no doubt that they succeeded. This is just another reason why we must get rid of these Fascist bastards."

Having gone over my cadet training, the general changed the topic of discussion. "Well, William, let's show this space alien what it is like to play in the ocean. On his planet they do not have oceans."

With that statement, we all headed for a plunge in the surf. Correction, we plunged; Caos slowly waded in. When a big wave hit him full force, he fell back and disappeared below the waves for a moment. When he surfaced, he did not look very happy. He looked downright scared. As my uncle and I played in the ocean, Caos stayed in the shallow part of the beach. Playing in an ocean was not his thing.

While we were on the beach, I paid a lot of attention to Caos. This was the first time I had gotten really close to an actual space alien who wasn't wearing a uniform of sorts. Even if he did look like an Earthman, he was from another world. I took the opportunity to take a closer look at this Nordic man. My observations did not come up with much. Caos had skin that was, let's say, on the pale side. His eyes were a little different. They seemed to be more brilliant than regular Earth people's. But other than that, he could fit right into a crowd of Earth people. I kept looking for a physical difference other than just slight eye differences and pale skin.

After my uncle called an end to our ocean adventure, we headed for the beach house to clean up. When we got to the back deck, my uncle took us over to the outside shower.

"Well, boys, strip off those wet suits and wash the sand off. The towels are on the back table. After you dry off, go upstairs and get some rest. I will start fixing our dinner. We are having salmon tonight."

I smiled and took off my wet trunks and headed for the shower.

I had the idea that maybe seeing Caos in the nude would reveal that difference that I was looking for. But no dice, he checked out. Now I knew that these Nordics were pretty much the same as us. Except for what my uncle told me later: "They have four fewer teeth than us, and their teeth are replaceable. They have no need for false teeth, as some of us do." This statement made the Nordics seem a little superior to the average Earthman.

After a great dinner—my uncle is a great cook—we settled in the living room to discuss what my uncle called "vital communications for our operations."

"Will, communications is the backbone of any intelligence operation. So, after much thought, Caos and I came up with a foolproof way for us to communicate. Because of your talents, it should work very well. Now, Will, I want you to close your eyes and mentally say, 'Caos one, two, three.'"

I did as asked, and suddenly I got an answer back. "Will, this is Caos. If you are picking up my communication, raise your right hand now."

I did as asked. The voice in my head then said, "Will, you can now open your eyes."

When I opened my eyes, my uncle and Caos were both smiling. The experiment was a big success. We now had a bug-proof method of communication.

"Will, we will be using this method to transfer vital intelligence. Caos will be our connection. I will talk to him, and he will talk to you."

My uncle noticed that I had a slightly puzzled look on my face. "Yes, Will, Caos can transmit messages to your mind when ever he wants to contact you."

"That's right, Will," vibrated in my mind.

Caos left us that night. A small spacecraft landed on the beach. As luck would have it, I was allowed to inspect the inside of the small spaceship. It had two human-size chairs and a big control panel. I got to sit in one of the chairs as Caos prepared the craft for takeoff. Man, I was a kid again. This was great stuff. My uncle and I watched as the small spaceship lifted off and quickly shot off into the night sky.

"Well, William, Caos has quite a ride."

"Yes Uncle, all I can say is, when can I get one of those?"

My uncle just laughed.

The next five days of my visit were mostly social in nature. I and sometimes my uncle visited local sites. I even had an offer from a pretty young lady, who I have known from grade school days, to do some serious fucking. But the memory of Nancy was still fresh. I didn't think any babe could equal her performance.

Chapter 10: Stanford

Getting into Stanford's grad school was easier than what I now faced. Getting the classes, working with my grad-school advisor, and finding a place to live were a nightmare. My advisor for the MBA program was an old fossil. He was a professor that should have retired at least ten years ago. Talking to him was a chore. I think he was in the first stages of Alzheimer's. Finally, after several appointments, I had a list in hand of the classes that I needed for my first semester.

An MBA from Stanford is highly prized in the business world, and they don't hand them out easily. I knew that I was in for a real challenge when I chose Stanford to get my MBA. This was another expected step in what I would need to reach the top level of command at the Federal Security Administration. To help determine the future course of The New World Order, I needed a high-level position and I needed to get there as fast as possible.

List in hand, I showed up for early registering for classes. Grad students get the first pick of classes. Even with this advantage, it can still get dicey. Class changes take place all the time. Many students had already registered for their classes before the doors even opened. The schedule I had my advisor make out may have to be changed. Sitting on the gym floor and looking through a schedule of classes booklet was a common situation.

The last class that I needed was already full. I could not at first figure out what to do. Then it hit me. The fear factor—use it. I got back in line and this time when the professor manning the table told me the class was full, I showed him my Federal Security Administration credentials and told him it was a matter of national security that I got in this class. I also gave him a very cold look. The professor turned a little pale. It was his class. He let me in.

The professor did manage a slight smile as he said, "Welcome to my class, Captain Andrews."

Housing was my next problem. The problem was there wasn't any housing left. I had arrived a week before the start of school and every decent place to live had been long taken. So for now, I was homeless. Well, there were some motels available that I could use as a temporary home. So, I moved into the motel that was close to Stanford.

The next day I had to check in with the local Order people. The Federal Security Administration office was in a federal building at 101 Market Street in San Francisco. I read up on this local branch and its personnel before my scheduled appointment. It was run by a woman officer, Major Evens.

After getting through security on the first floor of the massive office building that was the home of the federals that I was to be working with, I took the elevator to the third floor, room 323.

Major Evens seemed happy to see me. This was a good start for me, since I would be working in her office part-time for the next two years.

Major Evens started our conversation on a social note. "How are you doing with getting your needed grad classes?"

"I had some problems. I finally got the classes that I needed. But I still have a housing problem."

"I remember what that is like. But since you're a captain in the Federal Security Administration, it is an easy problem to solve."

"How, may I ask, do I solve this housing problem of mine?"

"Well, just buy a house, of course. I will give you a credit line to use and connect you with one of our contacts in the Palo Alto real estate market. You will have a house of your choice, completely furnished, within the week, and you of course will need transportation too."

She wasn't kidding. I had a furnished three-bedroom townhouse to call home and a new car four days later. The Order paid all the bills. All I had to do was put gas in the car.

After going over my duties in her office, which was mostly advising officials and using my psychic abilities, I was given a schedule (only ten hours a week) that fit well with my class schedule. I was starting to get the hang of my new position. The perks can be really interesting.

After moving into my new home, I took a walk through the Stanford campus. I wanted to find out the location of each of my classes and get a feel for the campus and what the social life was like. I found my classes without any real problems, but on the way back I came face to face with a new problem that had been developing: my cock problem. I had not exercised my cock (with another person) in the last two weeks. It was starting to get to me. I needed to hook up with some regular fucks, as I had at Harvard. I had the body, mind, and the pad to get all the pussy and boy ass that I needed. I just hadn't given any effort to solving this developing sexual problem of mine.

The next day, only three days before school started, I lucked out big time. Her name was Joan. She caught my eye as I passed several female students that were playing soccer on a playing field. I sat on a bench for two hours watching her play. She was strikingly beautiful. This woman of my dreams looked a lot like Nancy. She was about the same size and her tits stood straight out and defied gravity just like Nancy's. The only real difference was this girl had slightly olive-colored skin that turned me on to no end.

Every once in while she took a look in my direction and smiled. She knew that I was interested, and she seemed to like that fact. The next move would be hers, and it came in the form of a soccer ball. When the soccer game got close to the bench that I was sitting on, it happened. She made a sudden swift kick and the ball came flying straight at me. I caught it and I stood up.

As she approached me, I held the ball in my right hand and said, "Lose something?"

She just smiled and said, "My name is Joan."

I gave her the ball and said, "My name is William. You can call me Will if you want to."

"Do you come here often, Will?"

"No, I'm new on campus. I just got settled in. I'm still getting used to the campus and where my classes will be."

"Well, if you wait a little longer, my team will win this match and then I will give you a tour of the campus."

"It's a deal."

To cut to the chase, Joan gave me a two-hour tour of the campus, complete with campus history and the best places to eat. I could see from the start that knowing Joan was going to be a big asset in my studies at Stanford.

Joan was also working on an MBA degree. She was through with her first year's work, a fact that should help me since she had already covered the academic ground that I was just starting to work on.

Joan was also very high on the subject of being able to trust her friends. I sensed that she was a very honest and dependable individual and that I could be truthful with her. The old saying, that you cannot be really truthful to a woman because she will say that she has forgiven you but will later throw it back in your face, did not apply to Joan. In short, Joan, I found out later, did not think like the average woman. She thought more like a man. Frankly, this made my life easier. I've always hated not being fully truthful with a woman. Joan was a breath of fresh air.

It was a full month before I was able to get Joan into my bed. It was definitely worth the effort. Joan was a pure animal in bed. She was a young man's sex dream come true. She was the full package: a great mind in a fantastic body and great sex too. And the fact that I was bisexual did not bother her at all. So, naturally, I had to ask her to be my girlfriend.

Joan told me that she would be available only for the next year. She was mine until she graduated. This was okay with me. She was a great catch for a man like me. I told her that if only a year was available, I would be quite happy to make it a great year for the both of us.

Of course, for security reasons there are things that I could not discuss with Joan, but she understood this. So, over the first few months of our relationship Joan and I got to know each other better, in and out of bed. For me, a guy on a mission of sorts, she was a perfect mate.

I would see Joan three or four days a week. She had a great sense of humor and was one of the most affectionate people that I have ever met. I was completely content, and it was only to get better. The better was in two parts: she moved into my house, and we both decided to ask her gay brother, a freshman at Stanford, to move in with us. Joan and her brother Greg were very close. Greg was also a very good-looking, dark-blond young man of twenty years of age. Like Joan, Greg's skin was flawless and slightly tanned. Looking over his facial features, it was easy to see that he was related to Joan. As I turned my attention to the big bulge in his jeans, I could tell that he was also very well endowed and interested in me. Since Joan knew that I was bisexual, this arrangement provided some interesting possibilities.

Both Joan and Greg were, like me, trust-fund babies. Money was never an issue in our relationship. Money was spent freely, and no one kept records of who paid for what and who owed what to who.

The first time I met Joan's brother, we hit it off right away. Yes, I read his mind and he was available. Later, when I was on a date with Joan, we were walking home from the movies when she just suddenly said, "Hey, my brother is hot for your bod. If you want him, you can have him, as long as you do not neglect me."

The next time Joan was at the school library, Greg got royally fucked.

This was the best situation possible for a bisexual stud like me. I had the best of both worlds right in my own house. From that day on, it was like Harvard all over again. I was never sexually frustrated again that school year.

My job at the Order was as a psychic advisor the first six months. But nothing stayed the same. A mission was in the works, and I was chosen to be in on it. Major Evens introduced me to the team. They at first did not take to me.

One of the team members started to ask me multiple questions on different aspects of team procedure. I had studied the manual and knew it by heart. Finally, he got off the subject and just got to the point. "Captain Andrews, have you ever killed someone?" The fact that I looked so young and innocent was back causing me trouble again.

I just gave him a blank stare and said, "Yes, Captain Noel, I have killed thirteen people, some of them with a sword and some with my bare hands."

This seemed to impress him, especially after Major Evens confirmed that I was telling the truth. I was in and I intended to complete it.

The mission was in the Bronx part of New York City. The target was a street gang of mostly Puerto Ricans who were major suppliers of illegal drugs. The goal was simply to find a way to get them in the same building at the same time and then kill them. We were to make it look like an accident. People in the New York PD were in place to rubberstamp an accident report.

The gang, The Bronx Bloods, ruled a ten-square-block area of the south Bronx. Operating in the area was left up to the NYPD. At that point, our team would not go into the area under the gang's control; we would stand out too much. We would go in only when we were ready to send them all to the next world.

We had to figure out how to get them into just one building at the same time. The knock-out technology would be used in this exercise. The use of photos taken from a police helicopter, computer records, and interviews with the NYPD gang detail were our main sources of intelligence on the Lords of Blood.

After personally reviewing the gang's history and talking to some former and rival members, I got a good perspective on how the gang leadership thought. I and the team would have to figure out a way to get the gang leadership to assemble the gang members for the kill.

One member of the NYPD gang unit gave us the opening that we needed. It seemed that one member of the gang leadership (code name: Jesus) could be bought. We came to an agreement with the gang member that he would call a party at his house for gang members only. It was a reward party. Lots of liquor, coke, and good food would be present. Also, serious bonuses of cash would be given out. This wouldn't set off any alarms since the gang leader does this bonus party each year and it was time for another party.

To buy the loyalty of the gang leader, he was told that the whole event was to be a massive bust of the gang. For added insurance to ensure his help, he was informed that the country of Costa Rica had accepted him for citizenship. He would also be given a new identity and one million dollars to start a new life. At least that is what he was told. Officially, he would die in the house with his fellow gang members. Unofficially, he would die from a gunshot wound in the back of his head. His body would never be found.

The house in question was an old Victorian structure with two stories, five bedrooms, and a full cellar. The part that was interesting to me was the full cellar had a heating oil tank at one end, a big one. It was decided that the explosives would be put under the oil tank. C-45 would be used. It would leave no traces after use. The whole house would become a giant fireball. The knock-out device was to be used to knock out the people in the house and the guards that would be outside the house. Our team would then take the guards into the house before the blast set off the oil tank.

The job of setting up the charges was done by our team, at night, working out of a van that was painted to look like a New York Parks Department vehicle. As planned, the gang leader set up the party.

The party was already in high gear when we arrived at an empty building right across the street from the house. Two vans full of personnel were cruising around the area waiting for the word to come in and pick up the knocked-out guards and take them into the house.

The knock-out device was set up on the roof of the empty building across the street from the target house. With loud Latin music playing in our ears, we figured the area to be exposed to the technology and then pushed the button. It worked according to plan. The people inside the house and their guards outside dropped to the ground. Our two extra vans of personnel arrived in less than a minute. The guards were quickly taken into the house and dropped in different rooms. The whole house was silent except for the sound of Latin music playing on a boom box.

My part of the team piled into our van along with the high-tech equipment that we had just used to knock out the gang members. When our vans were outside the gang's turf, a helicopter flew over the area of the house and someone pushed a button to make the house blow up in one huge fireball. The job was done. Check off forty-two gang members.

The evening news went as expected. It was a terrible accident. "Stay tuned for more details as the story develops."

I slept well that night in a five-star New York City hotel, and I felt good about eliminating some more social scum that feed on decent people. At least that is what I told myself. Was I going over the edge? Was I becoming just as bad as the people I had helped to kill? Of course I was. In order to rid a city of sewer rats, you had to get down in the sewer. I knew that the only real differences between me and them were the reasons we killed. I prefer my reasons. I killed to save innocent lives and provide a crude form of justice for the victims of the scum that I have killed. Our so-called justice system had not provided such justice in this case.

I flew back to California on a private jet along with some other members of my team. Officially, all of us were working on an assignment in the federal office in San Francisco. We were never in New York City. Well, at least not during that time period.

When I was dropped off at my home I was eager to see Joan. That is, eager to see all of Joan. I was horny as hell. I found Joan in the kitchen wearing only a pair of red silk panties and one of my white T-shirts. Joan liked to wear the T-shirt that I slept in. It had my scent on it and it made her feel close to me when I was gone.

Without saying a word, I started to kiss the back of her neck as I ran my hands under the front of her T-shirt and started to massage her nipples. Joan started to softly moan as I worked my way up to lick and slightly bit her earlobes. In one fast move,

I lowered my hands and took off her T-shirt. I turned her around to face me and we began to passionately make out. Man, Joan had the hottest lips.

Joan had her back against the sink when I dropped to my knees and pulled her panties down. I buried my tongue deep into her snatch, which was warm, wet, and sweet. After only a few minutes, Joan had her first orgasm. This was to be the first of three intense orgasms that night. This was a great homecoming.

Joan was gone when I woke up the next morning. I had the day off from work and classes and I was still fucking horny. But as usual for my life in regard to sex, I lucked out. I could hear Greg getting out of the shower. When the bathroom door opened, Greg looked pleased when he saw me standing in front of him naked with a roaring hard-on. He just smiled and said, "Well, stud, want to take a wild ride?" One thing I can say about Greg is that he is a great fuck. Greg is what gays will call a power bottom. He loves to be fucked by a hung stud long and hard. In regard to fucking, he is very proactive. He does not just lie there. He moans loudly, at times he violently shakes, and in general puts on a great show. This is one way Greg is like his sister. Being a fantastic fuck must run in their family.

The next day I only had one class: ethics and management. I could only shake my head in amazement. How did a guy like me, doing the type of work that I do, get stuck taking a class on ethics? The only ethics my profession had was to do whatever I had to do to get the job done and not get caught. Well, as usual I could fake my way through this course, ace it, and later get some real use out of this class book. The idea of using it as a doorstop did come to mind.

The type of courses I needed were basic. It was a requirement of my first-year MBA program. The second year would be different because it was made up of electives. I could pick and choose what suited me. I sure wasn't going to get into any more ethics classes.

I could handle the coursework for my MBA program. It was hard work, but it was manageable. My talents as a psychic and my photographic memory helped cut down the amount of time I spent on mindless paperwork. Other grad students were not as blessed. Many cracked up, dropped out, or turned into different types of antisocial hermits.

Even with the hard coursework and the requirements of my job, I did manage a fairly active social life. Of course, Joan and Greg were my constant companions. We would go to different campus events together. I think I may have been the only grad student at Stanford who had both a girlfriend and a boyfriend. I'm not completely sure of that, but it could be true.

My best memories of Stanford involved my social life with my family, Joan and Greg. Just walking through the campus with them was a social event. They were both playful, creative, and very well educated. They kept me in good spirits my first year at Stanford, not to mention they took care of my cock problem.

One event we usually attended was Stanford football games. At the games that had chilly weather, I always wore my oversized Harvard football game coat. It was so big that I could get both me and Joan into it. This fact created a great opportunity for me to play with Joan. Joan knew this and she always wore gym sweat clothes.

Joan would sit in front of me, and I would wrap my big coat around her and zip it up. She would lean back against me and I would put my hands under her sweatshirt and cup her tits in my hands. It was a great way to keep my hands warm. If the game got a little boring, I could always start to play with Joan's nipples. Unlike most women, Joan was always ready to play.

If the game got more exciting and the fans were coming to life and not paying attention to us, I would put the fingers of my right hand in my mouth, get them good and wet, slide them into Joan's sweatpants, and start to finger-fuck her. At one game, our team made a big touchdown and the crowd went wild, and

Joan did too. She climaxed just as our team won the game. Nobody, except Greg, was even the wiser.

As my first year of grad school was coming to an end, I had to make some adjustments in my lifestyle again. Nothing ever stays the same in life, and my life was not an exception to the rule. Joan was graduating with her MBA, a fact that deeply depressed me. A new chapter in my life was opening up. The first chapter was Joan and the new chapter, it seemed, was to be called Greg. Joan was leaving, with part of my heart with her. I was later to find that she took more than a part.

On our last full day together, Joan, Greg, and I were walking across the campus, talking and joking mostly, when I grabbed Greg and asked Joan, "Joan, can I have your brother for my pet? He would make a good house pet."

Greg nodded.

Joan said, "Well, if you can train him, he's your property."

Greg then kissed me on the cheek and said, "Sir, I will be your property, if you will be my master."

Visions of my grandfather's two sex slaves came to mind. "Well, boy, I accept your offer to serve. This summer I will properly train my new pet boy."

Greg just smiled and said, "Yes, sir!" It was all in good humor, I thought at the time. But Greg was serious, and I quickly came to the conclusion that owning and training Greg would be a good learning experience for me and him.

Greg's summer training went very well. He was a natural. Greg seemed to love the idea of belonging to a good-looking, hung stud like me. The stricter I got with him, the more he seemed to enjoy serving me. This whole scene was new to me—being a master and owning someone—so I read books on the subject and asked some leather people, both gay and straight, for pointers. By the end of the summer, I was the owner of one well-disciplined and trained man slave, or naked houseboy.

Not that I had any problems with enslaving a hot young man, or woman for that matter. Greg was an extremely good-looking, blond, hung, muscular, pretty boy. He was a master's dream come true. After talking to about a dozen gay leather masters and researching an equal number of S&M books. Pretty, blond men like Greg could usually be found dancing their asses off in gay bars and playing pretty me games. I found that the S&M community considered such young men impossible to collar and train. This made Greg a very special and rare property.

Greg not only kept care of my needs, he also managed my household. I didn't completely give up women, of course. I fucked a dozen pretty women that year without any problems with Greg. I had trained Greg to follow my orders to the letter. I had developed such strict control of him that I actually ordered Greg to fuck three of said women and he performed well. After all, you do not need to be totally straight to enjoy fucking a hot chick.

I quickly got used to being a master. Imagine having a hot-looking roommate, male or female, that followed your orders to the letter. One that did his housework in the nude and was available to service your cock anytime you were in the mood. I was now, truly, the master of my house.

The second year of my MBA program was made up of elective classes. This is the part of the MBA program in which a grad student customizes his MBA to suit his academic and professional needs. I chose electives mostly from the leadership section of the program. My goal was to lead, not follow. I did not intend to be a small part in a big machine. I wanted to control the machine. Rising to a top leadership post in the Order was my goal.

When the end of my second year was fast approaching, Greg laid a bombshell on me. His sister Joan had given birth to twin boys. The babies, of course, were mine. I was the father. At first, I couldn't figure out why Joan did not tell me that she was expecting. But it seemed she did not know she was going to be a mother when she graduated. Joan was a very independent woman who didn't really believe in getting married. She wanted kids, but not a husband in her life, so she saw no need to tell me. Greg found out about the twins from a friend.

Both I and Greg saw the twins for the first time the next week. Joan drove up from her home in Los Angeles. They were the cutest little guys. Their names were William and Josh. Joan said she wanted me to be part of the boys' lives, but she did not need any financial support. What could I do except take on the role of a drop-in father? Was the addition of two sons to my life going be a plus or a minus? In my line of work, only time would tell.

Chapter 11: My Slave

Leaving Stanford and Greg behind was depressing in a way. Greg had one more year of Stanford and then grad school to complete. He could not follow me around to whatever assignments I would now be given. I asked if he wanted me to find him a new master. I had developed some solid contacts in the leather community in San Francisco, and I had met two good-looking young men that could be good prospects. But Greg turned down the offer. Serving me had been the experience of his dreams, and he was going back to being just a student for the next few years. He did add, with a smile, that when he got his MBA that he could be available, if I were still interested in owning a boy again.

After visiting the general and checking up on things in person rather than by e-mail, I decided to visit my aging grandfather in Saudi Arabia. My grandfather was getting on in years and I thought best that I should see him while he was still in good health.

The long flight from California to Cairo was an ordeal for me. I do not care for plane trips of over six hours. Long plane flights leave me extremely tired. My grandfather knew of my dislike of such flights, and he had arranged for me to stay at a five-star hotel in Cairo for two nights. I badly needed the rest and in two days was refreshed and on my grandfather's private jet to his palace in Riyadh.

Riyadh is the capital of Saudi Arabia. It is a former walled, desert town that has grown into a modern city. I visited Riyadh five different times as a teenager in order to spend time with my grandfather. These boyhood visits to Riyadh were a great way to learn about another culture. The cultural stuff, over time, just seemed to fade into my distant memory. The parts that stayed with me were the parts that affected my daily life, such as don't drive a car in downtown Riyadh; it is an open invitation to get into a traffic accident. Within a month of daily driving, you are almost certain to get hit. And I had learned to stay at home during dust storms. When a big dust storms hits Riyadh, you wouldn't be able to see ten yards in front of yourself.

My grandfather's palace was a modern structure of several hundred rooms with marbled hallways and every modern accessory. My grandfather was in such good spirits and health when he met me at the door to his home. I was glad to see the two slave boys, Sabao and Muhammad, standing in the reception line. They both seemed to be really glad to see me again. I had heard the usual stories about sex slaves being mistreated, sold, or even being killed by their Saudi masters. My grandfather had discussed the subject with me on one of my past visits, and he always said that such horrible practices had been stopped by the present king in the 2020s.

Sabao and Muhammad were put in charge of the baggage. They were both assigned to me, and they quickly took my bags up to the guestroom that I always used when I visited my grandfather.

Since my grandfather mentioned that he wanted to talk to me in his office, I followed him to the big guesthouse behind the palace. His guesthouse was bigger and grander than my townhouse at Stanford. My grandfather enjoyed going over the details of my stay a Stanford. He was especially interested in Joan, Greg, and the twins.

"It is good you had such a woman in your life, and I am very happy to hear that I have more great-grandchildren. I will set up a family trust for both of the boys. You must send me photos of them."

"Yes, Grandfather."

"And what is this you said about training a personal slave? If you wanted a slave, I could have bought you one. In fact, a man that I deal with has a property for sale that would be perfect for you. He is an American much like your Greg, a very beautiful, blond, young man. He was enslaved at age fourteen, with the consent of his uncle, who was his guardian at the time. He is now twenty-seven years of age. But due to the youth drugs that are available today, he looks more like he is seventeen or eighteen. He has accepted his fate as a slave, and he is very content in serving his master. You must look at him, William."

"Yes, Grandfather. If you like, I will look him over. It will be an interesting experience to visit a modern slave dealer and to look over his stock."

"Then the matter is settled. I will make arrangements for your visit as soon as possible. This slave is due to be put up for sale in three days. I will get you an appointment before then."

After my conference with my grandfather, I decided I could use a shower and a good massage, etc. I had told the house manager to have the boys, as I called them, take my bags up to my room and unpack them. They were then to wait in my room until I felt a need of their services.

When I walked into my bedroom suite, I was pleased with what I found. Both boys were naked and kneeling on the floor. I ordered them to stand up. Both of them were sporting roaring hard-ons. It was apparent that they both were really eager to please me, which I had dreamed about for the last two years.

"Well, boys, it is time to inspect each of you again to see if there have been any changes that I will disapprove of."

I proceeded to physically inspect every inch of their naked, shaved bodies. The whole time, I could see that both of them were smiling. They were in better shape than during my last visit. It seemed the house manager had followed my advice and put the boys on an exercise schedule.

"Sabao, get my shower ready."

"Yes sir!"

"Muhammad, set up the massage table."

"Yes sir!"

As I got undressed in front of the full-body mirrors, I noticed that both boys were watching my little strip show with great interest.

After I took a quick shower, the boys gave me a great, full-body massage. I had waited two years to get another massage by these two talented slaves, and it was worth it. After a second brief shower to wash off the massage oil, I had the boys towel-dry my naked body.

After sleeping for several hours with the two slaves, I woke up with my cock at attention and an overpowering urge to fuck. An hour and a half later, I had finished power-fucking both of the slaves. I was very pleased with their performance.

A representative of the slave dealer arrived early the next day. I met him in the conference room downstairs. He handed me a photo album of the slave in question. I asked him to please be seated. I could see by the expression on his face that he was eager to make a sale—a good sign, if you are a buyer.

The first three pages were face shots of the slave. He was, as grandfather had said, a very beautiful young man. I was surprised to see that the remaining photos were full nudes, since the Saudis are uptight about nudity. But of course, I had forgotten that Saudis do not consider slaves to be fully human. The young slave that I was reviewing was, by Saudi standards, not a man. Saudis view slaves as nothing more than subhuman livestock.

I had expected the slave to have a swimmer's build, much like Sabao and Muhammad. Instead, he was very well developed and defined. This slave had spent some serious time in the gym. He was well hung (about eight inches) with a beautiful round ass that Americans would describe as a bubble butt. His body was completely smooth—no body hair—and last, but not least, the end of his cock had been ringed. This slave was developed as if he had had an American master. He reminded me of Greg. The combination of a gym-toned male body, with smooth, healthy-looking skin has always been a big sexual turn-on for me.

I looked up at the dealer's representative and said, "Tell me the history of this property."

I said property because in the eyes of this man, that is all that he was.

"Mr. Andrews, this property was acquired when he was fourteen years old. He was sold into slavery by his uncle, his guardian at the time, since both his parents are dead. Both the slave and his uncle are Americans by birth."

At this point, I held up my hand as a gesture to stop talking. "Why was he sold into slavery?"

"It was because the uncle knew he was, as you Americans say, gay, and the uncle needed money at the time."

"Proceed with your presentation, sir."

"My employer, who is the dealer who is presently handling his current sale, sent him to the best slave trainer in Saudi Arabia. The man employs the most up-to-date technical methods. He not only trains the slave's body, but his mind as well. The end result, you will see, speaks for the effectiveness of his methods.

The slave has completely accepted his position in life. He is a slave, and that is Allah's will."

"What is his ownership history?"

"He has been owned by two previous masters. Both masters thought very highly of his abilities and talent. He has been intensively educated. The boy can speak three languages: English, Arabic, and French. He has been taught the most modern methods of how to please his master, both sexually and socially. He is extremely well disciplined. He can be termed to be the perfect man servant."

"You said that this slave has had two masters. Tell me about them."

"He was sold to his first master when he was fifteen years old. A rich businessman bought him in a private sale to please his two teenage sons. The sons were very strict masters and made good use of him, both for themselves and their close friends. The slave learned a lot about serving a master from these teenage boys. When the businessman's sons went away to college in America, the slave was sold to his second master."

"Now tell me about the second master."

"He was an Arab American who lived in and did extensive business in our country. He is related to the House of Saud. He built up the slave's body and had him permanently shaved and ringed. He also bought me in a private sale."

I raised my hand to stop again. "You used the past tense word was to describe his second master. Is his second master dead?"

"Yes, sir. He died in a plane crash in Europe a few weeks ago. His estate is the seller of the slave property in question. His second master was very pleased with this slave. If he were still alive today, I have no doubt that this slave would not be for sale at any price."

"I have one big concern about this slave, and it concerns trust. Can I trust this slave to remain loyal to me if I take him out of Saudi Arabia?"

"All I can say is that one reason his second master was so pleased with him is that he could travel the world with him and he would not have to worry about him running away. His former master spent half of each year outside our country, with this slave, during the nine years that he owned him, and he never had to worry about his loyalty. This slave worshiped his second master. He knows that he is a slave and that is his fate in life.

"Sir, in regard to being able to trust this slave outside our country, my employer has taken some measures to ensure a higher level of security with the slave properties that he is currently offering for sale. The boy in question has been chipped. He has had a computer chip implanted under his skin, so his master may know his location at any time."

"You can tell your employer that I will come to visit his establishment at 1:00 p.m. tomorrow to review and make a decision on this property. Does that sound reasonable to you?"

"Yes, sir. My employer will be happy to welcome you to his establishment."

The slave was the property of a dealer who had his establishment outside Riyadh, at a small oasis. The place was a guarded, walled compound. My driver made the arrangements to enter the fortress-like structure. As my car pulled up to the front entrance, a tall black man opened the door and in Arabic welcomed me to his master's home.

I was glad to get inside the air-conditioned main building because the midmorning sun was getting unbearable. It must have been at least one hundred thirty degrees outside.

The main entrance was like walking into an old Arabian palace. The floor and all the walls were tiled. A fountain sat in the center of the room. The climate of the room was very cool, which was a big contrast to the terrible heat outside.

I was greeted by an old Saudi gentleman. He introduced himself, in Arabic, as Muhammad Abdula. He was the slave dealer that I had come to see. After a little social conversation, I was shown into an upstairs bedroom and asked to sit down. The slave would be brought to me for inspection and use.

After I sat down in an overstuffed chair, I took a mental inventory of the interesting items that the room contained. In the middle of the room was an elevated, round platform. This is what is termed a slave block. In the back of the room was a king-sized bed, with only a sheet on it. On one wall hung several S&M play toys: collars, handcuffs, and several types of whips. I recognized one of the whips as a cat-o'-nine-tails.

This room was designed not only to physically review a slave, but also to test his or her talents. It didn't matter whether a master was in the market to buy a sex slave, a house servant, a work slave, or a torture slave—the means to inspect and test a slave's talents were all available in this room. I looked at the slave block in the middle of the room and wondered how many slaves had stood on that block. I wondered what fate had in store for them. How many of them ended up brutalized, beaten, starved, tortured, and murdered at an early age? How many human bones bleaching in the Saudi Arabian desert belonged to slaves that once stood on this slave block? The whole idea of what has happened to said former slaves started to get to me. Maybe I should buy this slave for his own health and safety. How long could even a good-looking slave last until some crazed master decided to have him thrown out of a helicopter naked while it was flying over the desert at three thousand feet? The more that I stared at the block, the more of a bleeding heart I became.

My morbid chain of thoughts was broken by the arrival of the slave that I was interested in buying. It was a good beginning in that the slave was not bound in any way. He was naked and he followed his master into the room, with his head bowed, in a proper, submissive fashion.

The slave was ordered to stand on the slave block. He obeyed and showed no emotions. He stood on the block, head bowed and his hands behind his back. This boy, as I was told, was well trained.

"Mr. Andrews, we will now leave you with this slave for as long as you need for you evaluation. A guard will be posted outside the door. When you are done, please tell the guard. If you are interested in purchasing this slave, let me know. Your grandfather has already agreed to the price. He is yours if you want him. Do you have any questions, sir?"

"No, I will let you know my decision."

After that, I was left alone in the room with the slave. I decided to mentally test him. For the next fifteen minutes, I just sat in that overstuffed chair and stared at him. The whole time, the only movement on his part that I could notice was his breathing. This was one well-disciplined slave. I was starting to be impressed.

I got up and started to walk around the slave block, visually inspecting every inch of the slave's naked and permanently shaved body. His skin was flawless—no pimples, scars, wounds, or burn marks. This boy had been a slave for twelve years and his body showed no signs of being physically abused.

I now started with my physical inspection. I ran my hands over his muscular legs. His only reaction was that his cock got rock hard. He was horny, and I intended to make use of that fact. With his cock rock hard and throbbing, I started to lightly massage his firm, hairless balls. His body began to mildly shake. He was horned up all right. I then ordered him to stand on the floor.

He said, "Yes, sir!" and stepped off the block.

I now continued my inspection of his chest, back, arms, neck, cock, which was ringed, ass, and even his teeth. I then stood behind him, wet my fingers, and started to play with his nipples. He moaned and started to squirm. His cock throbbed up and down. To the feel of my fingers massaging his nipples, I added kissing and licking his neck and lightly biting his earlobes. He started to moan louder and louder. When I thought he was close to climax, I backed off until his breathing stabilized again. Still he did not smile.

It was time to change my game. With the slave standing on the floor with his cock still hard and throbbing, I walked over to the chair and began to strip. This should be quite a show for this slave. He was going to see his new master naked for the first time. Maybe this time he would smile. But one thing I was sure of was that the person or persons that were watching this performance from hidden security cameras were going to get an eye full. This fact was the real reason that this slave had not reacted so far; he knew they were watching his performance.

I now sat down naked in the overstuffed chair. I ordered the slave to get on his knees. He quickly dropped to his knees in front of me with his head still bowed and his hands behind his back.

"Now, slave, I want you to lick my feet and suck on my toes."

"Yes sir!"

The boy had talent all right. He did a great job of massaging my feet with his tongue. My cock got rock hard, which was quite a feat, considering last night I had gone several rounds with my grandfather's pleasure slaves.

I told him to stop and to sit up with his hands on his knees. I then stood in front of him and ordered him to tilt his head back and open his mouth. He did as ordered. I stepped forward and put my balls into his mouth, with my big hard cock covering the middle of his face. At this point, he could see my whole naked body and he actually showed a slight smile as his eyes got bigger. I flipped my big cock against his face several times before I said, "Now, slave, lick my balls." His warm, wet tongue went to work and he soon had my balls dripping wet with his saliva.

I said to him, "Suck my cock, slave."

At this point, he put on a great performance. The boy had no gag reflex. He could swallow most of my big cock. I was soon moaning. Best of all, the boy seemed to really enjoy what he was doing. He had a real hungry animalistic nature to his cock-sucking method. He started to actually smile. The boy was really into what he was doing, a good sign.

After about ten minutes of his expert methodology, I shot a big load down his eager throat. He then proceeded to lick my cock clean and then he said, "Thank you, sir!"

I did not have to scan his mind to know that he really meant it.

But I wanted more. I grabbed the slave by the hair on the of his head, walked him over to the bed, and bent him over. A jar of lube was on the nightstand. I greased up, put some lube on his asshole, and slid my cock in. With each stroke, I moved deeper and deeper into his ass, until he was taking all of me and acting like he was really enjoying this fucking. He moaned and squirmed more and more as I started to power-fuck him. In only a few minutes, I had him ready to climb the walls. I then turned him over and put his legs on my shoulders and I began to shove it to him. Between short sessions of power-fucking, I would slow down, bend over, and make out with him. He had very sweet and moist lips. By the time I ordered him to cum without touching himself, he was well primed and smiling. When he shot his big load all over his torso, he was smiling ear to ear. I had in thirty minutes accomplished what I wanted to. I was not just buying him as my slave; he wanted me to be his next master. This was a good beginning to a new chapter in my life.

My limp cock slid out of his ass and I lifted the slave to his feet. I put my hand on the back of his neck and led him into the bathroom. After cleaning up, I told him to give me a massage on the bed.

He smiled and said, "Yes, sir, my pleasure, sir!"

That up to now was the most I had heard him say. He mounted my naked ass and began to lovingly massage my back.

The boy was an expert at giving a deep tissue massage. My body relaxed and a lot of tension disappeared. What made it even better was that he would lean down, every so often, and whisper into my ear. "Please, sir, buy me, please. I will do anything to have you as my master." I can read minds, and he was completely truthful.

When the slave was through with my full-body massage, we both jumped into the shower. The boy was very attentive. He soaped down my body, massaging each muscle as he worked his way down my naked body until he was washing my feet. This boy was working hard to please me.

After our shower, the boy went to work toweling off my body. When he was done, he dropped to his knees and asked, "Sir! Is there anything more you want me to do for you?" The slave dealer in charge of selling this slave was right when he referred to him as the perfect manservant.

I told the slave to follow me into the bedroom. I ordered him to get on his knees in front of the chair. After putting on my boxer shorts, I sat down in the chair in front of him. It was time to ask him some personal questions. Since he may become my property, I wished to know more about his background.

"Boy!"

"Yes sir!"

"I am going to review your past history. I want you to fill the gaps. Your file says that your uncle sold you into slavery when you were fourteen years old. Explain what happened."

"Sir, what the file says is true. My uncle was not happy with me. My parents had been killed in a plane crash in North Carolina, and he was the only relative available to take me in. My uncle was an engineer for oil companies, and he lived and worked in this country. He was a very conservative Christian and hated homosexuals. When he found out that I was gay, he flew into a rage. He gave me two choices: either he would sell me into slavery, or he would strip me naked, tie my hands behind my back, throw me into the trunk of his car, and drive far out into the desert. He would then take me out into the sand dunes and put a bullet in the back of my head. I knew my uncle, and he was deadly serious. The choice was easy. Selling me into slavery was his way of sending me to hell.

"My uncle took me down to the slave dealer, the same dealer who is currently selling me now. My uncle warned me again of what would happen to me if I fucked up this sale. I was not to crying, complaining, or begging. I was ordered to stand naked with my hands behind my back on the slave block in this very same room. The dealer inspected my naked body. He gave me a brutal physical and sexual exam. He grabbed and squeezed my nuts, twisted my nipples, fondled me, shoved his greased fingers and hand up my ass, and severely whipped me. The slave dealer then had one of the guards whip out his cock and he ordered me to suck it. I tried to give the guard the best blowjob that I could. After about five minutes of pleasing the guard, he backed off, stripped, threw me on the bed, and started to fuck me. The fact that my cock got hard and I did not cry or complain in any way the whole time seemed to greatly impress the slave dealer.

"He seemed pleased with my performance and also with the fact that I was a very pretty boy with beautiful skin, a nice ass, and a big cock. I believe he saw me as a good commercial property, if trained properly. I don't know the price that I was sold for; it was not mentioned. I just know that when my uncle finished signing papers that enslaved me, he left with a smile on his face. So, I suspect that he got a good price for me.

"I was then put into a yearlong slave-training program. It is during this training that I came to realize that to be a slave suited me. Later I came to believe that I was, as my trainer had said, born to be a slave. Fate had led me to my enslavement."

"Tell me your birth name, place of birth, and some facts about your childhood and schooling," I said.

"Sir, my birth name is Jimmy Rose. I was born and raised in Wellington, North Carolina. I attended local school until the age of fourteen. My school grades were straight A's. School was easy for me. Since then I have been educated by my masters and some tutors. I can speak three languages: Arabic, English, and French."

"Boy, what type of master would you like to have?"

"Sir, as a slave I am trained to serve any master. I have no standards for a master."

"Boy, what training and talents do you bring to your new master?"

"Sir, I have been extensively trained to please a man sexually. I can swallow a soft twelve-inch cock. I have no gag reflex. My slave ass has three times the anal tissue of a regular person. I am designed and trained to please a master. I am trained to the whip and can take a severe whipping if my master finds a need or reason to punish me. I am well disciplined. If my master does not need me, I can kneel and remain mute for hours at a time. I have also been trained to manage a household and I have completed classes to be a chef. I am an excellent cook. I have also graduated from a british butler school and I have been trained to be an excellent masseur. Sir, do you wish to know more about me?"

"Boy, you mentioned that you have three times the anal tissue of a regular person, explain that statement."

"Sir, part of the slave training program was taking shots in the anus to cause the growth of more anal tissue. I believe stem cells were involved. The result is that more tissue grew and now I am better able to please my master."

"Yes, slave, you are one fantastic fuck." This answer also explains why my grandfather's slaves are great fucks. They probably had the same treatments.

"Boy, tell me about your last two masters."

"Sir, my first master was a very wealthy French Muslim businessman. He bought me to entertain himself and to service his two teenage sons. My master and his sons taught me a lot about pleasing most any man and how to be a well-disciplined slave. My master told me that he bought me in a private sale to avoid having me put on the general market.

"My second master was a rich American businessman. He was a close business associate of my first master. Again I was sold in a private sale, not a public one. My second master was about forty years old when he bought me. He taught how to cook and he sent me to chef's school. My master also had tutors teach me the art of massage, and one summer, while we were in London, he sent me to butler's school.

"My second master worked hard with me in his gym and began to remold my body into what you see today. My master also had my body shaved and my cock ringed. He said it made me look like an American slave. My late master took me with him on trips to over thirty countries. He taught me two new languages, Arabic and French. I worshiped my second master. Do you wish to know more, sir?"

"No, that is enough. You have impressed me, slave, and I wish to find out more about you. But I will need several years to do that. So I will buy you, boy."

"Thank you, sir. I will never disappoint you. I will work hard to please you."

I was very impressed by the slave's answers. His answers were will organized. His formal education had ended when he was only fourteen years old, but he was an educated person. He really impressed me. Physically he was perfect, sexually he was extremely talented and experienced, and mentally he was far more intelligent than I had expected him to be. This slave was really too good to be true, and it was only going better. Also, I couldn't help but think that some guardian spirit was looking after this boy. He had been sold twice by a Saudi slave dealer in private sales. If he had be sold as a boy of fifteen years in a public sale, an abusive, child-loving Saudi prince would have bought him and he would have been used up and disposed of in the desert years ago. This boy was one lucky slave. He had been lucky enough to avoid a public sale three times now. He may have avoided an early and brutal death.

The details had been worked out by my grandfather. I never knew the price he paid for my new slave. He was mine and he was devoted to serving me. That is all that mattered to me. I was given the slave's file and his American passport. I was driven back to my grandfather's palace with my new property kneeling on the floor, with his head in my lap. I had been given a handheld device to track the chip that was implanted in my new property. The device showed the right location, the middle of Riyadh, Saudi Arabia. Hopefully, I would not have much use for the device.

As my driver drove through the streets of Riyadh, I looked through my slave's file. It was arranged according to time. The first few papers were the slave contract that I had just signed. It listed me as the boy's third master. The next section concerned the sale of this slave by his uncle, Earl T. Rose (that SOB had sold his fourteen-year-old nephew for just thirty thousand dollars). The file contained nude photos of the boy. Jimmy, according to his file photos, was a very pretty boy. I could see why a Saudi slave dealer would buy him. With the right training,

Jimmy could be sold to a wealthy child-loving Saudi for a large sum.

After one year of training, the then fifteen-year-old boy was sold to his first master, Mr. Pierre Beaumont, for the sum of two hundred fifty thousand dollars, and four years later the then nineteen-year-old slave was sold to his second master, Mr. Martin Reese, for the sum of three hundred fifty thousand dollars.

The rest of the file also had nude pictures of the slave each time he was sold. It also listed the medical changes: the anus shots to grow more tissue and the new youth drugs that caused a person to age only one year for each five years of life. This explained why my slave, who was twenty-seven years old and had been enslaved for thirteen years, still looked like a teenager.

This boy was amazing. How he managed to exist in Saudi society as a slave and not end up being owned by an abusive master was hard to figure. Why he was still alive was the hard question to answer. I know one thing for sure: this boy had someone looking after him.

Nothing in the file would give me a reason why Jimmy had become such a devoted slave. The only reference was a section titled "Mind Changes," followed by the time it took and what it cost. My American-born and raised mind could not fully understand how this was done. But remembering how well trained my grandfather's pleasure slaves were, it seemed someone in the slave-training business had a secret. This was something that I needed to look into at a later date.

Most people born and raised in the American culture cannot understand how a slave can be happy and content. Even if you quote history books for examples of happy slaves, they won't change their views. Freedom is everything to them. Funny, as a member of The New World Order I know how stupid that idea is. Americans have never really been free. There have always been forces controlling us and telling us what to think and do. Even our presidents are not really elected by us. The powers behind the curtain pick the person that we the people will elect. As FDR stated, "Presidents are not elected, they are selected." The big banking interests of America picked FDR to be president because he would bring big government, and big government means big taxes and big profits.

Slavery did not end with the American Civil War. Only one form of involuntary slavery was ended. Does a prisoner in a country or state prison thinks that he is free? A prisoner is just as much a slave as any slave in the old South. How about the term wage slave? Does it strike a nerve? Most working people are no more than wage slaves. They survive from check to check. Do such people really have an employer, or a master? What about the US military? Is it a form of slavery? Just ask a person that was drafted into the military. Both the state prison systems of America and the US military can produce paperwork that says that a person belongs to them for a certain amount of time. Does that sound like slavery? Voluntary slavery and involuntary slavery are still very much with us; they just go by different names today.

It took me a while to figure out Jimmy's attitude. Shouldn't he fight to be a free man? But in the end, the only facts that matter are that he was happy and content with his station in life. One can look at it his way: he did not have to worry about making a living, having a career, paying taxes, serving on a jury, etc. His master, who he was devoted to, took care of all his needs.

Sabao and Muhammad did not seem to be pleased that I had bought my own slave boy. It was like I was cheating on them or something. But after I gave them a chance to play with my new boy for a night, they forgave me.

The flight back to California was much easier than flying in a commercial jet. My grandfather let me use his private jet. Most of the flight I spent sleeping and bonding with my new play toy.

CHAPTER 12: CHANGE

———————— 🗡 ————————

Since I was now a graduate of Stanford's grad school, my rank was raised to major and I was given a new assignment. Because of my education and my ability to predict markets, I was transferred to Chicago. The Federal Security people wanted more accurate projects on commodity prices. Control of the world's commodities was a goal of The New World Order.

The Order bought me an old two-story, four bedroom, three-bathroom house, in the Lake Shore part of Chicago. My boy and I moved in the same day that we arrived. The federals also completely furnished the place and equipped the place with the most up-to-date electronics. One room in the basement, a place I called my cave, had a computer system that was top secret. It was a secure facility. In short, anyone that went in there better be me. The room and the tech were married to my body, so to speak. My boy was forbidden to go down to this room. He knew he was not to mess with what was in that room.

Did the federals like the idea of me owning a slave? Well, they never asked me, and I did not tell them. My boy was listed as my houseboy. No one ever asked me to explain how I had such a pretty and talented person managing my house, when I did not seem to pay him anything. Frankly, I doubt that any of them would care, considering all the shit that they were involved in. Since my boy was part of my household, he was listed as my house boy, and he was covered by my agency health insurance.

My job was to work with a team of commodity professionals to basically punish the Chinese. China was at the time a pain in the side to The New World Order. They did not like the idea of having Western banking interests control their country's economy. The New World Order could not allow China to remain fully independent. The Order wanted China to come into the fold, or to be busted up into several smaller and easier to manage pieces. The plan was to control the flow of raw commodities to China and thereby gain tremendous influence on its economy and its political system.

Contrary to public opinion, China was not a stable country. The population was mostly young people who wanted the same standard of living that the West had. The social pressures in China were heading in the direction of causing the country to fragment into several different countries. The New World Order wanted to help this process along. A broken China would be easier to manage than a united country.

My basic job was to find the time periods in which different key commodities could be shot up and down in a drastic fashion. If I found that a big up move was due in wheat, my team could cause the price to rise even higher and that would drain China's foreign currency reserves. This would cause China to be less and less independent and an easy mark for the Order.

This project would take years to accomplish. We all knew that our organization could not steal a nation's treasury all at once; it had to be done slowly in order to cover our tracks. I knew that this assignment was good for a few years at best, so I already had my uncle, the general, looking for my next assignment that would take me up the ladder of power within the Order.

Both I and my boy loved my new house. He was a real homebody. Jimmy was not very social. He knew that people would not understand his choices in life, so he did not socialize much. He would not leave the house without me even to shop for supplies. In my opinion, the good part was that when I was home, my boy was almost always available to me.

My boy craved strict discipline. He was owned property and liked to be treated as such. To follow his master's orders was a pleasure to him. It made him feel wanted and needed. When I was home, half the time my boy was kneeling naked on the floor awaiting his next order. Sometimes I think that owning my slave was like having a puppy that needed constant attention. I quickly got used to managing my boy. Considering his contributions to my life, taking the time to manage him was a small problem to deal with.

Most of my daily work I could do in my cave. My job only required me to go downtown when I needed to converse with my team members and plot our next moves. So far, we had been very successful. We had cost the Chinese several hundred billion world dollars. Luckily for us, we had avoided detection by the Chinese. How do I know this? Well, my job put me in contact with many members of the Chinese staff in Chicago. Yes, I read their minds and vibes.

Since my team only advised others to make trades, they, not us, were on the firing line. If the Chinese got really pissed off, they, not my team, would take the hit. When you were involved with stealing a ton of a nation's treasury, things could go down the toilet rather fast. I operated behind the scenes as much as possible. I did not wish to put a target on my back.

As a cover for our operation, we were organized as a private commodity fund. We were a closed, not public fund. During the years we were in business, our firm had a financially successful record. Yes, we frustrated the hell out of many very wealthy people. They could not invest in our private fund.

Chicago can be a great place to live, except during a bad winter. My first year in Chicago saw the city experience a severe winter. I tried to work at home as much as possible. When I had to work with my team, they either came to my house, or our downtown office would send a car to pick me up. Frankly, I did not care for snow. I am more of a beach person. My boy, on the other hand, just loved it. After so much time living in a country like Saudi Arabia, he loved to play in the snow. If I let him, he would go into the backyard and jump in the mounds of snow and roll in the nude. I let him do this at times as a reward. It was fun to watch.

I had little experience in owning and managing a real slave when my grandfather gave me my boy. There was Greg of course. But Greg was more of a daddy's boy than a slave. Slaves take more time to manage. Since my slave liked strict discipline, I bought a book on how to train and discipline a dog. Yes, a dog. It worked out very well. When my boy was not pleasing me, or following an order that I gave him, he was kneeling on the floor. My boy had gotten used to simple dog-training commands like "Boy, come here," "Good boy," and "Kneel, boy," which was the same as saying, "Sit." This is what my boy as used to, and he seemed to like it. He smiled and seemed quite happy when I ran his life.

My team was made up of only five people: three men and two women. Brad was the oldest member. He was fifty-two years old and a veteran of the pits, as he would say. Brad knew commodities, a game that he loved. He had gotten very rich working commodities. Brad, it was said, was worth several hundred million dollars. He was a graduate of Northwestern University and the University of Chicago. Yes, he was a local boy.

Susan was a woman of about thirty. She wouldn't tell us her real age, which meant she was older than we thought she was. She was also a commodities expert and, like me, a graduate of Harvard.

Kevin was a veteran of the spy wars. He was ex-CIA. He worked with intelligence agencies and he kept us informed about what was going on behind the scenes. He was involved in the type of stuff that never got close to being printed or broadcast in the American media. Graduated from what? Kevin's whole background was classified.

The last team member was Jane. She was forty-eight years old and a pits veteran. Jane knew commodity cycles, and she could estimate crop and herd production down to the last hog or bushel. She was quite accurate.

With my team's experience in the commodity markets and my psychic abilities, we never lost money on a trade.

Together, we caused some of the biggest up moves in commodities. Well, when you had my team, my talents, and a shit pile of money, you were a major player. The best part of my job was that I and my team members could trade in the commodities that we targeted. Yes, we all made a pile of cash in the commodity options markets, not that any of us needed the money since we were all very wealthy before we joined the Order.

My life was very simple at this time. My work did not take up much of my life. So my social life improved. My social life was centered in two areas: my house and boy, and getting to know the wealthy and powerful people of Chicago.

My boy managed my house and part of my sexual needs. Yes, I still fucked pussy. I had hooked up with three hot chicks so far in Chicago. My boy was a good companion. We went to a gym nearby and to local restaurants. The gym was 50 percent gay male. We attracted a lot of attention, and we made several good friends. One game that we liked to play at the gym after we worked out was when we headed for the shower. Seeing me and my boy in the buff greatly upped our popularity. I attracted a lot of envy and attention in the nude, but my boy attracted attention and questions that led to gossip. My boy's body was hairless and his cock was ringed. When I gave him an order he said, "Yes sir." This, coupled with the fact that my boy would not talk to anyone without my permission, added a little mystery to us. I think the gay guys at the gym had figured out what the scene was—I got some really interesting offers from good-looking guys at the gym.

Sometimes when we went to the gym, I liked to play head games with the members of the gym. One of them I called my steam room game. The game was a tease. After taking a shower, my boy would follow me into the steam room. Usually, several gay guys and some straights from the shower and the locker room followed us. I picked a spot away from anyone in the room. I sat down and said, "Boy, kneel and put your head on my lap."

He would say, "Yes, sir."

My boy would put his towel on the floor in front of me, get on his knees, and put his arms around my waist with his head on my naked crotch. At times, to keep people's attention fixed on us, I would massage my boy's wet back and slap his bare ass. The show was simple, and we attracted a lot of attention from the people in the steam room. No one complained.

The gay gym scene was not the only strange game in town. Some of the parties that I got invited to could get dicey. One that is fixed in my memory was the wrestling club event. A male friend of mine, Richard Westly from my Harvard days, took me to a wrestling club. Fight club would be a more accurate term for this event. I suspected that I was in for a wild ride when my friend told me to wear gym shoes and sweats. He knew that I had been an all-state wrestling champ in high school and that I was extremely strong. I had no idea what type of game Rick was running. No, I did not try to read his mind. I figured it would be more interesting to let the game unfold in a natural way this time.

The event was held in an old warehouse close to Lake Michigan. The crowd was a cross section of young people and a few old people. Just after we got through the security people, Rick started to introduce me to his friends, including one anti-social dude with an attitude problem. I scanned him when Rick introduced me to him and his really smoking hot lady, Linda. His name was Ben, and he was the top dog at this event. I also found that Ben was a fellow slave owner. Linda was his property. She was a hardcore submissive and Ben won her at this event. Rick I could read without my talents. He really hated this dude. I think you have figured out Rick's little game by now.

This was an organized event, in some ways. Dudes and some chicks would challenge each other and the spectators would make side bets on who would win. Some serious money could change hands at this event. Ben, let's say, lacked social skills. Rick filled me in on Ben and Linda. Ben was an in-your-face high school dropout, a hardheaded Irishman, and an ex-marine from a poor section of Chicago. Rick introduced me to Ben and he threw in all of my educational history. Rick knew how to bait this guy. I just let the action develop. I could have figured every move and word that would follow. At that moment, Ben was just a sideshow act. What really caught my eye was his girlfriend. Rick had told me before I was introduced to the sterling Ben that Linda was Ben's slave.

Linda was strikingly beautiful, if you got past the fact that she had on too much eye shadow, her dark red hair was cut short like a marine's, and she had hair tattoos that looked like tire tread marks on both sides of her head. She was dressed in short shorts and a halter-top that showed off her great body. Her skin was flawless and slightly tanned. I had the urge to put a bag over her head and fuck her right then and there. While Ben was engaged in his first match, Linda made eye contact with me and smiled. It was on.

Right after this Ben dude wiped the floor with his first opponent, he was up in my face. "Dude, you think you are better than me, don't you?"

I didn't respond. I let him dig his own grave.

"Well, pretty educated dude, you came to this party dressed right. Are you going to have the guts to dance, pussy boy? Just as I thought: no guts."

After that, we engaged in a stare-down situation until I broke the ice by puckering up and throwing him a kiss.

"You fucking faggot!" he shouted. "You think you're tough. Put it on the line, tough guy!"

I looked at him and said, "You want me to challenge you in a match?"

"Yes, pretty faggot dude, if you have the guts."

Rick was just eating up the whole scene. His plan was working. He had brought me to this event to destroy this guy.

Now was the time. "You know, Benjamin, we have not yet come to terms on the wager."

"Oh, you want to lose some money tonight. How much you got?"

"I wasn't thinking just money. I was thinking my one thousand dollars against ownership for one week of your slave girl Linda."

I looked straight into his eyes and said, "You got the guts, dude?"

"Let me get this straight. If I win, and I will, I get one thousand in cash, and if you win, you get to fuck my slave girl for a week and you will return her. Is that the deal?"

"Yes, that's the deal."

He then shoved his hand in my direction. We shook.

This guy was way overconfident and of course stupid. A smart person would have watched me wrestle first and sized me up before making a challenge, but not Ben. He was in for a rude wake-up call.

I could see the match before it took place. Ben was going to come in overconfident and attack me hard and fast, just like he did in his first match tonight. I was going to kick the shit out of him. He would get a worried look on his face and he would start to fight dirty. At that point, I would destroy him and claim my prize. He would have the nerve or desire to welsh on the bet that he made in public.

Everything went as planned, except that I broke his right leg. This fact did not stop him from calling me names: "You fucking faggot! Next time I will kill your ass!"

Rick was smiling ear to ear.

Linda not only was smoking hot to look at, but she was also a great fuck. I sort of gave my boy a little vacation that week. He did not seem to mind. He and Linda became like soul mates. My boy actually liked to talk to her, and they worked well together around my house. Maybe it was just two slaves exchanging their secrets. Whatever it was, it worked.

The local restaurants were quite good. My favorite was a family-run Mexican restaurant. The place had the best Mexican food. I tried to get my boy out of the house at least once a week. He needed to learn social skills. Jimmy already had excellent manners, but going one on one with other people in social conversation was still difficult for him. My boy needed to know how to operate in general society.

Having an easy and very profitable job, plus a good social life in Chicago, did not mean that I had forgotten about Joan and my twin boys. I talked to Joan several times a month on my visual phone in my cave. Being part of their lives was something that I needed. Joan wanted me and Jimmy to visit this summer. I also phoned Greg once in a while. He was close to graduating from Stanford and was looking for a grad school. My instincts said he would enroll at the University of Chicago. He knew about my boy, but I think he wanted his daddy back. That was a problem that I would have to find a way to manage.

Greg showed up to look over the U of C's grad school program, which was predictable. I found a way to turn him off. I left town for two days on business and I ordered my boy to entertain my guest. Greg was great sex, but he could not come close to matching my boy Jimmy. He quickly came to the conclusion that the competition was too tough. He decided not to attend grad school in Chicago. We are still close friends.

The three years that I spent in Chicago were great years, both personally and professionally. My team's project was half-successful. We cut China's reserve currency pile in half, and China is now more willing to work with the leadership of The New World Order. They still do not trust us, but it was a start in the right direction. My twin boys were now four years old and as cute as a button. I saw them as often as I could find the time.

The Project China, as I called it, was terminated. Thanks to the behind-the-scenes activity of my uncle, I was promoted to the rank of colonel and given a new assignment that could change my life for the worse. The assignment was the establishment of a Federal Security Prison and a high-class resort on an island in the northern Pacific Ocean. It was to be much more than what I was told in my briefing on the subject.

Chapter 13: The Urge to Kill

Have you ever had a burning, almost overpowering, desire to kill someone? I don't mean just getting pissed off at someone, for whatever reason. What I mean is having a powerful, reoccurring urge to torture and kill a fellow human being just because you would like to see a person suffer and hear him plead for his life before you decide it is time to end his miserable existence. Maybe it is because you believe that the act of murder will set you above the average person and possibly even make you feel like a god. If you are one of these people, you have probably already justified this line of reasoning to yourself by pointing to the average history book. History is littered with examples of men and women who butchered their fellow humans, and the writers of said history books referred to these people as heroes and at times even added the title of great to their names.

If you are like most of the human race, you are afraid to act on such animalistic instincts out of fear of being caught and punished by the proper authorities. Perhaps your own educational background has been mined with all sorts of social and religious taboos that forbid killing another human being. But what if the proper authorities gave you permission to kill someone? Would you take such an opportunity if you could?

Historically, common persons and those of high ranking have been given the power to kill. Soldiers, judges, policemen, and assorted types of executioners have had such power given to them by the state throughout history. But not until the year 2040 was this power given to the rich and powerful of our world by the people behind the curtain. Sure, rich and powerful people have been involved in the mass killings of human beings for all of history, usually to make profits or to gain power. But did they ever really have the power to butcher a person face to face for their own amusement and it was legal?

On March 20, 2040, at the urging of several senior Fascist members of the Order, a facility for the sale and execution of condemned prisoners was to be established on an island in the northern Pacific Ocean. I was appointed to be in charge of its creation and operation. I was to learn later that my uncle went along with this project idea for reasons that he did not share with me at the time.

This island facility would provide the opportunity for very powerful members of the Order to enjoy the most decadent of pleasures, the opportunity to torture and kill another human being of their choice, while enjoying the comforts of a four-star resort.

This was the reason that the facility was built. It was not the reason that I wanted to be in charge of this operation.

The island was selected because of its warm weather, beautiful beaches, and good fishing prospects. The facility was to have its own airfield, which would be capable of handling jetliners. The services would be first-class and the recreational opportunities, you could say, would be unequaled anywhere in the world.

The island was also selected to be an intelligence center for the Order. Top-secret information was to be stored on the island, and intelligence operations were to be run out of a complex one hundred feet under the airport.

The facility's primary purpose was to allow members of the Order to bid on the right to execute convicted felons who had been given the death penalty. Murderers, child molesters, rapists, and street gang members would be offered up for bid at an auction on a secure Internet site.

In view of the possibilities of such a concept getting out of my control, I set up a list of guidelines for the operation. There were two: no persons under the age of eighteen and no innocent people. In short, no one, no matter how powerful, could choose to execute his spouse, neighbor, business partners, or someone he just didn't like at any particular moment.

The site of execution would be an extremely well-guarded prison located on the opposite end of the island from the hotel resort. It would be a massive, gray-stone building that would stand on a hill overlooking the beautiful Pacific Ocean. It would look like a regular prison, but in fact it would be a monument to pain and death.

The prison facility would be constructed as a perfect assembly line of death. The prisoners would be brought to the island by air. The prisoner transports would land at the island's own airfield. From the airfield, the prisoners would be taken to the prison for inspection. The prisoners would be stripped naked and go through a lengthy medical and physical inspection before being herded naked to their individual, top-security cells. Prisoners would then be given inmate overalls and tennis shoes to wear.

From this point until the moment of execution was just a matter of days to weeks. The prisoners were nothing more than cattle being prepared for slaughter.

The people who had been pre-selected to be bidders would receive complete case histories and photographs of each prisoner. Once a month an auction would be held on the Internet for the right to torture and kill any one of the prisoners that a client took a shine to. After buying a prisoner, or two, or three, a client was provided with whatever special rooms and equipment that he or she requested. The only real rule was that the client had thirty days to depose of the property. The bodies were then to be sent to the prison crematorium, which had the capacity to burn thirty bodies a day. The ashes would then be dumped into the sea without ceremonies.

Yes, I know this story sounds like a plot from an old horror movie, but, sadly, it is the reality that I had to deal with on a daily basis. In order to do my job, both the official and the secret version, I had trained myself to not give a damn what happened to these criminals. In my opinion, they were no more than human lice that fed on decent people. My new opinion of said prisoners would set me in good standing with the Fascist Element, which was my target.

How was it possible to take condemned prisoners from different countries throughout the world and not be noticed or have prison officials complain? The New World Order enacted new laws governing condemned prisoners. Under the new Penal Law System, anyone who had been given a death sentence would legally cease to exist. They were legally dead already; we only finished the job.

The legal systems that provided such prisoners received a 40 percent share of the selling price of the condemned prisoner. This share of the profits was used to compensate, in part, the legal system for the cost of the legal action against said prisoner. Did all the money go for said purpose? I cannot answer that question. We dealt with a lot of legal systems in over one hundred countries, and the chances that people dipped their hands into this pile of cash would always be there.

With the trend of letting corporations run prisons, which had become well established over the last fifty years, the idea of execution for profit could not be ruled out. Corporation mentality had slowly taken over most of the penal system. Now I was preparing to use this trend to entertain and fight the Fascist Element's attempt to dominate The New World Order.

Chapter 14: The Transition

The island was at the time known as Rica Island, after the family that owned it. The island was three miles long and two miles wide. It was in the northern Pacific Ocean, in what is called Micronesia. These islands are US property and are managed by the United States from Hawaii. The weather is tropical and the island has several nice beaches.

The Federal Security Administration, as advised by the Fascist Element, had decided to use the island to solve jail overcrowding in the United States and make a huge profit at the same time. Hundreds of jail systems in America and later the world would be sending condemned prisoners to our new facility.

You may be wondering how building a new prison facility would help make a huge profit. It might not seem to compute.

It does compute if you review the changes in the death penalty laws in the states and many other countries. It probably was not on the evening news, but the law was changed concerning the death penalty. Now, anyone convicted and sentenced to death had only one appeal. The appeal was heard within six months. If the prisoner lost his appeal, he, according to the new law, was officially dead. What happened to him from then on was not recorded. Such people could be sent to Rica Island. The prison facility on Rica Island killed condemned prisoners with a new and very profitable twist.

The basis for the commercial venture known as Rica Island reads like an old horror movie. The idea was that legally the condemned prisoners were dead. Once they were past their only appeal, they ceased to exist. There were no more legal battles and no paperwork that would tell you where they were being held. You say, "What if the person is found to be innocent later? DNA evidence showed that he is not guilty." Well, in such cases, and they did happen, the state was legally responsible to pay damages to the man's relatives. I had no problem with that; mistakes do happen. The condemned prisoners disappeared into the prison system, never to be heard from again. Rather than pay the cost of caring for these condemned prisoners for the rest of their lives, it was decided to make a profit off them to counterbalance the cost to the state of convicting them.

It would be done simply, by selling the condemned prisoners to the highest bidders at an auction, who could than kill them in any way that they saw fit. We are talking about a blood sport concept here. How much would you pay to have the right to torture and kill a convicted murderer? Would you pay to have the personal right to rid the world of a well-known serial killer or a child rapist? How about a child molester? How about the man who raped and killed your fifteen-year-old daughter or granddaughter? Have I mentioned someone that you would like to kill yet?

Everyone has run across people that they would pay to have whacked, hanged, shot, etc. It is all about basic human nature. Men, and to a lesser extent women, are all potential killers. The recent changes in the capital crimes law in the United States have made the building and operation of Rica Island possible.

How would such prisoners be sold and the public not complain? Well, this is where it got good. The public could not bid on these prisoners. Only members of the Order could submit a bid. The

Fascist Element in the Order would be especially attracted to said blood sport. I was counting on it.

How would the bidding take place? It would be run on the Internet and only approved members of the Order would have the right and the proper codes to access the site. The auctions would be held once a month. Information on the prisoners to be sold would be available at the same site. Due to advanced technology, the site was considered to be hacker-proof. No member with the right to bid could share information with any nonmember. Penalties for breaking this rule were quite severe.

Whose brain child was this whole concept? It was the brainchild of the Fascist Element. I, with the help of my uncle and several powerful Fascists on the governing council of the Order, developed, proposed, and got approval of this business concept. If run right and profitable, it was my ticket to the top of the ladder in the Order. Yes, I was going to climb to the top on a pile of dead bodies. To me, it was all one big trade-off. Thousands of people, who were no more than human scum, would die in order to save billions of innocent people. The clock was ticking, and the Fascists were at the door. It was time to make bold moves. The war against evil now required me to look and act like a Fascist in good standing. In the end, God would decide who was right.

Getting to the top of the Order and stopping the Fascist Element's drive to dominate the Order were the two most important reasons that I accepted the appointment as manager of the Rica Island project. Many of the top Fascists in the Order would show up on the island, and I would be able to scan their brains for vital information and, most of all, their finances. Such information would enable our side in this conflict to gain a big advantage over the Fascists. If the Moderates could knock out most of the heavy financing of the Fascist Element, their efforts to take control of the Order would be seriously hurt, if not destroyed.

After my appointment and promotion to colonel came through, I was required to fill the administration slots for the team that would run the island. For this task, I needed more seasoned advice: my uncle. After conferring by phone with the general, he agreed to meet me in New York City in one week to discuss who my team would be. The general knew all the animals in the jungle. He could tell me who I could trust.

I had one week to take a vacation before I had to oversee the construction of the facility on Rica Island and hire my team. A trip to Los Angeles, California, seemed to be in order. I wanted to see my twin boys before I moved to the island. That night, I phoned Joan and got her approval. I then ordered my boy to pack up our personal stuff. I had to have it shipped to the island. A guesthouse on the beach, a structure that had been the family home, would be used by me and my boy until my villa was finished.

The idea of living on a tropical island had my boy psyched up. He loved the idea of living in a house on a private beach. The three years that I owned my boy had been fantastic. Fuck the morality crap. Jimmy was the best thing that I had ever bought. I wouldn't know how to live without him.

My boy and I flew to Los Angeles two days later. I instructed my slave that during our stay he was "my valet" and I would call him Jimmy. Joan was at the airport to pick us up. When I kissed and hugged her again, it was like old times. I had flashbacks to our days at Stanford. Joan took one look at Jimmy and her eyes lit up.

As she walked over and held out her hand, she said, "Hello, you must be Jimmy."

Jimmy smiled, "Yes, and you must be Joan. It is nice to meet you."

The ride to Joan's place took almost an hour. LA is a big place. You really need a car to live in LA. Joan's house was a surprise. I had expected a basic family home, but her place was more like a mansion. I had forgotten that she came from a wealthy family. When we pulled up to the front door a nanny was waiting, with the twins, to greet us. The boys had grown a lot, and, to my surprise, they were glad to see their daddy.

After getting two hours of rest in the guesthouse bedroom, with two kids and one small dog named Corky piled on top of both me and my boy, someone yelled that dinner was ready "next to the pool." The twins knew where that meant, and they led us to Joan and the very welcomed food. Both Jimmy and I were starving.

The dinner table was a spread of meats, salads, and mashed potatoes. Milk was provided for the twins and wine for the rest of us. I started off the dinner conversation with a toast: "To Joan, a great mother who is doing a good job of raising our two sons." The adults and the twins then clicked our glasses. With two four year-olds, this took a little effort, but we managed.

During the dinner, Joan gave me and Jimmy a review of the twins' life so far. It seemed that they were little rascals always getting into things and not putting their toys away. Yes, they were my kids. They were a lot like me as a young child. The twins kept quiet and smiled at what was said about them.

Just looking at their two smiling faces gave me another reason for fighting the Fascists. I don't want my two boys living under Fascist rule. I doubt many American parents would say anything different.

The rest of our three-day stay was involved mostly with getting to know my kids. Joan was right that they were rascals, and to my relief they were a lot of fun too. During our stay, Jimmy came out of his shell. He thought that my boys were a lot of fun, and he seemed to enjoy playing catch with them and teaching them how to swim in the backyard pool. Jimmy and Corky seemed to bond. Jimmy liked playing with Corky, and the dog followed him around Joan's house. After seeing how Jimmy reacted to Corky, I was reminded of what a friend of mine had said about why he got a second dog: "A pet needs a friend to play with when I am not at home."

I concluded that I needed to get a pet, possibly a dog, or maybe another slave. I needed a companion that could keep my boy company when I was not home. My job on the island was going to take up a lot of time. It was time that I had enjoyed spending with my boy. Those days were over.

The second night Joan was a little frisky, to say the least. We revisited our Stanford arrangement three times that night. It was a great feeling waking up with Joan's naked body next to mine.

Our stay was too brief. In reality, I wanted to take Joan and the twins home with me, but then I realized what my life had become and that taking care of Joan and the twins was not possible on my new assignment.

The flight to New York City was uneventful. I slept most of the time. My uncle sent his car to pick us up at the airport. The drive to the Trump Towers apartment complex only took an hour. My uncle welcomed us to his "city cave," as he called his ten-room suite. I introduced him to my boy. I used the term boy because my uncle knew everything about my life and it seemed he approved of my taste in slave boys.

"Will, you sure have an eye for good-looking, stud slave boys. You were very lucky to buy this boy before one of the Saudi princes saw him. He will be much happier and safer with you as his master."

He was right about that. If I hadn't bought my slave, he may not be alive today. My boy just stood submissively and did not speak.

To give my boy something to do, I convinced my uncle to let him greet people at the door. I added, "Uncle, if you want my boy to greet your guests in the nude, it will be all right with me."

"No, no, Will that will not be necessary. But later, after the meeting is over, your boy can work in the nude if you like. You both will be staying here for the weekend, and I would like to get a full look at the slave that you have bought."

"Uncle, you can also physically inspect him and use him for your pleasure if you want."

He just smiled. My uncle is a big pussy hound.

I took one final shot. "Uncle, you should get in your reservation as soon as possible. My boy has the most incredible ass. Fucking him is like fucking a tight, warm pussy."

He just smiled again and walked into the dinner room that was to be used for our meeting. I was just messing with him and he knew it, or was I?

Yes, the game was on. I and my uncle had been playing games with each other since I was a kid. The general usually won such games. My uncle was far more experienced than me. I hoped to make major points this round. The game was simple: could I get a pussy hound like my uncle to fuck my boy? My boy had an extremely beautiful body. He looked far better naked than he did with clothes on. Add to this the fact that he was very talented in bed, and I had a shot at winning this game. After all, my uncle already admitted that my boy was a beautiful, young stud.

But I don't want to give you the idea that my uncle was not attractive. He was only fifty-five years old, but he looked more like forty. I suspected that he had been using the new youth drugs. The guy was a real athletic man. He had a very muscular, gym-toned body, and, last but not least, he was equipped with the family big cock. But could I get this very straight, older stud to fuck my slave?

My boy did a good job of greeting our guests. The main reason for the conference was to get a team together to run the island. My uncle helped me sell the idea and develop the concept further. Now I needed to team made up of experienced and talented people to put the plan into action.

When fifteen men and one woman were seated, I started off with the basic question, as I called it. "Since all of you have read the materials concerning this project, I must ask if you have any reservations about what we are going to do."

The attendees remained silent, which was a good sign. "Then we are all in agreement." I turned the presentation over to my uncle.

My uncle went over the details of who got what job, etc. I now had a team of people to run the island and help fight the Fascist Element in The New World Order. Would the whole plan work? This project was only available to the Fascist Element in The New World Order. Would this project get me the intelligence that our team needed about the Fascists? The people who would come to the island to engage in this blood sport would be mostly a cross section of the Fascist Element of The New World Order. We would be able to chart how far the tentacles of the Fascist power extended. We would find out who their allies really were. Would it get me the information that I needed to stop the Fascists from ruling the world? Would the Fascists figure out our plan and put a stop to it? Hell, would I be able to stay alive long enough to matter in this fight?

After the team left, I needed a mental break from the subject of the island. The game was on again. I ordered my boy to strip and follow me into the conference room. My uncle was still reading a section of the master plan. He did not look even slightly startled when I entered the room with my naked slave. It was not a good start.

"Uncle, you said that earlier that you wanted to inspect my boy."

My uncle got up from the table walked around the naked slave, taking mental notes. This was a head-trip that I learned from him.

"Will, your boy is an extremely pretty, well-built young stud. You were lucky to buy such a rare find. I don't think that he would have lived much longer. The Saudi princes are not kind to their slaves."

"You may physically inspect him if you chose," I said.

Now he did the unexpected. I had expected this very straight uncle of mine to say, "No, thanks." But instead, he stood in front of my boy and fondled him. My boy started to squirm and his cock got throbbing hard.

"Good reaction, Will." He then ran his hands over every inch of the boy's naked body before he said, "Bend over, boy!"

"Yes sir!"

My uncle now inspected the slave's anus. His inspection had only taken a few minutes. When he was finished, he ordered my boy to stand up.

"That is one beautiful property, Will. You must feel very lucky to own this boy."

"Yes, Uncle, he is a real find, and I am proud to own this slave."

With that, he smiled and said, "Will, it has been a long and hard day." He patted me on the back and said, "We did good work tonight. I will see you in the morning."

I didn't know yet, but I think I was the one that got played.

The next day was spent in reviewing the project and the contracts that had been issued for the construction of the facility. The home office of the project was at present Honolulu, Hawaii. All the construction companies working on the project were from Hawaii. All supplies and materials were shipped from Honolulu.

The advertising for the services was already being e-mailed to the Fascist Element of the Order. Well, e-mails were sent to known members of the Fascist Element. The list of such elements would continue to expand. The grand opening was scheduled for June 5, six months from now. My team was at work lining up the condemned prisoners of our choice to be offered for sale. The team was instructed to find the most notorious and, if possible, the prisoners with the best bodies possible. Finding a condemned prisoner with a great body was, as I could already see, going to be a problem.

As I and my uncle did our work, my boy kneeled naked on the floor of my uncle's living room. He stayed motionless for hours, until even my former military man uncle had to say, "Will, your boy is sure disciplined. I have known very few professional soldiers in my life that had his sense of discipline."

"Yes, he is well trained and experienced. If you wish him to do something, feel free to order him around."

My uncle walked over to my kneeling boy and said, "Boy, get up and fix us some chicken salad sandwiches. The makings are in the refrigerator."

"Yes sir!"

When my boy served us the sandwiches, I told him to make one for himself. When he left the dining room, my uncle eyeballed his beautiful ass. This was a good sign. My uncle knew that I had seen him take a look, and he smiled.

"Well, Uncle, any time you want to take his ass for a ride, he is yours."

My uncle again did not respond.

The next morning was our last day in New York City. I had to take a meeting in Manhattan at 10:00 a.m. After showering and putting on an expensive suit (God, I hate suits), I ate a quick snack. Before I went out the door, I told my boy to kneel on the front-room floor and do what my uncle ordered him to do.

The meeting took up the rest of my day. When I got back to

my uncle's Trump Tower suite, it was dinnertime. My boy had fixed a dinner of corned beef and cabbage, a favorite of my Irish uncle. The dinner was fantastic. You could cut the tender corned beef with a fork.

My uncle was impressed. "Will, your boy is one great cook."

"Yes, that is one of his many talents."

"Oh, by the way, I took you up on your offer. Your boy is also one really great fuck. With your permission, I would like another round with him tomorrow morning before you leave."

"No problem. He is yours any time you want him."

For the first time in years, I had scored points against the pro himself. I learned it all from the best, my uncle. I knew that something had happened when I walked in tonight. My boy acted very happy and he was smiling. This is his usual state right after he has been royally fucked.

Before leaving for the airport, I had a brief conversation with my uncle. Two questions were on my mind. "Uncle, I would like you to find out some things for me."

"Yes, Will, anything that's in my power to do."

"I want to know the answers to some questions. The first is, who is them? I heard the term many times, and my own roommate at training camp was one of them. The second question is something for your Saudi contacts. My slave, when he was fourteen years old, went through slave training. I have seen his records, and his mind was worked on—you have witnessed the result. I would like to know how this mind change thing works. Such a method could be useful to us in some way."

My uncle wrote down both requests. "Will, these people called them are probably bio-robots of some sort. I will track down the details and get back to use by way of Caos."

Yes, if Caos did not know the answer, it was going to be tough to find out who or what they were.

I was due in San Francisco in one week, time enough to complete the packing of my personal stuff in the Chicago house. There was also one unfinished matter to attend to: getting a pet to keep my boy company during my long absences at work.

After spending a night in the Chicago house, I ordered my boy to spend the day packing our personal stuff and getting it sent to the island. The Federal Express truck was due to arrive at 2:00 p.m.

I put on my Federal Security uniform, with my new colonel rank, and then went over my game plan one more time. My car arrived 9:00 p.m. with a driver and two uniformed police officers. After going through the usual social greetings and briefly telling the policemen what I expected of them, we left for our destination, a junkyard outside Chicago.

As I walked into the main building, I saw him and he saw me. At first, he looked startled, then a little mean.

I said, "Benjamin, I need to have a word with you."

He looked at the two cops and my Federal Security Officer's uniform and quickly obeyed. He wasn't quite as dumb as I had figured.

"Okay, what do you guys want me for this time?"

"Well, Benjamin, I just need to have a chat with you. That can turn out to be very bad or good for you. Follow me."

I walked outside and told Benjamin to have a seat in what looked like the employee lunch area.

"Benjamin, I am here to make you an offer, an offer that you would be smart to take. I want you to sell me your slave, Linda."

I took a fat envelope out of my pocket and threw it on Ben's lap. "That is thirty thousand dollars in cash. Do we have a deal?"

Benjamin went through the contents of the envelope, smiled, and said, "Hell, yes. The bitch is yours."

I had Benjamin call Linda and tell her the news. When I talked to her, she seemed pleased that she now belonged to me. I told her I would be over to her place of employment in about an hour to pick her up. She was to quit her job and tell her boss that she was going to work on a resort in the Pacific Ocean.

After I picked up Linda, we dropped by the place that she had shared with Ben and she threw what things she owned into a suitcase. On the way back to my house, I had the driver take the both of us to the Federal Security office in downtown Chicago. I wanted to use the bio-pulse machine to knock out any pathogens that Linda may have picked up in service to her two former scumbag masters.

When I got back to the Chicago house, my boy was upstairs packing stuff. I ordered my new slave to strip and kneel on the floor, like a proper slave. She smiled and obeyed.

When I walked into the upstairs bedroom that my boy was working in, I told him I had bought him a pet to keep him company on the island. "I bought Linda as a second slave. She will be your slave. You will help train her properly. During her training, if you want to fuck her, or have her suck your cock, you have my permission. Linda will be known as girl and she will be your assistant. You will be the house manager, cook, and butler. She will be the housemaid."

After going downstairs, I explained everything to Linda: her position in my household and the fact that we were going to live on an island in the Pacific. I then left the two alone. From my downstairs office in the cave, I could hear both of them talking like fifteen-year-old girls. These two were well suited to each other.

The next two days my slaves had very little to occupy their time. My personal stuff had been shipped and I needed only to tie up loose ends in my office. I ordered my boy to start training the new slave.

At times during the first day I could heard my boy saying such things as, "Get moving bitch, faster, faster," and "That's not a good way to lick my feet girl, try again." It was good to hear my boy training the new house slave, and a little funny to boot.

To add my own style to Linda's training, I would, when I encountered her working in the nude, grab her by the shoulders, back her against the wall, and start to kiss her as I finger-fucked her. First, I shoved one finger up her cunt, then two, and finally three. I would work my way down her neck and massage her nipples with my tongue.

After she climaxed, I withdrew my fingers, kissed her one more time, and said, "Good girl." This was treating her the way she liked—in a less brutal manner than Ben.

Linda had served two masters so far in her brief twenty-two years of life. Both masters misread her. They both thought that she liked to be whipped and beaten. But during the week that I owned her, after I had won her in the wrestling match, I learned that she was a hardcore submissive, but not really masochistic by nature. She needed a dominant man who firmly controlled her and would provide the security that she craved so much but never found with her first two meathead masters.

The beating crap was part of the needs of her past masters, not her needs. In short, Benjamin and Linda's first two masters did not know beans about what they had, or how to develop this property. I did not intend to make their mistakes. Linda will be trained properly. She will become a prized property of me, her new master, and in the end, she will be happy with her life and I will be proud to say that I own such a beautiful and well-trained female slave.

My last day in Chicago was uneventful, except for the mental contact that I got from Caos. It was an answer to the two questions that I had given to my uncle. "Will, this is Caos. In short, the bio-robots known as them are spies created by the people you refer to as the Lizards. The Lizards are the allies of the Fascist Element, but allies do not always trust each other. The Lizards developed them to keep track of their allies in the Order."

That explains why the Order wanted to know who they were but did not want to take action against all of them at this point in time.

"In regard to your questions about the Saudi slave-training method for mind change, I can only say that only one Saudi slave trainer knows the secret: Omar Saud. He trained your slave Jimmy Rose. The method is very effective in making a submissive person even more submissive like a slave."

Next time I visited my grandfather, I would have him set up a meeting with this Omar Saud. If his method was for real, I would find a way to get control of it. It could be useful to our side.

Chapter 15: The Island

The flight to San Francisco was short and easy. I used the time to catch up on my paperwork, which for this project was increasing at a fast pace. Luckily, I had hired two assistants. But they were already assembling my office on the island.

A private corporate jet was waiting at the Honolulu airport. But it could wait. I wanted a few days to relax in Hawaii before taking on the construction project, or nightmare, that was the current reality on the island.

My staff had booked a suite at the Royal Hawaiian Hotel right on the beach. The old hotel had been the US Navy's headquarters during World War II. It had just been remodeled. Walking through the first floor was like walking through a page of history.

After unpacking, I realized that the one thing that we did not pack was swimsuits. The desk clerk gave me directions to a good retailer. Picking out a suit for me was easy. My usual boxer trunks type of swimsuit was standard for me. I never liked the idea of thongs. I did not feel the need to advertise the size of my cock, which is big.

But for my slaves, my standards were different. I bought two pairs of thong suits for my boy, one black and one blue. For my girl I bought two thong bikinis in the same colors. Both purchases would come in useful later on, I was to find out. But for now, it was back to the hotel and then out to the beach.

The beautiful blue Pacific Ocean was almost as warm as bath water. Playing in the mild surf can be fun, especially watching my slaves. It was like I had two children. I don't think either of them had ever played in the ocean before.

Sleeping with my naked slaves that night was very relaxing. They were so warm and comfortable to cuddle with. In the morning, my boy taught my girl how to give their master a full-body massage. Linda was new, but she was eager to learn how to do a basic massage. The massage had given me a roaring hard-on and I proceeded to fuck both of my slaves that morning. Linda was first and, God, she could moan and squirm. Jimmy put on a second show that I was sure would disturb whoever was in the next room. Both of my slaves seemed very content with being my property, and I felt blessed to own such perfect servants.

It was about a five-hour flight to the island. The jet landing strip had just been completed. The control tower was not in operation, but that did not stop us from landing safely. As my plane taxied to a stop, a black Lincoln Town Car pulled up alongside the plane. My ride was here.

The driver was Major Reid, my island security chief. He was a retired marine officer and an expert on security, high-tech or basic. Major Reid was to be my right hand man. His unofficial job was that he was the project chief of intelligence. He would try to put the pieces of information that I supplied together and come up with a picture of the present projects and future plans of the Fascist Element of The New World Order. If we were successful, our side would be able to shut down the Fascists' plan to take over The New World Order and establish Fascist rule over the whole world.

My official residence, a villa on a cliff overlooking the ocean, would not be completed for several more months. I was to use a temporary house. It was the home of the family that had formerly owned this island. The house was a two-story Victorian with five bedrooms and a wraparound porch. It was built on a small mound about one hundred feet above water level, just off a private beach.

If you thought this sounded like paradise, you would be close to the truth. Perfect? No. It was a nice, roomy house and a great location, but the house was old and it did not have modern air conditioning. Instead, it had those old-fashioned, big ceiling fans to cool down the house.

After my slaves brought our baggage into this vast beach house, I told them to walk around the house and to get to know the place. Since they would be taking care of this house, it seemed practical for them to know every inch of the house. Since the house was fully furnished, including food, I got myself a beer from the fridge and found a nice, cool part of the porch where I sat down to enjoy a cold one. In the background, I could hear my two slaves running around the house like a bunch of kids getting used to their new home. I thought, *Sometimes, a master, sometimes a dad.*

The next morning my driver, a new guy named Tony, picked me up for the ride to the newly completed administration building. My nightmare had begun. Before leaving, I instructed my boy and girl to get to know the place and to draw up a plan for running the household. I also instructed my boy to spend half the day in training my new slave.

My two office assistants had done a great job in getting my office together. We spent my first day with me being briefed on the progress and problems of the project. The project was on schedule; several of the main buildings were nearly ready. Only one building was completed: the prison.

The prison was on the opposite end of the island. I scheduled my visit and inspection of the facility for early the next morning. My first day was a little boring.

When I got back to the beach house, I was glad my two slaves had unpacked all my stuff and the house was shipshape. They must have worked their asses off, so I wasn't surprised to find them both naked and asleep in the master bedroom. Being beat myself, I stripped naked and lay down between them. Feeling the bed move caused them both to wake up. They did not say a word. They just smiled and cuddled up to me and we all fell asleep.

When I awoke early the next day, I looked over to see the clock on the nightstand. It was 7:30 a.m. I rolled out of bed. I did not have to wake my two slaves. They had gotten up before me and were already fixing my first meal of the day.

As usual, I had a throbbing hard-on, so I yelled downstairs, "Boy, I need you up here!"

I could hear a voice from the kitchen yell, "Yes, Sir, right away!" and the sounds of running.

As I sat down in an armchair, I placed a call to the office. When my boy entered the room, I pointed to my hard-on. He smiled and dropped to his knees in front of me. He knew the drill. So as the operator connected me with the motor pool, my slave gave me a great waking up head job. By the time I had confirmed that my car would be at my house at 9:00 a.m., my whole body was squirming as I shot a big load down my boy's throat.

I ended the phone conversation, bent over, and gave my boy a long, deep kiss. "Good work, boy."

I had owned Jimmy Rose for three years and couldn't be more pleased with his progress and devotion. When I bought my boy, he was a very well-trained and experienced man slave, which was not up to my personal standards. Well-trained slaves show no personality, and they never have an opinion. They just follow their master's orders. In short, a well-trained slave can be fucking boring.

In the previous three years, I had slowly retrained my boy to act more like a daddy's boy than a slave. So far, I had been fairly successful at this. My boy was developing an individual personality. He even at times had an opinion or would offer some advice when I asked for it. He became more of a playful companion than just a slave. This was the same way that I would train my new girl. I found out with training my boy that if you allowed a slave to act human, rather than as just a piece of furniture that you use for your pleasure, he, or she, will be more devoted to you and more interesting.

The trip to the new prison was tricky. The road was still not paved. It was a two-mile road trip on a gravel road. The prison soon appeared in the distance. It was a massive two-story, gray stone building with a high wall topped by barbed wire. Security cameras were everywhere. The guard at the main gate checked our papers and then phoned the new warden, Mr. Gilbert.

When my car pulled up to the front of the prison, Mr. Gilbert was there to greet me. After a brief social get-together in the warden's office, I was offered the chance to be the first person to inspect the newly finished prison. The prison was built in an open tier fashion with a security tower in the center of the building. The guards that manned the security tower had an open view into every cell in the building.

The building was getting ready for the first shipment of condemned prisoners, which was due for delivery in three months. The warden expected to have all the cells full by the time the first auction was run. That would mean three hundred prisoners for sale. What happened to a prisoner if he or she did not attract a bid? Since the minimum bid on a prisoner was thirty thousand dollars, a no-bid result was a possibility. The new rules said that the prisoner would be hanged the next day.

Who made these rules? The Fascists that were involved in planning this project make the rules.

When I got back to my office, I looked over the list of bidders. So far, over five thousand powerful people had signed up for this auction. The total even shocked me. The list was a who's who of the most powerful and wealthy people in the world. Most of them no one would suspect would harbor such murderous desires, let alone be members of a Fascist plan to control the world.

In less than six months, this project would be up and running. I felt confident that I would get the intelligence that I was seeking. But this was a situation that could easily get out of control and end up taking the shape of something that I had not envisioned. When people start to kill other people, things can take a strange turn really fast. Could I ride this horse to the finish line? Only time would tell.

When I got to the beach house, it was about 6:00 p.m. My two slaves were kneeling on the living room floor. Dinner was ready. We were having baked chicken, mashed potatoes, and a salad. After dinner, I told my slaves to fuck the clean up for now because we were going skinny dipping in the ocean. My boy and girl smiled and then they both helped me to get out of my work clothes really fast. My slaves followed my naked ass out the door, down to the beach, and into the warm water of the Pacific Ocean.

Later that night, I sat naked on the living room couch with my naked boy at my feet and my naked girl beside me. We watched TV and ate buttered popcorn for several hours. I was thankful for such a relaxing home life. I would be needing just such an emotional release a lot in the near future.

As the months passed, my project was nearing completion. The main buildings were up. The resort was hiring staff and the prisoners were arriving at the airport.

I decided to inspect the final building to be completed: the execution building. The building was near the prison. It was split up into about sixty specialty rooms. Each room was outfitted with a special means of torture and execution.

The first room I inspected was the gallows room. Inside this two-story room was an actual wooden gallows. This room was designed for the person who wanted to administer justice to a condemned prisoner in an old-fashioned manner.

The purchaser of a prisoner could act as the official hangman. Guards would be provided to help. Said person would have the option of either hanging a prisoner fast, or slow. The first method would mean placing the knot of the noose against the prisoner's right ear. When the prisoner dropped through the trapdoor of the gallows for several feet, the noose would quickly break his neck. He would be dead in a few short minutes. The second method would mean placing the knot of the hangman's noose behind the prisoner's neck. In this case the prisoners would drop through the gallows trap door, his neck would not break. He would be left to strangle. He would kick for twenty to thirty minutes before he finally died. This was considered to be a very cruel way to execute a prisoner.

The second room that I saw was the headman's room. It was also two stories high. In the center of the room was a raised platform. On the platform was a block of wood with a headman's ax next to it. This was for the purchaser who wished to dispose of a prisoner by cutting off his head. A basket was placed in front of the block.

The third room was the most blood chilling of them all: the impalement room. It was a two-story room, but with a small difference. In the center of the room were several steel pole holders. A three-inch by six-foot-long fence post had been locked into one of the steel post holders on the floor; the exposed end of the post had been sharpened. In this room, a buyer could witness the guards shove a greased fence post up a prisoner's ass. People impaled like this usually took from three hours to three days to die. It was considered the most brutal and cruel method of execution ever invented by man.

This method of execution was reserved for those who wanted to dispatch a prisoner with extreme prejudice. Someone would really have to hate a person to do this to them.

The other specialty rooms were of the same nature. Most could be adjusted to suit any request, no matter how strange.

The facilities were ready; the auction was scheduled for next week and rooms at the hotel were being booked—so far, so good. The chips were all falling into place. My intelligence team was ready to figure out the full extent of the Fascist and Lizard influence on The New World Order.

This was also the week that I moved into my new cliff-top villa overlooking the beautiful Pacific Ocean. The villa was to be the residence of the commander of the island, who of course was me. The villa had eight bedrooms, four being spacious suites. It had a huge outdoor pool, which I had outfitted with an oxygen system for keeping the water bug-free rather than with the usual chemicals. Sitting in one of these pools was refreshing. Little oxygen bubbles formed all over your body. The oxygen content of your blood was raised, and you would feel more energized and clean.

The villa's kitchen was state of the art, along with the tech room, which had all the latest high-tech toys. My den was my favorite room in the villa. My second favorite room was the fully equipped gym in the basement. I and my slaves worked out three times a week. My den was my office at home, and it was equipped with the best communication devices available. The den was furnished with leather couches and chairs, a pool table, a fully equipped bar, and a one-hundred-fifty-inch HDTV.

My two slaves seemed startled when they first saw the villa. But they both got used to the fact that they would be living in this home and taking care of it. Managing the house and me were going to be a time-consuming task for the both of them.

As for my girl, her training was complete. She was now a well-trained slave. Well, she was trained to suit my needs. She had adjusted to serving me, her new master, and I was proud of her progress. But one thing suddenly came to mind about her that started to bother me. It seemed, because of my heavy workload, I had not realized that my new girl had not had a period the whole time that I owned her. I called her into my den to find out the answer.

As she knelt on the floor I said, "Girl, I have overlooked something about you these last six months. It's your period. You haven't had one. Why?"

She looked a little startled. "Yes, I hope that the fact that I don't have periods will not make you want me less. I have a problem that is call amenorrhea. I don't function like a normal female, and I cannot have children. I hope that you are not disappointed in me."

"No girl, this is not a problem, in fact, not having periods once a month makes you more valuable to me."

"Thank you, sir."

I didn't need a slave girl to have babies with. I already had two sons. I was soon to find out that I was mistaken in that assumption.

During my twice monthly vision-phone conference with Joan and the twins, the twins let slip that their mommy was going to have a baby. I thought right away, Oh, boy! Yes, it was mine. She had tricked me again. But she and the boys were happy about it, so why should I feel down? After all, it was not the only time a woman had conned me.

Since everything was in place for the first auction, I took two days off. I finally had time to rest so I and my slaves spent the whole time in the nude. I now found out what it is like to walk around a three-million-dollar villa in the nude and molest, or fuck, my slaves anytime I wanted. I did some serious fucking those three days (twelve times) and got three great and relaxing massages from my boy. Throw in the good food and wine, and you get what I mean. It was a great three days.

Chapter 16: The First Auction

The first monthly auction went well. All but twelve prisoners sold for the minimum bid or above. Some prisoners sold for much more than we thought they would. The twelve that did not sell, I had to dispose of. I was responsible for carrying out their death sentences.

The day after the auction, the twelve unsold prisoners were brought to the gallows room to be hanged. They were kept hooded, in shackles, and under armed guard. None of them was aware of what was going to happen to them.

Several handpicked guards would conduct the executions. I was the witness for the state. The first prisoner was a murderer. He had killed his wife and two small daughters. I was surprised that someone did not bid on this prisoner, since child murder usually attracted a lot of attention. Maybe it was the fact that he was butt ugly. He acted startled when he learned that he was about to be hanged, but he walked to his death like a man.

Most of the men went to the gallows that day without complaint. One prisoner even looked like he welcomed the chance to die. But three of the prisoners became very angry, and they had to be physically dragged to the gallows.

After the executions, the prisoners' bodies were sent to the crematorium for burning. The crematorium is in the back of the execution building. It has the capacity to cremate thirty bodies a day. Today, it performed its task without any problems. The ashes were later thrown into the ocean.

In a few days, the hotel was 92 percent full. The guests were settling in and starting to make their reservations at the execution building. Most of the requests for rooms were fairly basic. The gallows room was booked by twenty-seven successful bidders, the headsman room by twenty-two, and the impalement room by two. The rest of the successful bidders booked the other rooms, mostly with the intent of torturing their properties before they let them die.

I was thankful at this point of the operation for my ability to see this venture as just a business enterprise, instead of what it was: a murder factory. This ability of mine helped to keep me sane.

To start off, at the opening of the facility the hotel guests were all invited to my villa for cocktails and the usual expensive food. My two slaves and added help prepared the food and the villa. Some of the most powerful and wealthy people in the world had shown up. I was mainly interested in just seven of the guests, with one being Mr. Cole, the chief financial officer for the Fascist Element of The New World Order. He was a wealth of secret information on the financial dealing and bank accounts of the Fascist Element. Scanning his brain would be a major achievement for our side.

The guests filed into my villa, wearing the most expensive clothes and jewelry. Looking at these people, one would believe that they were going to a charity event instead of the blood sport that was in the works.

When the guests were assembled in the living room and surrounding areas, I grabbed a microphone and welcomed them to my home. I made a few announcements and then added that my own personal house slaves, Jimmy and Linda, would be their waiters tonight. Both Linda and Jimmy were almost naked. They were wearing only their black thong bikinis and black slave collars. As they mingled with the guests, I could see that they were attracting a lot of attention and quite a few looks of approval.

Just walking around and getting to know my guests was quite an education. It was like taking a course in who ran the world. Most of these people were not known to the general public. They operated behind the curtain, and they didn't like personal publicity. I found them to be very open with me about what they wanted from the facility that I ran. The theme that I had feared would surface kept appearing. The question, in different forms, was this: when are you going to offer younger and prettier subjects? I feared that in the near future someone above me in the chain of command would give in to these requests.

One very wealthy lady, Mrs. Weiss, was a welcomed relief. She just asked me, "Are your house slaves really your slaves?"

"Yes, I own both of them."

She looked fascinated. I would guess that she has trouble getting and keeping a good maid.

"Well, where did you buy them?"

I just laughed.

"Well, I bought Linda from her master in Chicago, and Jimmy I bought from a slave dealer in Saudi Arabia. They are perfect, extremely well-trained, and loyal servants. I am proud to own both of them."

Jimmy overheard what I told the lady. His eyes lit up and he smiled at me.

"You mean that people like me can't buy one, don't you, Colonel?"

I smiled. "Mrs. Weiss, it is not just a matter of money. In my case, it is because I am a rich, dominant, well-built, hung, male stud. You are a nice lady, but you are only rich."

She laughed a little.

As the evening wore on the crowd thinned out. I had instructed my two slaves to please the guests. I wish that I had phrased those instructions better. As the party neared a natural end, I walked around the house looking for my slaves. I found Jimmy in my den. He was standing naked among six middle-aged women who were physically inspecting his body. Mrs. Weiss was talking to him and at the same time fondling his balls, and two of her friends were playing with his bare ass. Her friends, as she, seemed to be fascinated with looking at and touching Jimmy's naked body. Well, granted, Jimmy has a fantastic body, but the scene was a little surreal even for my tastes.

I walked over to them and said, "Ladies, I'm sorry to say, since you all seem to be having such a great time with my boy Jimmy, that I now need him to start cleaning up after the party." The wealthy ladies looked sad as their boy toy left. They followed me into the kitchen.

Linda was in the same type of situation. She was naked and in the pool with a man's head stuck between her beautiful, firm tits. He also seemed sad to lose his girl toy.

Next time, I would give my slaves better instructions on what I meant by the phrase, "Please the guests."

That night I started to work on Mr. Cole, the CFO of the Fascist Element. I used my subconscious to subconscious method of intelligence gathering. It has worked for me many times in the past and I hoped to be successful this time. A lot depended on this working. The information that Mr. Cole knew was vital to our side's success.

I could see the front of the main hotel at the resort from my patio. I knew which room Mr. Cole had been assigned. It was one of the top floor suites. The lights were already out. But was

Mr. Cole in the room and was he asleep yet? I did not have to guess. The whole hotel was bugged and equipped with infrared scanners. I could tell if Mr. Cole was in the room and whether he was asleep.

Using the computer in my den, I punched in the needed passwords and focused on Mr. Cole's room. The scanners could read a person's heat pattern and physical state. Mr. Cole was asleep in his room. I then looked up Mr. Cole's reservations and his auction records. It seemed Mr. Cole was planning a five-day stay on the island and that he had purchased two prisoners to execute. Both prisoners were women in their twenties who had committed murder. So, I have five days in which to extract the needed information.

I prepared myself mentally to scan Mr. Cole's subconscious. The process took over five hours. I wrote down, on a legal pad, detail after detail of the financial dealings of the Fascist Element. It covered over five hundred bank accounts and the financial interests in hundreds of top worldwide corporations. It named names, the names of people who were links in a vast corporate worldwide empire. This had been my first time out gathering intelligence on the island, and I had struck gold big time. But it was not the end of the information.

The morning came too fast. I was dog tired. I needed sleep badly, so I phoned my office and left a message that I would be working at home and to not disturb me, unless it was very important. The office crew would probably just think that I had a hangover from the party the night before.

I locked my extensive notes on the financial inner dealings of the Fascist Element of The New World Order in my safe. I would type them up later when my mind was not fried. I headed upstairs to the master bedroom. My two slaves were still asleep. I stripped and crawled between them and quickly fell asleep.

I woke up about 10:00 a.m. with my arm lying on my boy's chest and my girl cuddled up against me, with her nice firm, warm tits on my chest. I lay there for a few minutes with my eyes wide awake, wishing I could just stay in bed with my two slaves. It would be much less stressful than facing the real world. But as usual, as most people do, I convinced myself that I had to get up and go to work. As my house slaves prepared breakfast, I shaved and took a quick shower.

It was a beautiful, sunny day on the island. A slight breeze cooled the island and our guests were already torturing and dispatching their purchases. My office kept track of such activities and they informed me, as I entered my official office, that fifteen prisoners had already been sent to the crematorium. While it seemed, so far, that it was becoming a productive day in the execution-for-profit business, I could not say at that time that our customers were pleased.

I walked into the security room in the back of the administration building. The security room monitored the cameras in all the execution rooms. The customers did not know of this back-up system. It was meant to provide security to our clients in case a prisoner caused, or was about to cause, them harm. I sat in front of the screen that was monitoring Mrs. Weiss. Mrs. Weiss had purchase a child molester and murderer who, according to his records, was thirty-two years of age. He was also overweight and not very good looking. This helped explain her question to me about when people could buy a young, good-looking man or woman to work on. She had chosen to torture him with red-hot pokers and a whip with a small nail in the tip of each length of leather.

Mrs. Weiss had already done a hell of a lot of damage by the time I had tuned in. The prisoner had bleeding cuts and bruises all over his body. Now, she did something that startled me. She took out a metal clamp-like device from the equipment bag. She fastened it to the prisoner's nuts and proceeded to crush them. The prisoner screamed and then passed out. Well, I think he passed out. Mrs. Weiss then took out a knife and cut the prisoner's throat. That settled that—I was not going to let Mrs. Weiss fondle my boy again, ever.

Mrs. Weiss was a good example of the Fascist Element. She could be a delight to talk to in public, but in a situation like the island offered, she could be a cruel, stone-cold killer. I was to meet hundreds of such people on the island. There was just something about them that was not human. These people had a warm and friendly exterior, but none of them had what I would call a heart. They thought of themselves as some sort of ruling class that was above those other creatures, above the rest of humanity. It became easier and easier to understand how the Fascist Element could come up with a plan to kill most of the population of the planet and justify such thinking by saying that they were saving mankind from itself.

That night I put my slaves to sleep as soon as Mr. Cole went to bed. When the scanners indicated that he was asleep, I went into my trance and my subconscious paid his subconscious a visit. As in the night before, I got a ton of detailed information.

I finished my work about four in the morning. The sun had not come up. I put my notes in the safe and I slipped into to bed with my slaves and fell fast asleep. I woke up about 9:00 a.m. My slaves were already awake. They were just waiting for me to awake. My slaves never get up without my permission. I sent my boy downstairs to start breakfast. My girl I told to stay in bed as I shaved. Fucking my girl that morning was a great way to relieve the stress that I had built up the night before. After eating breakfast, I had my boy give me a full-body, deep tissue massage.

It was a great way to start the day. I had been bred and fed. It was time to go to my office and type up the results of the night's snooping on Mr. Cole's mind. It took me three hours to type up the notes. I had to do the work. This type of information could not be entrusted to anyone but myself. I then headed over to the resort hotel. A special dinner had been prepared and all of the element's elite would be attending. I had to go make nice to a large group of extremely rich and powerful Fascist bastards and a few non-Fascists.

The spread was lavish. Only the most expensive food and wines were placed on the serving tables. I filled my plate with a cut of prime rib, a potato, and some salad that looked interesting. With my plate and a glass of expensive wine in hand, I sat down at an empty table. I wanted to see who, among the elite, would consider me a good dinner companion.

It wasn't long before my table was full. I had the pleasure of the company of a very rich former police chief, a Texas billionaire, a Japanese billionaire and his eighteen-year-old son, and a CEO of a major worldwide corporation. I knew that the main topic was going to be my island and its attractions, let's say.

The Texas billionaire seemed very satisfied with his experiences on the island. "I can't remember when I have had such a great experience on one of my trips. This place has great food and the hotel is first class. But the part I like best is the extra special side activities that are offered. It feels good to be part of administering justice. I've already administered justice twice today."

I asked him about his favorite method of justice. He replied, "I'm old-fashioned. I prefer the hangman's noose. It is fast and not very messy."

The former police chief, Mr. James, who had inherited a big fortune, was a little more involved with his style of administering justice. He liked to get physical. He would not go into details at the table—thank God—but he did invite me to be his guest the next morning to witness how he administered justice to two gang bangers who had raped and killed a twelve-year-old girl. I accepted his offer.

The Japanese businessman, Mr. Akito, and his son, Ichiro, were like the Texas billionaire—traditional in their method. The samurai sword was their weapon of choice. After I told them of my own experiences with a sword, they showed much interest. They also invited me to witness a performance of how to administer justice. They had purchased two murderers that they intended to execute the next day in the afternoon. I accepted their offer.

It seemed my social calendar was now full for the next day. I was starting to get the guests to open up to me. I needed information, and this social angle was a good way to find out who had information that could be useful.

That night was my final scan of Mr. Cole's mind. I now had over one hundred pages of information on the financial dealings, bank accounts, properties, and future plans of the Fascist Element of The New World Order. The information was too sensitive and valuable to risk sending it to my uncle by the usual computer methods. I would have to hand-deliver it to my uncle in New York.

Meanwhile, I had two appointments to witness new ways to kill people. It was a social requirement. My first stop the next day was with Mr. James and two gang bangers, rapist and murderers. I met Mr. James at the hotel and we were driven over to the execution building a few miles away.

Mr. James had booked a large torture room that had been cleared to provide a large open space, with a bare cement floor. I was shown the equipment bag. It only contained a few items: a set of brass knuckles, a six-inch knife, a policeman's nightstick, a jar of lube, and a baseball bat, simple stuff, but effective. Mr. James said that he was ready to inflict some serious pain to his two purchases before he cut their throats.

The two subjects of this game, Jose and Francisco, were brought into the room by guards. They were child rapists and murderers. They were both naked and handcuffed behind their backs. The guards threw them on the cement floor and left.

They both started running their mouths with the usual shit. "You bastards are going to pay for this. Our lawyer is going to roast your nuts."

Jose looked up at the both of us standing on the other side of the room. "What the fuck you two faggots want?"

Mr. James had put on a pair of overalls and steel-toed work boots. He approached the two bangers just after they had gotten to their feet. The first one, Jose, went down with two brutal punches to his guts, and Francisco crumbled to the floor after he was kicked in the nuts. The show was just beginning.

Jose was either not as hurt as Francisco or he was just more stupid. Jose got on his feet and ran at Mr. James. Mr. James quickly stepped aside and tripped Jose. The banger fell face first into the cement floor.

While the two thugs were getting their wits back, Mr. James put on a pair of brass knuckles with spikes on them. Mr. James then bypassed Jose to work over Francisco. The spikes on the knuckles took a heavy toll on Jose's body and face. In only about fifteen minutes, Mr. James had hit Francisco with over fifty punches. The result was Francisco bleeding and out cold on the floor.

Jose had managed to sit up during the whole thing and he witnessed what happened to his friend.

He started to act scared. "What? You two are crazy. I am going to sue the shit out of you both."

Mr. James now took out the policeman's stick. He put some lube on it and then turned around and looked at Francisco. "Remember, asshole, what you two did to that twelve-year-old girl before you killed her?"

"I didn't kill nobody."

A few moments later Mr. James had put a hammerlock on Francisco and had shoved the greased nightstick up his ass. When Francisco started to scream and cry, Mr. James shoved the nightstick in harder and deeper. When Mr. James finally withdrew the nightstick, Francisco lay bleeding from his ass on the cement floor.

Now it was Jose's turn. The end result was the same.

Mr. James now stood looking at both bangers who were crying and bleeding on the floor.

"Well, assholes, how did it feel?"

Those were the last words Mr. James spoke to the gang bangers. He took the baseball bat out of the equipment bag. Francisco was to be the first target. He was now on all fours and crawling toward the door in a vain attempt to get out of the room. The first blow hit him in the lower back. I heard bones crack. Francisco fell to the floor screaming in severe pain. The next several blows were to his back, legs, and arms. Again I heard his bones break. The end came with two hard blows to his head. There was blood all over the floor around Francisco. To make sure Francisco was dead, Mr. James took out the six-inch knife and slit his throat from ear to ear.

Jose got the same treatment, except he survived the blows from the bat—but not the cutting of his throat.

Did the show shock me? Of course not. Creeps like Francisco and Jose deserve a lot worse than what they got.

I could only think of how many people affected by their crimes would have loved to witness what happened to them. Hell, even a few rival gang members would have liked to be in on this kill.

My second stop, on what was to be a bloody day, was a demonstration of the use of the samurai sword. After a relaxing lunch at the resort, I was driven back to the execution building to witness the use of the samurai sword. Mr. Akito and his eighteen-year-old son Ichiro were my hosts.

The torture room had been prepared as they had requested. It was bare, except for two five-foot tall wooden posts. The posts were placed at opposite ends of the large, two-story room. Rings for holding shackles were inserted in different areas of the posts, as well as iron rings in front of the posts to hold shackled feet. I sat down in a folding chair on the side of the room near the entrance and waited. In only a few minutes, Mr. Akito, dressed in a business suit, and his son Ichiro, dressed in sandals and a Japanese robe, entered the room. Each of them was carrying a samurai sword. Ichiro's hair was fashioned in a bun, a traditional samurai style. I stood up. Mr. Akito and his son greeted me traditionally with a slight bow.

I bowed to them.

"Colonel, we are pleased that you could make it," Mr. Akito said.

"Glad to be here, Mr. Akito. It should be an interesting show."

"Yes Colonel. My son will do his best to entertain you today."

Mr. Akito's son now took off his robe. He was wearing only a sumo wrestler type of underwear, if you can call it that. To me, it looked more like a little white diaper. Ichiro had an athletic build. He stood about six feet tall and weighed about one hundred sixty pounds. His body was muscular and well defined. His skin was slightly tanned and smooth.

The two prisoners were now brought in. Both of them were naked and blindfolded. Each of them also had a ball gag inserted into his mouth. One of them was a very muscular Japanese man in his late twenties. He stood about six feet two and probably weighed at least one hundred ninety. The prisoner had several Japanese gang tats. Looking at his face told me right away this guy was a hardcore Japanese gangster.

The second prisoner was a white American man also in his twenties. He was not as muscular as the first prisoner, but he looked to be in fairly good shape. He was about six feet tall and weighed about one hundred sixty-five. He had a semi-hairy body. I knew the story on the first prisoner. He was a gang member and a multiple murderer. The second prisoner I had no memory of. I had read all the files on the prisoners, but this one did not stick in my mind. I used my hand pod to look him up. Yes, as usual, he was a murderer. He had killed his wife and their three kids because his wife was going to divorce him.

The guards shackled the prisoners to the posts, with their feet shackled to iron floor rings and their arms shackled behind the posts. A four-inch leather belt was fastened around their waists and the post.

Ichiro now started to prepare the prisoners for execution. He assembled two small, wooden bench-like devices and placed them in front of each prisoner. Both benches stood about two and a half feet tall and each had strings and a small wheel-like device at the end. I had no idea what it was used for. That was to change.

Ichiro bent down in front of each prisoner's privates. He fastened one end of each bench to the pole. Ichiro then tied the prisoner's cock and balls together. Then he fixed the strings in the device to the tied prisoner's balls and cock, and he started to twist. The prisoner, who had just been shaking a little during this procedure, now started to violently shake. He tried to scream but to no avail. When Ichiro was through, the device had the prisoner's balls and cock pulled straight out from his crotch. I could envision the reason for doing this.

The other prisoner was equipped in the same manner. Being blindfolded, both prisoners were probably confused as to what was in store. They would find out in just a few minutes.

After doing warming up exercises with his samurai sword, Ichiro was ready to work on the two prisoners. He chose the Japanese gangster as his first subject. First, he took the prisoner's blindfold off. He wanted the man to see what was happening to him. His first two sword strikes cut the prisoner's nipples open. Drops of blood started to run down the prisoner's chest. The gangster did not show that he was in pain. The next blow cut open his upper lip. Still he did not show that he was in pain. He stood motionless, without any expressions on his face, just a stone-cold look.

Ichiro now started a quick series of cuts that left over twenty large cuts on the prisoner's front torso and his legs. Soon, the front of his body was half covered in his own blood. This severe torture got no physical reaction from him.

The next sword blows would prove different. Ichiro now cut off both of the prisoner's ears. This got a reaction. The prisoner's body shook and his muscles tensed up. Ichiro now stopped for a few minutes and watched the Japanese gangster bleed.

I could sense that the end was near. After his rest, Ichiro got deadly serious. With one fast blow, he took off the prisoner's cock and balls. The Japanese gangster's body shook violently and his muscles tensed up. He tried to scream, but, because of the ball gag, he could not. Blood was all over the floor around the gangster. The man was bleeding to death. The end came with a heavy sword blow from the side. The gangster's head came off and fell to the floor. Ichiro turned and bowed to his father and to me.

The American prisoner was in for a different type of show. Ichiro tied heavy string around his lower legs, just above the kneecaps. He also did the same with his arms, just above the elbows. Again the prisoner's blindfold was taken off. After the usual small cuts, with good reactions, the end came fast. First Ichiro cut off his cock and balls and then both of his lower legs. The pain caused the prisoner to try to yank his body off the post. The veins in his face and upper body bulged and his body violently shook. Next came his forearms. Ichiro now rested for a few minutes to watch the prisoner's body shake in pain. The only thing holding the prisoner's body to the post was the four-inch leather belt around his waist. The man's torso fell forward. The end was the same as with the first prisoner. His head was soon lying on the cement floor. It was over. They were over.

Ichiro was now covered with his victims' blood. He looked content. He had administered justice and pleased himself and his father.

The drive back to the villa was relaxing. I had the air conditioning turned on, and I used the time to think. I was getting to the point where I understood why the people who staff this facility and many of our guests now refer to this island as Slaughter Island.

The next day I spent completing the file on the Fascist Element's financial system, which I had lifted from Mr. Cole's subconscious mind. The information was extensive. The bank accounts alone amounted to over seven trillion world dollars. These accounts were not supposed to exist. The Order had a banking system. Secret accounts were illegal. This information was really hot stuff. Now, my strange life was entering a new phrase: big-time bank robbery. This was going to be the biggest bank heist in history.

I contacted my uncle and told him the code phrase, "Uncle I've just bought your birthday present. I want to deliver it in person." He knew the phrase meant that I had acquired the needed information from Mr. Cole.

I decided that on this trip, I would take my girl with me. She smiled when I told her that we were going to New York City. She loved to travel with her new master. Plus I wanted my uncle to have an opportunity to meet my girl. You know what I mean. On this trip, I could hand-deliver the package of financial information and go over the details of how it was going to be used.

I put my boy in charge of my house. While I was giving Jimmy instructions on what I wanted done while I and my girl were in New York City, I heard a dog bark. The sound came from the backyard. Jimmy looked a little nervous. My boy followed me outside.

In the backyard, I found a medium-sized, short-haired female dog. Jimmy said that she had appeared on the property today and looked hungry and unkempt. So he fed the dog and gave it a bath. The dog was very friendly and playful. It was easy to figure that the dog had some training and had been someone's pet.

Then it hit me. This was the same stray dog that I had seen twice while I was overseeing the construction of the island facility. Several construction workers had befriended the dog and kept care of it. The story was that the dog belonged to the late owner of the island. After he died, the dog took off. It seemed the dog just did not want to leave his island. Now this dog turns up on my doorstep and gets adopted by my boy.

My boy seemed to really like his new toy and I was not in the mood to tell him to get rid of the dog. I later learned that the dog was a dead ringer for a dog that he had had as a kid in North Carolina.

Yes, I folded. I told my boy he had to care for and train the dog. My boy's eyes lit up and a big smile appeared on his face. I had said the magic words.

Jimmy grabbed and hugged the dog and said, "Sir, I will take good care of Princess."

Well, I now assumed that Princess was his childhood dog's name. That assumption turned out to be correct.

I took the company jet again. I was going to visit the Federal Security Administration building, in Washington DC, for a conference, and it was just a short hop from New York City. Visiting my uncle was going to be my first stop.

My uncle sent his car to pick me up. The ride to the Trump Towers was easier than usual. The difference was that I had arrived at the airport at 2:00 a.m. My uncle was eager to talk to me. I introduced him to my girl. My uncle had prepared a meeting with several of his associates, the good guys in the Order, for me to meet and plan a course of action. My girl I ordered to go to bed and get some sleep. I said that I would join her in a few hours.

As people were getting seated for the meeting, my uncle whispered in my ear. "Will, is that pretty lady your new slave girl?"

"Yes, she is devoted to me. If you are a good boy, Uncle, you can take her for a ride sometime tomorrow."

My uncle smiled. "It's a deal, Will."

I took three hours to go over the information and the possibilities it offered our cause. The plan was simple. We were going to steal the money and then transfer it to accounts controlled by our side of The New World Order. We would take out a few billion for our team as a handling fee. My uncle and his friends would set up new accounts, hundreds of them. The money would be transferred out of the original accounts to new accounts and then into the accounts of the Order. The financial alarm bell would go off big time the next day. So we had twenty-four hours at most to make the money disappear.

Our team had the benefit of an inside man in Mr. Cole's office in Chicago. With the information I had brought, our inside man could make the transfers from Mr. Cole's computer using his passwords and codes. When people started to trace where the money went, they would find out the whole thieft had started with Mr. Cole. Mr. Cole was our fall guy. But there would be no formal charges filed. Mr. Cole would be hunted by the Fascists. They would never find him, unless they searched the bottom of Lake Michigan.

The plan was to transfer the money to new accounts, then to other accounts, then to still other accounts, and to finally start to transfer the money to the Order accounts. It is a lot like the shell game: which cup is the pea under? Hopefully, the Fascists would not find any of the peas before we had the money safely in the Order accounts. The Fascists could not try to claim the missing money to the Order. They were not supposed to have these funds.

When the game was done, my uncle would visit the island to engage in the social activities that it offered. At least that would be the cover story. He would even buy a prisoner to execute. The real reason would be to go over what had happened after the plan was put into action. Seven trillion dollars. That was sure a hell of a lot of cash. My uncle estimated that the loss of such a sum to the Fascist Element would put them behind schedule by at least ten years. That was an extra ten years for our side to use to outmaneuver them and maybe put a stop to their plans.

After breakfast the next morning, my uncle, having been a very good boy, had a go at my girl. The way he was smiling the rest of the day gave me the impression that he rather enjoyed himself.

My girl said that my uncle is a real stud. "Sir, he really knows how to fuck."

The conference in DC was more routine stuff than educational. Sub-boring is the rating that I gave it. The boring conference did give me an opportunity to rub shoulders with some of the most powerful people in the Order. Several of these people I had already met on the island.

My second day in DC was spent with my girl in shopping (girl stuff), sightseeing, and trying to find the impossible in DC. The impossible task was finding a restaurant with good food. Washington, DC, was one of the centers of power in the world. You would think that you could find a place with good food, but I soon found out the DC was not known for good food.

The flight back to the island took several days. I do not like long plane flights, even if I have a private jet, a bed, etc. We stopped off for a day in San Francisco, which had good food, and a day in Honolulu, which had decent food.

When we arrived on the island, it was a little past midnight. I had not phoned ahead to tell my boy I was coming back. I never phoned him. I knew that I could trust him, and I usually did not know my own schedule. My schedule could change fast and only my office staff knew when I would return.

As I and my girl were driven up to the front door of the villa, all the lights were out. My girl handled the few bags that we had and I walked into the big house, turning on lights as I went. I found my boy sleeping on the front room couch, with his arm around his new pet, Princess. I smiled. My boy was happy, and that made me happy.

I gently woke him up. He opened his eyes and smiled. "Master, you are back."

"Okay, boy, it is late. Now get your slave ass up to bed. I will put Princess to bed."

"Yes sir. I am glad to have you back home."

I just had to clap my hands and Princess followed me to the laundry room in the back of the villa. I motioned for her to lie down on her blanket and she obeyed. I covered her over and petted her several times. I then unlocked the doggie door so she could go out if she needed to during the night. I had the doggie door installed when the house was built, just in case I wanted a dog.

CHAPTER 17: THE SECOND AUCTION

The second auction was ready to hit the Internet. We had acquired a better selection of prisoners. What I mean is we had a better idea of what our clients wanted to bid on now. In-shape gang bangers with lots of tats were in. Decent-looking, young (if possible) child molesters/killers were big sellers. If we could get a good-looking male lawyer, he would bring a high price. A lot of people hate lawyers. But at this auction, I was to sell two prisoners that would change almost the whole inventory of what the auction offered. Their names were Helen and Carlos.

Helen Campos was an extremely beautiful and deadly twenty-six-year-old female. She had a nasty habit of subduing rich young men with her beautiful body and her many charms. Her game plan was to drain the men of as much cash and expensive jewelry as she could before she killed them. Why kill them? Only she knew the answer to that question, and she never talked. She was one extremely sexy nut case. But she had one value that she did not know about. As was said in the stories that described her crimes, she owed a debt to society and we on the island intended to collect it.

Helen was marketed differently from former prisoners. Her Internet ad showed nearly nude and full frontal nude pictures of her. It listed her crimes and her sexual talents. When the second auction was held, she topped the list for the highest price paid. She brought in six hundred thousand world dollars. This of course was the highest price paid so far for any person on the auction, and the buyer intended to get his money's worth out of her before he dispatched this super bitch to hell.

The buyer was one Mr. Herbert Stone, and I was soon to learn that his last name described his heart. He was a wealthy, forty-six-year-old oilman from Houston, Texas. Mr. Stone was a big, stocky man. He was six feet four and he must have weighed at least three hundred pounds. His nickname was Long Horn. You can figure out what that means on your own.

Mr. Stone had brought along two relatives of his, a brother and a cousin, to help him get his money's worth, as he said, out of this crazy bitch that he had just purchased.

I met Mr. Stone and company at the main restaurant at the hotel. It was not a good beginning. When I walked into the room, I held out my hand to Mr. Stone.

He just stared at me and said, "What is that, boy? I don't socialize with the help."

I looked straight into his eyes and said, "Well, let me introduce myself. I am Colonel Andrews. I am in charge of this island and the auction."

He looked a little startled. "You mean the Order lets punk kids run a facility like this? God damn, that is stupid."

"What's stupid, Mr. Stone, is your attitude, and if you don't start copping a more polite attitude, I will have your big ass thrown off my island."

He now smiled. "Don't get your dander up, boy. I was just messing with you."

The conversation did improve after our brief conversation. But I have better taste in friends, and he was not going to be on my social list. But hell, if he wanted to pay a small fortune to off a very beautiful but crazy cunt, that was all right with me.

I had one of my assistants make his arrangements for him and I got as far away from that fat bastard as I could. I told myself that I wasn't going to have any more contact with Mr. Stone.

Mr. Stone and company decided to take three days to finish Helen Campos. Even if I had a bad opinion of Mr. Stone and his total lack of basic social skills, I had to admit that being raped, tortured, and killed by the likes of Mr. Stone and his relatives was a fitting end to her life.

I watched the action on the security cameras at the administration office. The first day Mr. Stone and company had Helen tied naked, spread-eagle, to a four-poster bed, in an almost empty torture room. For hours, the three men drank beer and raped Helen. I counted twelve times, but I did not watch the action the whole time. The security crew said it was fourteen times. One thing was sure: Helen probably walked bowlegged after that night, if she could walk at all. Mr. Stone and company didn't seem to mind all the foul names that she called them before they put a sock in her mouth.

The second night, Mr. Stone and company entertained themselves with more beer and a few snacks while they whipped the shit out of Helen. Again, she called them all sorts of foul names, some of which were new to me. This time they just let her mouth off. I think they were judging how effective their whipping was by how loud she screamed insults at them.

The third night was the end game. Helen was going to die. The boys, that is what I was now calling these three boneheads, were ready to finish her. But first, she was going to bleed. The cat-o'-nine-tails whip that they had used the night before was now equipped with small nails on the end of each strand of leather. Helen was soon bleeding over half of her body.

But this whipping was not to be the end of her. The boys were more creative; they brought along their own twelve-foot bullwhip. Mr. Stone, all lubed up himself, proceed to cut Helen to pieces. She bled out in less than twenty minutes. The clean-up crew carted her corpse over to be cremated. She was ashes and history in about three more hours.

Carlos Juarez was a good-looking Mexican American. He stood about six feet tall and he had an extremely muscular and well-defined body. This guy was a stud. But the Catholic Church had fucked up his mind. He had sexual problems, let's say. He had bought the crap the church taught him about homosexuals. The whole subject fucked up his mind. He was a convicted serial killer from LA. He would pick up gay guys and kill them. He hated them, but he just could not keep his hands off them. Yes, he was a real head case.

This was one time that it was personal. It seemed the father of one of the gay guys that he killed was a powerful member of the Order. Revenge was the game. Carlos was sold for five hundred thousand world dollars. The buyer was Mr. James Heller, the father of one of his victims. I was to find that making it personal added a lot of spice to the mix and a much higher selling price.

Mr. Heller scheduled an interesting series of events that Carlos would never forget in the brief time he had left. The first event I called sexual humiliation 101. Carlos was stripped naked and his hands were handcuffed behind his back. He was then led to a holding cell with twenty brutal convicts in it. The cons were bribed to rape him and teach him how to suck cock a dozen times. Carlos, it seemed, was a real screamer and mama's boy. He kept screaming for his mama. It was very unmanly of him.

The second night, Mr. Heller was present and it was not fun to watch. Carlos was severely whipped before Mr. Heller cut his balls off. I had to turn down the sound when he lost his balls. His screams hurt my ears. But this was not the end.

Carlos was taken back to his cell to live a ball-less life for another two weeks. Man, that must have been one hell of a head-trip for a man with a fucked-up mind like Carlos. During those two weeks, he stayed in his cell, eating very little and crying a lot.

After two weeks of me wondering what the next chapter was going to be, the final night was booked. It was an unexpected shocker. Mr. Heller had booked the impalement room. The last day for Carlos was going to be very painful.

That day and the next two, the crew, and sometimes I, watched Carlos slide down the post, until the sharp tip of the post was coming out of the center of his chest. He lasted two and a half days of the most intense pain a person can suffer. Three hours later, he was ashes.

What I called the saga of Helen and Carlos would in the end change the island's auction forever. Convicts did not pay as well as pretty people and revenge. Murderers, rapists, child molesters, etc. paid the bills, but the big money was in offering up a new type of product. Beautiful people and revenge were going to slowly become the big-ticket items. This is what I had feared would happen. Market forces were now starting to take control of the process. I just hoped that I could keep under-aged people out of the action. That is one line that I had decided I would not cross.

My uncle phoned me just after the fourth auction. He had bought a man on the auction, a murderer. He was flying on his private jet to dispatch his purchase. Well, that was the cover story. In reality, he needed to talk to me and tell me what progress had been made on our little project.

He showed up at the administration building early. I had been told he was not due for another three hours. He likes to surprise people. We took a long walk on the beach. It was a beautiful day. After exchanging social talk and going over the activities of my island, he stopped walking and gave me a very serious look. "Will, it is ready. Monday morning, Mr. Cole will disappear. Our boys have arranged for him to sleep with the fishes. Our man in Mr. Cole's office will make the transfers. The whole thing will be blamed on the missing Mr. Cole. While the Fascists are looking for the missing Mr. Cole and trying to figure out what is going on, the money will be in our accounts."

Would it in some form be on the evening news? I could not say. The effects of moving seven trillion dollars might have unforeseen reactions on the world economy.

Monday morning was tomorrow morning. My uncle was going to ride out the storm, if any, with me on the island. I asked him what he intended to do with his purchase. He just shrugged and said, "Well, we could just hang the creep. It would not be too messy."

So the next day, Mr. Oliver Hurt, murderer, was dropped to his death from the gallows in the execution building. My uncle and I spent the rest of the day at my villa watching news reports to see if what was happening behind the scenes in the world of high finance would be mentioned.

Reports from our people in the field kept coming in coded form from my uncle's home office. Everything was going as planned. No problems surfaced during the day. The game was in play and our team was winning, big time. Finally, we got the word. It was done. We had the money. Now it was up to us to see that all evidence of the crime was erased. We had the best computer and financial people available in the world. If something went wrong, it would have to something completely new.

Dinner that evening was great, as usual. My boy was a really good cook, or I should say chef. That evening, the four of us watched old horror movies on my new, massive one-hundred-fifty-inch HDTV. Both my boy and girl served us snacks and drinks in the nude. Both my uncle and I enjoyed seeing Linda and Jimmy in the nude and playing with them at times. I was their master and they existed for my pleasure. I kept saying that to myself because I had never gotten used to the fact that I actually owned two such perfect human, physical specimens.

I slept in the nude with Jimmy cuddled up against me and

Linda entertained my uncle. The entertaining went on and on. I didn't know that my fifty-five-year-old uncle had it in him. They stopped at about three in the morning and finally the house got quiet. I thought for a moment before falling asleep that maybe I should give my uncle a new nickname, such as Rabbit.

The next few days bought good news. The deed was done, and apparently we were not traced. I could tell by reviewing communications with different parts of the Order that not all was well. A lot of security lockdowns were ordered. My island was out of the loop and was not affected. The staff at Mr. Cole's Chicago office was interrogated.

I received a phone call from a general in DC that my services were needed in Chicago. What a setup. I was the person that was to scan the brains of Mr. Cole's office staff to see if any of them knew anything about the heist of the Fascist cash, as I called it. Score one for our side.

I took my boy to Chicago with me. It was his turn to travel with me. My girl was left to care for the villa and Princess. She welcomed the responsibility. It showed that I trusted her, and that put a smile on her face.

It was winter in Chicago. The city had just experienced a heavy snowfall. The Order had booked me into my old house. The Order had kept the house, which I and my boy had lived in for three years, as a guesthouse. It was good to step into my former home. My boy, having lived on a tropical island for the last six months, was eager to play in the snow. I gave him permission, and he stripped and ran naked into the backyard. My boy really likes to roll naked in snow banks. I stood on the back porch and watched the fun. After Jimmy was done having fun, I told him to go upstairs and take a hot shower.

After unpacking and doing some paperwork and making needed phone calls, it was dinnertime. I and my boy walked over to a local Mexican restaurant, one of my favorite places in Chicago, to have something to eat. The food, as usual, was great. We talked to a couple who had been our close friends when we lived in the city. It was great to see Jimmy start to come out of his shell and for a moment act like an average person. In the past, he seldom said anything in public. He was becoming the daddy's boy, in public, that I wanted him to be.

The next morning a car picked me up and took me downtown to the offices of the accountant to the Fascist Element, the now missing Mr. Cole. The offices looked like they were in a lockdown mode. No member of Mr. Cole's staff had been given permission to leave without two armed guards with them. They all were under close watch.

I introduced myself to the guards at the door to the offices. They asked me for my credentials, which I provided. They seemed satisfied, and one guard led me into an office to meet the head of security, Major Wells.

Major Wells went over the situation with me in a broad overview fashion. He did not cough up any details. I had to say, "Major, you failed to mention exactly what it is that you are looking for."

"Yes, sir, I can only say that some money is missing."

Hell, it was a mountain of money. "Major, how am I going to interview and interrogate the staff if I don't know what I am looking for? Some money is missing, Major. You would not apply such methods on an office staff unless a lot of money was missing."

"My orders, sir, do not give me the authority to tell you more than I have."

"I understand, Major. I will do my best with what I have been told."

I stayed at the accountant's offices for the next six hours, interviewing the staff, including the man who had helped my uncle to transfer the funds. I then spent another two hours typing up a detailed summary of my interviews and whether any of the staff was lying. The lying part was the only thing that the security people were actually interested in.

I faxed my report to the general that had recruited me for this job. It was now time to go back to my former Chicago home. The general would get back to me. I had laid the blame for the heist squarely on the shoulders of the now dead Mr. Cole. When the Fascists found out that their hidden cash was safely in the accounts of the Order, they wouldn't be able to do anything about it. The blame would be fixed on Mr. Cole, and the Fascists would make a vain attempt to find him. Their attempt would last years. They would never find him.

The plane flight back to the island was a mini vacation. I ordered the pilot to stop in Honolulu for a weekend. My boy and I enjoyed playing in the surf again and relaxing on the beach.

I got the word during my monthly vision-phone session with Joan and the twins: I became a father again. My daughter, Joan Elizabeth Andrews, was born while I was in Chicago. Joan sent me pictures of her all wrapped up in a pink blanket and a pink cap. The twins seemed overjoyed to have a baby sister. I now had a new addition to one of my two families. My family life was a little strange by average standards, but I was content with the way things were at present. Happiness was what mattered in the end.

The moderate side of The New World Order, or as I describe them the good guys, were very pleased with our team's heist of the Fascist Element bank accounts. Rewards and bonuses were approved. I was promoted to brigadier general in the Federal Security Agency. The members of our team were given financial bonuses, slush funds as they are called, which we could use for further activities against the Fascists. All such funds were in top-secret accounts. I was floored to see that my secret account had three billion world dollars in it. The members of the team had full authority to use the funds as they saw fit. In short, the funds were ours.

My uncle, the general, received five billion in his account. His reaction was, "What the fuck am I to do with this pile of money?"

He was already a rich man. The addition of several billion dollars would not make any difference in how he lived his life. The accounts were untraceable. Our names were not on them. With codes and passwords, our team could transfer funds to anybody, business, political party, or project that we wanted to fund in an effort to stop the Fascists from gaining control of The New World Order. In short, we were going to use the funds in the same manner as the Fascists had done. We were going to bribe people and influence the flow of world and regional events.

Our festive moods were dampened by my next communication from Caos. He informed me that the Fascists were not down and out. They were hurt, but not fatally. The repairs would take years, but the Fascists would recover. We had bought some time to organize and prepare. Caos indicated that we could expect the Fascist Element, along with their Lizard allies, to be more aggressive and cruel. Up to now, the Fascists had been using the tactic of bribery and economic pressure to bring people into their fold. Now they lacked the needed funds for such a tactic and they could be expected to get down and dirty, even to the level of using the Lizard military forces.

The possibility of facing the Lizard military put a whole new slant on the situation. The island and other friendly Order facilities were not really prepared to withstand a military assault. I would have to look into the security situation of the island.

As the next auction date approached, the pressure to add beautiful people and to allow revenge killings mounted. I had thought that this issue was to be my next problem. I was way off course on this one.

Her name was Mrs. Elizabeth Hollows. She was the widow of a billionaire businessman. She also served as a member of the governing boards of directors of The New World Order. She had power, and she knew how to use it.

The event that caused Mrs. Hollows to push for a change in my job description, and to dictate what my next project was going to be, was when I was to investigate the disappearance of her daughter, Pauline Hollows, age seventeen. She was a very pretty, blond, blue-eyed high school honors student. She was president of her high school student government and well liked at her school. Her loss was considered a great tragedy.

Her body was never found, and her mother was determined to find out what happened to her and to punish the person, or persons, responsible. The police investigation led nowhere. It seemed that Jane Hollows had just vanished off the face of the Earth. Add to this situation the fact that Mrs. Hollows was pretty sure that she knew who had taken her daughter, and you have the makings of a revenge killing.

Mrs. Hollows was referred to me because of my talents. My abilities were only known by a few people, mainly my uncle and the members of the team that pulled off the big heist of the Fascist trillions, and a few select members of the governing board of the Order. Mrs. Hollows was one of those board members. The woman was powerful and one of the Moderates on the governing board of the Order, so I agreed to help her.

The island project was running well and it did not need my constant presence. My teams were out all over the world looking for good-looking, condemned prisoners for the next auction. If they were successful, the rising tide of pressure to snatch people off the street could be stopped.

Mrs. Hollows was so determined to find out what happened to her daughter she took leave of her duties to the Order for a week in order to fly to my island and discuss the whole case with me personally. She would bring all the police files and the files of her own private investigators. I had my own ways of getting information.

Meeting Mrs. Hollows was an experience for me. She was a combination of a very pretty and feminine middle-aged women and an experienced, no-nonsense administrator. This woman had balls. She had power and she knew how to use it to get things done.

After the usual social gestures that such dire situations dictated, Mrs. Hollows presented me with the files that the police and her own private investigators had compiled. I was happy that the files contained numerous photos of her daughter and the leading suspects. I can get a reading from such photos.

After completing what was to be our first meeting, I had to ask, "Mrs. Hollows, may I ask what this project has to do with my island facility?"

"General, if my instincts are right, John and Gary Welsh killed my daughter and I want them brought to your island so that I can personally make them pay for what they did to my daughter. I will pay any needed cost, up to five million dollars, for your services."

She started to walk away, and then she turned around and said, "I want these bastards, General, so I can cut their balls off and kill them." With her point made, Mrs. Hollows left my office.

After reviewing the files, which took the rest of my day, I had come to the conclusion that Mrs. Hollows could be right about the Welsh brothers. In fact, my instincts told me that Mrs. Hollows's daughter was not the only victim. Was I sure? I wish it was that simple. No, I had to get close to the brothers in order to confirm that they were guilty of this crime.

The Welsh brothers were trust-fund babies. They were worth about one hundred million dollars. John was now twenty-seven years old and his brother Gary was twenty-five. They were sent to the best schools. Hell, John Welsh had been at Harvard only two years behind me. His brother went to Princeton. They spent their lives as party boys. The brothers were well known for throwing rowdy parties at their LA mansion. They were playboys. Their only goal in life seemed to be racking up a high score of babes that they had bedded. In college, the Welsh brothers would have been my type of people. That is, without the murdering teenage girls part of the picture.

The standards for selecting people for execution on the island had been changed by Mrs. Hollows and a vote of the high council of the Order. I could now execute people who were just suspects in a crime like murder, if I had investigated them and judged them to be guilty. Yes, I was now the only person entrusted with such authority. I was now the judge, jury, and executioner for never tried or convicted suspects.

I scheduled a dinner meeting with Mrs. Hollows in the main restaurant of the resort. Mrs. Hollows seemed very interested in what I had to say. "Mrs. Hollows, I am sorry to confirm that your daughter is dead. She was murdered, most likely by the Welsh brothers. Your daughter's murder may not have been the only murders committed by these men. My report to you tonight is not conclusive. I will have to get close to the Welsh brothers in order to confirm their guilt and the details of their crimes."

Mrs. Hollows looked relieved to know that her instincts were right and she had found the likely killers of her daughter. But she wanted to be sure the brothers were guilty.

"Thank you, General. I will be happy to help you in confirming their guilt in any way that I can."

"The first order of business, Mrs. Hollows, is to get me in a social situation with the Welsh brothers, and then I will need to be near them when they are asleep." I did not explain the reasons for such requests.

Mrs. Hollows agreed. "I will have my private investigators make the arrangements, General."

Mrs. Hollows left the island the very next day. She seemed eager to finally close this very painful chapter in her life.

I was now on call, it seemed. Until this matter was resolved to the satisfaction of Mrs. Hollows, who was my superior, I was basically her bitch.

Mrs. Hollows's private investigators lined everything up in just a week. They found out the Welsh brothers would be at a private pool party at one of their friends' Palm Beach, Florida, estate. Mrs. Hollows had great social connections, and she got me an invite for two to the party.

Since I was a very good-looking, hung stud and only twenty-nine years old, I should have fit into this crowd. Hell, I should really have stood out, especially since I had decided to take my girl to this party. Private pool parties like this one, with young good-looking rich people, end up with some nudity involved. Linda looked great in the nude. She would attract the Welsh brothers and give me the introduction that I needed to read the minds of the brothers.

Mrs. Hollows had also arranged for me to sleep in the room next to the brothers at their hotel. This assignment should be wrapped up in two days. My girl and I could spend an extra few days in Florida socializing with some old friends of mine, while my pick-up crew from the island arranged to snatch the brothers and make it look like an accident.

The flight to Florida went smoothly. When you have a private jet, long flights are more bearable. If you get tired you can just go to sleep in one of the bedrooms on the jet. Sleeping with my girl is always relaxing.

The weather was beautiful in Florida, a nice eighty-five degrees. My girl and I checked into the hotel room that was said to be right next to the Welsh brothers. We were in luck; the Welsh brothers passed us as we were walking to our hotel room. The brothers checked out my girl, and she smiled at them. This was a good opening. I had instructed my girl to flirt with the Welsh brothers if she got a chance. Mission accomplished.

The party started in one hour. I did not want to be one of the first couples to arrive, so Linda and I went shopping. In my opinion, women of any type, including devout slaves, like to shop. My girl picked out a pink thong bikini for the pool party. The bikini was designed to cover very little of my girl and to show off her natural physical assets. I called the suit Welsh brothers bait.

We arrived two hours after the start of the party. The place was packed with mostly good-looking, young people in various stages of dress. I could already spot several girls swimming nude in the pool. Such girls were either trying to impress their current boyfriends, or they were fishing for new rich boyfriends. After putting on our suits in the changing room, a room that had an attendant dressed as a butler, my girl followed me out to the pool area. I picked up two cocktails from a waiter and we were in business. Finding the Welsh brothers was easy. They had set themselves up in a choice location: a big table in the center of the social action. They had several hot, young babes with them.

The brothers eyed my girl, and she flirted with them with her eyes. Our opening came fast. The brothers sent a girl over to invite us over to their table. After basic introductions, we sat down.

The brothers were interested in my girl, so they naturally wanted to know whether we were a couple. I confirmed that Linda was my date; we were not a couple. Since Linda was, let's say, possibly available, the brothers took the bait. They now were much more social. They even acted like my friend.

In conversations with both of them, I tried to fit into their lifestyle. Names of colleges were exchanged. John asked me questions about Harvard. He wanted to check me out and see if I was a phony. I passed. All the while, I was reading their minds. Unfortunately, the brothers were both dicks and were just thinking about pussy. Linda seemed to really attract both of them. My girl was a great asset in this game.

The brothers' vibrations and the scan of their minds told me they were guilty. But I wanted details, and I could only get them with a talk tonight with their subconscious minds. We left the party early. I had made the contact with the brothers that I had come here for. The main event would be late tonight. The brothers would probably come back to their room with some hot babes and fuck away a few hours before they were ready to sleep. I figured 2:00 a.m. would be the hour.

While the brothers slept in their room, I would talk to their subconscious minds. They would sleep soundly not knowing that they were on trial for murder, and by the time they awoke they might be convicted and sentenced to a very painful death.

My girl and I used a rental car to visit a few local sights, and we had relaxing and delicious dinner at a Cuban restaurant. We then attended a local movie theater and saw a popular sci-fi movie. We got back to our room at about midnight. As we slipped into bed, I started to listen to the party boys next door. The brothers finally fell asleep with their current girlfriends about 1:00 a.m. By 2:00, I was able to get inside their sleeping minds to talk to their wide-awake subconscious minds.

What I learned that night was a horror story of how two rich, well-educated, and good-looking young men, who had every good thing that life could offer, had turned into serial killers. The reason was simple. The brothers had everything a normal person could want—money, women, and the time to do whatever they wanted—for as long as they wanted. Like many rich young people who never had to work a day in their lives, they had become bored. They were jaded. They wanted what money and physical good looks could not get them. The brothers wanted forbidden fruit. In their case, this was the pleasure of raping and killing innocent, pretty, teenage girls. They wanted to play God.

The brothers had raped and murdered fifteen teenage girls in the last three years. The routine was always the same. Kidnap a girl by using a tranquilizing gun. Then they would tie up and gag her and take her to their sailboat. The boat was a forty-two-foot-long pleasure craft that could sleep six people.

They would set sail and later anchor in a secluded bay along the coast of southern California. They would spent most of the night repeatedly raping and physically abusing the young girl. In the morning, having bound and gagged the girl again, they would set sail for deep water.

When the brothers were so far out to sea that they could not see the coast anymore, they would weigh down the still living girl before they would remove her gag, kiss her good-bye, and then dump her body over the side. When the bubbles stopped rising to the surface they would set sail for harbor.

The routine also included the complete cleaning of the sailboat and the changing of the van's license plates. The phony plates were taken off and disposed of and the real plates put back on. The van was also cleaned and sometimes repainted by the brothers themselves in an old warehouse that they owned.

Mrs. Hollows came back to the island to find out what my investigation had uncovered. When she read my very detailed report, she flew into a rage. She screamed, "I want to crush their nuts in my hands. Get them for me. I will pay you five million dollars to bring those two bastards to this island. I will dispose of them for good."

I agreed, and we then discussed how long it would take.

"Mrs. Hollows, I have a team of experts working on arranging a fatal accident for the brothers."

She interrupted me. "No! You do not understand. I want the pleasure of ending their lives."

"Yes, I understand, Mrs. Hollows. You see, when we snatch them, we have to make it look like they had an accident and their bodies were never recovered."

She now smiled. "Yes, I can see what you mean, General."

"My team believes that the brothers' sailboat is the key to having them disappear, as if an accident has happened. I will call you when we have the brothers in custody. Then you can take as long as you want to dispose of them."

My conversation with Mrs. Hollows now entered a more vengeful phrase, the brothers' method of execution. I described the facilities available on the island. But Hollows was more interested in my experiences. I went over several different very painful methods that I had experience with. Mrs. Hollows did not make any decisions about methods that night, but she did seem really interested in my story about how Carlos Juarez was tortured and killed. It was almost painful enough to suit her.

The team sent to snatch the brothers was comprised of Federal Security Officers. They could operate out in the open with the knowledge of the local police department. The locals, as federals called them, did not interfere in any way with the operation. To them, it was a national security problem.

It was weeks before the brothers actually went sailing alone. Three times they took groups of friends with them. Then everything came together.

One weekend with only fair weather, the brothers set sail alone. The weather report was mixed. There was a possibility of stormy weather. This was the perfect situation to set up the snatch. The team set off in a cabin cruiser that they had borrowed from the coast guard. The cruiser was outfitted with satellite radar. The team kept track of the brothers and when they were out of sight of land and no ship or boats were nearby, the team moved in. The brothers were arrested, cuffed, and put below deck. Their sailboat was struck with explosive charges.

Officially, the Welsh brothers were lost at sea. Even the stormy weather had helped out in the effort. The brothers were given a shot that would put them to sleep for twenty-four hours. Within hours, they were on a private jet to meet their fate on Slaughter Island.

When I phoned Mrs. Hollows, on a secure line, she was overjoyed, and, as with her commanding nature, she faxed me instructions on what to do with the brothers for the next month. She would arrive after we did, as she called it, the spade work. I did not realize it at the time, but the term spade work was a code.

Mrs. Hollows wanted the self-centered, cold-hearted brothers to be humiliated, abused, and raped. She wanted them to know what her daughter went through.

The first day the Welsh brothers spent on the island, they were naked and sitting in a prison cell. The cell was in a private section of the prison. The private little cell block held three cells and a big exercise room. Mrs. Hollows wanted the brothers to get some exercise, but not the type of exercise that average people engage in.

The first day I went over to the prison to visit our new arrivals. When I walked into the cell, wearing my general's uniform and carrying a file folder, both brothers recognized me instantly.

John was the first to speak, "Will, I am glad to see you. There has been a big mistake. We didn't do anything wrong. Can you help us out?"

I just looked at both naked brothers and forced a small laugh. "Yes, if you don't consider murder to be a bad thing."

Hearing my opening words sent a chill down their spines. They seemed a little scared. "We all know why you are here. You have committed the murder of fifteen teenage girls in the last few years."

John was the first again to speak. "We did nothing. I want my lawyer."

"Well, John, both you and your brother will not need a lawyer.

You have already been tried and convicted and there is no appeal process. You both have been sentenced to death."

Now Gary got mad. "Look, you fucking asshole. Stop playing this sick game and let us out of here. Our family lawyer is going to have your ass for lunch if you don't let us out of here right now!"

I didn't reply. I sat down in a chair that had been set up in front of the cell the brothers were occupying. After opening the file, I got started. "Let's start with the first teenage girl that you and your brother murdered, one Miss Linda Owes, only fifteen years old."

I proceeded to read off the story of how they found and kidnapped the young girl and I finished with the method of murder. Both brothers looked a little nervous. They looked at each other, as if one of them had confessed and ratted out the other.

To shouts from the brothers, of "Cut it out, you will never prove any of that crap," and the often repeated, "Fuck you, asshole" with the usual finger salute, I proceeded to outline the brothers' whole little reign of terror.

When I was through, they just sat in their cells, staring at each other. They were royally fucked, and they now knew it.

The brothers' first week was termed their exercise week. It was not a full-body exercise program; it was selective in its approach. Only two main parts of their bodies were exercised: their asses and their mouths. The guards taught them several new talents, including how to take it up the ass and how to properly suck a cock.

At first, they put up a fight, but they were no match for the big, muscular guards who were their teachers. They received their instructions twice a day. By the time a week was up, the two young men were starting to get good at what they were assigned to do, or who they did.

All of their instruction by the guards was filmed and sent to Mrs. Hollows. She at times would send back instructions on how a guard was to properly instruct one of the brothers. It was almost like Mrs. Hollows was directing a gay porn movie. She was really enjoying the whole scene, and I was making brownie points with a very powerful official of the Order.

The next week was considered a new level of instruction. The brothers were handcuffed behind their backs and taken naked down to one of the main holding cells. The cell at the time held twenty hardcore felons. The game was on. The brothers were repeatedly gang-raped, all filmed of course. The next few days John seemed to walk a little bowlegged. Both brothers complained of having sore assholes. It seemed the cons were not as gentle as the guards.

This gang rape was repeated two more times. The second time the brothers came out of the holding cell crying and begging not to be put back in that cell.

The following week, Mrs. Hollows arrived on the island. The end was near. She quickly ordered the brothers into a torture room. When she and I walked into the room, we saw that the brothers had been properly prepared. They were both naked and hanging by chains from the roof of the torture room. Their feet had been securely shackled to the cement floor.

I introduced Mrs. Hollows. "Well, boys, I would like to introduce you to your new master. Mrs. Hollows has just bought the both of you and she intends to get her money's worth out of your hides today."

Gary's face turned a light shade of red and he said, "Well, bitch, if you want me to fuck your old pussy, you are out of luck."

Mrs. Hollows stared directly into his eyes and said, "No, it is you and your brother who are out of luck and out of business."

Mrs. Hollows never spoke to the brothers again that night, regardless of what they said. She just whipped the shit out of them. By the time the guards took them down, they were both heavily bruised and cut up. They also had both passed out.

Mrs. Hollows was now in the mood to smile a little and enjoy the finer things that this island resort had to offer. She spent the next week getting massages, swimming, and socializing with the other hotel guests. It seemed she wanted the brothers to have some time to heal before her next session with them.

Mrs. Hollows asked me to accompany her in her next session with the boys. I sensed that the iron lady herself had some doubts that she could pull it off.

The brothers were again hanging naked from the ceiling by chains, with the usual torture room shackles on their bare feet. This session was to be short. My job was to teach Mrs. Hollows how to double-tie each brother's ball sack. I gave Mrs. Hollows two strands of heavy string. "Just do as I do, Mrs. Hollows." I got down in front of Gary's naked body, grabbed his balls, and yanked them down hard a few times. I then tied the first strand of string around the top part of his ball sack.

The brothers started to squirm and complain. "What are you going to do to us? Stop it!"

"Now tie the second strand a half inch lower."

Mrs. Hollows followed my directions. She was starting to smile.

I got up and went over to the equipment table. I gave Mrs. Hollows a six-inch cutting knife. "You cut between the knots. Do you want some privacy, Mrs. Hollows?"

She nodded, and I left the room. Before I was halfway down the hall, I heard John scream, and then a few seconds later Gary screamed really loud. After that, all I could hear was crying and bitching.

The next day, I had breakfast with Mrs. Hollows. She actually seemed to be in high spirits. "Well, General, in three days I will finish them both. The world is a better place without those two perverted bastards."

I agreed.

The last session was in the impalement room in the execution building. The brothers were brought in naked, gagged, and blindfolded. They offered no trouble to the guards. They had no fight left in them. I believe that the two brothers had held onto the hope that somehow they would find a way out of this mess and they could go back to being rich playboys and fucking hot chicks. That meager hope had vanished.

After the guards took the boys out of their cell, they used a police stick to grease up their assholes. They offered no trouble. The brothers had big bags under their eyes and a sickly pale look to their seriously bruised and wounded skin.

But the spark of life came back fast just after the guards mounted the boys on their individual poles. The blindfolds were now taken off so the brothers could watch themselves slide down the greased poles in the mirror in front of them. Mrs. Hollows wanted them to suffer and to watch their own painful deaths.

I left right after the boys were mounted on the poles. This form of torture and execution was not my cup of tea. Mrs. Hollows spent the rest of the day watching the two suffer as they slid further and further down their poles.

At this point, I wasn't worried about the two assholes on the poles but about the effect that this was having on Mrs. Hollows. Since the auctions were started, there had been people who displayed mental problems after executing a prisoner.

It was the old saying, sometimes people bite off more than they can chew.

The auctions now had more physically appealing young men and women. We had to get more and more prisoners from foreign countries, but the quality improved. In fact, if I was sent a young, muscular, defined, tattooed gang banger, I could get two hundred thousand world dollars for his naked ass. I was really surprised to see how many women members in high standing of the Order bought muscular, young hoods to butcher. Twenty-five percent of the buyers at the auction were women.

The numbers of prisoners offered at these auctions was down. We now put on the block fewer than one hundred prisoners per auction. The physical standards for the prisoners had been upgraded, which proved to me and my staff that this blood sport craved young, quality meat. Ugly cons were out, except well-known cases; young cons with good bodies were in.

The new section of the business, revenge killing, started to grow as word got out to the members. I had to hire new staff on the island and around the world to check out each new request. Most of the requests did not meet the needed standards. If a person passed through the system and checked out, I was left with the final responsibility to make a decision. Judging guilt was my business.

Two days each week I spent on this new process, holding to my standards that only people who were guilty of a capital crime would be picked up. But how long I could hold the line on this was a constant worry to me.

I was very grateful for my home life during this period. My slaves and Princess provided an oasis away from the storm. The pressures of my job kept expanding, and then there was always the threat from the Fascists and their allies the Lizards to contend with. We fought the Fascists' influence on the Order more and more as they became more aggressive in their tactics. Lack of funding had forced them to use muscle more and cash less as the struggle continued for control of the Order.

The thought in the back of our minds during these years was always the same question: When would the allies of the Fascists, the Lizards, get so frustrated with the progress of their allies that they would choose to commit their military forces? Caos told me several times that the Lizards were making plans. Over a year ago, I started preparations to defend the island. Using the island's natural cave system, a secret underground defense system was being built. We were not yet prepared for such an assault, but with the help of our allies, the Nordics and the Grays, we were making rapid progress.

Judging the guilt of a person who was referred to me for evaluation required a lot of travel. I tried to take along my girl or boy on these trips. Having one of them with me helped to steady my thinking, plus Jimmy gave great full-body, deep tissue massages. It was the best way for me to relax after a stressful day.

One such trip was to Los Angeles, California. An evaluation of a beautiful blond lady was required, and I took my girl with me. Since the best youth doctors in the world lived and worked in LA, I decided to get my girl and me the youth shots. The new shots were stronger than in previous years. Any person who took the shots would only age one year for every seven years lived.

I was now thirty years old and looked more like twenty-five. I had kept myself in excellent condition. Linda was twenty-four, and, frankly, she looked more like twenty. It was a good point in our lives to slow down the aging process, so we both could get more out of our limited time on this world.

The youth shots took a week to administer. The physical affects were minor. I and my girl at times felt a slight fever and at times a little light-headed feeling. This procedure did not in any way slow me down in doing my evaluations.

My reason for being in LA was a request for revenge, to approve the execution of one Miss Coy Bennett. She was a beautiful, twenty-six-year-old blond lady. The request said that she was a major con artist and murderer. Was she?

I was set up to meet her in the bar of the Beverly Hills Hilton.

She looked better in person than in her photos. This was one hot chick. My cover was that I was a potential investor in southern California real estate. Raw, undeveloped land was my game.

This lady liked to seduce and con wealthy married men. So far, two of her marks had ended up very dead. The brother of one of the dead men wanted to personally torture and kill this lady. On this trip, my girl posed as my wife. She was in on the scene, except for the part where the lady con artist is put to death. I like to keep my slaves out of my true business. My girl was devoted to me and she really enjoyed her little acting job.

Our meeting in the hotel bar was fruitful. In an hour-long conversation and three drinks each, I was able to determine that this beautiful lady was extremely dangerous. Yes, she was guilty, and this murderous bitch had to be put down.

The team was put into action. The lady in question just disappeared without a trace. The local police, who had investigated her several times in the past, were not surprised. The police had been building a case against her when she left town. She never turned up again.

The man who had made the request was very happy. He had paid half a million dollars to get his revenge. My staff said that the man enjoyed torturing the pretty lady before he personally strangled her. It was not the standard form of justice that Americans are used to, but it was justice.

Chapter 18: The Saudi Project

I was surprised as hell with the new revenge project that I had been handed. It was marked "Top Secret." The proposed project concerned the disappearance of the granddaughter of a powerful member of the Order. This man, Mr. Schulze, was also a person who was on our side of the fence. This project was to be given my full attention.

Investigations of the disappearance of the member's granddaughter got nowhere. The police detectives had followed all the leads and the leads pointed at a Saudi prince as the prime suspect. Having diplomatic status, the prince was untouchable. The trail went cold.

News of Saudi princes kidnapping girls and boys from America and Europe was not a new story. My grandfather told me that it did happen and that only a few Saudi princes were involved. He called the whole affair a curse on the House of Saud. My grandfather also was of the opinion that the current king of Saudi Arabia had put a stop to such practices. He was wrong.

My uncle had another, more political, reason for approving this new project. He wanted to publicly embarrass two Fascist Element members of the governing board of the Order. Both men were Saudi princes who were, according to his intelligence, involved in this child slave ring in Saudi Arabia. Such bad publicity would give him the needed power to kick the princes off the governing board. My uncle wanted to fill their two seats with Moderates of his choice.

To me, this new project was a dream come true. Since I was a child, I had dreamed of being a hero in just such a drama. Now I had the go-ahead and all the power and money that I needed to crack open the whole dirty affair and push two Fascists off the Order's governing council.

Did the fact that I owned two slaves have any effect on my mind at this point? No. This was to me not a moral issue; it was politics, pure and simple. I and my uncle were going to make a lot of political gains out of this project.

In order to hopefully free the member's granddaughter, and I believed a lot of other sex slaves, I first needed to do some field intelligence work. I decided that I needed a trip to Saudi Arabia to visit my grandfather and to interview the slave trainer that had trained my boy.

I phoned and arranged a visit with my grandfather at his Riyadh palace. I asked my grandfather to arrange the meeting with some special people that I would need to talk to in order to get the information that I needed to focus my investigation. I was soon to learn that my grandfather would get me more than I needed.

When I got home, I told my boy to pack my and his stuff. We were going to Saudi Arabia. Jimmy's reaction was unexpected. He dropped to his knees and said, "Please, sir, don't sell me. Please don't sell me."

"No, boy, I have no intention of selling you. You are far too valuable to me and my household. I would never sell you."

He looked up at me and smiled. "Thank you, master."

When I and my boy arrived in Riyadh, my grandfather and his car were waiting to pick us up. This was an unexpected honor.

My grandfather seldom greeted people at the airport. He had something on his mind that could not wait.

I sat in the back of the car with my grandfather and my boy rode up front. My grandfather seemed eager to talk about the purpose of my visit. In order to secure our conversation against prying ears, he pushed a button and a thick window slid into place, separating the front seat from the back.

"William, I am thankful that you have chosen to undertake this assignment. It is a subject that is dear to my heart. I have formally asked three kings of Saudi Arabia to intervene in this matter and I have gotten nowhere. I have only been told official lies. Hopefully, you can end this cruel practice of kidnapping children off the streets of foreign countries, abusing them, and then killing them. It has been a personal burden on me to know that this practice is going on and I have not been able to stop it."

As with the Koran, the Muslim holy book, my grandfather is on both sides of the issue when it comes to owning slaves. My grandfather believes that it is permitted to own a slave that was sold into slavery by themselves or their family. It is the will of Allah, according to my grandfather, that said person was to be a slave. But my grandfather believes that the Koran does not permit a master to abuse or kill his slave. So, while he is a slave owner, he treats his slaves well.

"As you have asked me to do, William, I have arranged two interviews for you. The first is with the slave trainer that you wished to talk to about his methods of mind changing, as you termed it. The second is with a former helicopter pilot and bodyguard for one of the most powerful princes that is involved in this crude affair."

At this point in our conversation, I had one very important question. "Grandfather, I need to know if you have told anyone about this project, especially your son Omar."

My grandfather smiled and said, "No, William, you told me it was top secret and I have told no one." My grandfather's word was all that I needed on the matter.

The car took us to my grandfather's palace in Riyadh. The palace was my grandfather's main residence and the home of Grandfather's branch of the House of Saud. The structure was the size of a big hotel, several hundred thousand square feet. The palace had beautiful marbled hallways and vast rooms for entertaining. The staff needed to run the palace numbered over two hundred.

Looking at my grandfather's home again could only make me think, *This is one hell of a shack.*

My grandfather's two pleasure slaves, Muhammad and Sabao, helped to unload our baggage. They both seemed happy to see me again, and they even greeted my boy in a friendly manner.

After having our bags unpacked by the two house slaves, I decided to get a few hours of sleep, so I and my boy stripped and we got into the room's king-size bed. When I awoke, I had my boy give me a massage, and later he soaped me down in the shower. I felt like a new man. As I and my boy stood naked, toweling off in the bathroom, Muhammad announced that a meal would be served in the main dining room in thirty minutes. Food—just what I was thinking of.

The food was a simple meal of chicken and lamb in rice, with dates, coffee, and flat bread. My boy followed me around not knowing how to behave at such an event. Frankly, I did not know if my slave was permitted to eat with me and my grandfather. The problem was solved when my grandfather noticed the problem.

"William, why don't you have your slave help with the meal? He can eat later."

"Yes, Grandfather. Grandfather, since this is the first time you have seen my boy, would you like him to help serve the food in the nude, so that you can see why I bought him?"

"Yes, William, that would be interesting. I will order Muhammad and Sabao to do the same."

That is how my grandfather met the slave that he had bought for me. My grandfather looked at my naked slave often during the meal. He seemed to approve of my taste in pleasure slaves. My grandfather was at the later stage of his life. He was not much interested in sex anymore. The pleasure slaves that he owned were more for his guests than for himself.

My grandfather had married three wives and had nine children. His second wife was a blond French lady and the mother of my mother, my grandfather's fourth child. My mother later married my father, an American of Irish descent, and they had me. My grandfather at the time did not approve of his daughter marrying an Irish American Catholic, but my mother was in college in the United States and married my father anyway. After I was born, my grandfather started to accept the marriage more and more as the years passed.

Two days later, my interview with the slave trainer was arranged. I took my boy with me. He was actually happy about seeing the man who had enslaved and trained him. Our driver drove us outside the city limits to an oasis that sheltered a large white-walled compound. An armed guard at the main entrance checked our credentials. He than checked his appointment list before he let us proceed.

A young, half-naked male slave led us into the main building. The structure was built around an open-air garden with a big fountain in the middle. The man I had come to see greeted me. My boy bowed his head in respect for his former master. The man noticed my boy and smiled.

"I see that you brought your slave with you. He was one of the best boys that I have ever trained. It was the will of Allah that sent this boy to me. General, has this slave performed up to your standards?"

"Yes, I am very proud to own such a devoted and well-trained slave."

The man smiled. He seemed to take a great deal of pride in his work.

"Before we proceed with our business, General, may I have permission to inspect your slave?"

"Yes, you may inspect my boy."

The slave trainer then ordered my boy to strip.

"Yes sir!"

The slave trainer then proceeded to caress, fondle, tickle, and grab every inch of my boy's naked body. He even inspected his teeth and asshole. My slave seemed to enjoy the attention he was getting from his former training master.

The slave trainer looked very pleased with my boy. "You have taken very good care of this slave. He looks much better than the day that I sold him to his first master. I like masters that treat their slaves well."

He then ordered my slave to kneel naked in a shaded area of the courtyard.

I was now asked to follow the slave trainer. As I walked into the building, I took a quick look around the courtyard. I wondered what memories my slave had of this place and his training. I would have asked him what had happened to him in this place. This place and the man that I was about to interview drastically changed his life, and I wanted to find out how it was done.

I was led in to a room that looked like a cross between a den and an office. I was asked to make myself comfortable in a lounge chair. The slave trainer sat down in a chair opposite to my own.

"General Andrews, I am Omar. My last name is of no importance. I have been told by an old friend of mine, your grandfather, that you want to know how a slave's mind is trained."

"Yes, that is true."

"Well General, it is a simple procedure. I developed a chemical compound and electric approach that allows me to reprogram the dominant/submissive nature of a slave's mind. It works best on slaves that already have submissive personalities. It will seldom work to any great degree on a very dominant personality. Slaves that are much like your boy are perfect subjects. Your boy was born to be a man's slave."

The rest of my interview I tried to get the slave trainer to go into more details, but he would not give up his secrets. All that I could get him to say was that the chemical compound relaxed and opened up parts of the slave's mind, and specially designed subliminal tapes slowly trained the slave's mind to make the new slave a person who was eager to please his or her master. I have lived with the result of such training for four years now, and I can testify to how effective this method is on the right personality. The slave trainer admitted that he and his associates were always on the lookout for good-looking, young males and females that fit the description of a perfect subject. Such slaves sold for a high price.

Because of my ability to read a person's mind I was able to uncover the fact that the chemical formula that was used was not developed by the slave trainer. He did not know the formula. I decided that finding out more about this formula and the person who owned it would have to wait until another time. I did not have the needed time at present to look further into this subject.

After the interview, I thanked the slave trainer for the information that he gave me. My boy was still kneeling naked in the courtyard. He had been there for two hours. During the ride back to my grandfather's palace, I gave my boy a short quiz. "Boy," I said.

"Yes sir."

"What did you think of seeing your old master and training school again?"

He smiled. "It was great, sir. I learned a lot at that school. I learned what is important. Like what God wants me to do with my life. I learned that I was born to be the property of a perfect master like you, sir."

Now it was my turn to smile.

The Saudi slave master did not have what I was looking for. The methods that he used were not anything new. What was I looking for? Well, a story that I read as a child has always stuck in my mind. It was the story of alien bodies. The bodies had been found at the site of an alien spaceship crash. They had been examined by American scientists. They found that the aliens had no digestive or reproductive systems. Their conclusion was that the aliens were not the aliens. They were biological robots. Bio-robots like my former training camp roommate Fred.

As a boy, I could not help to wonder that, if they were robots, then they must have a system to program these robots. The human mind is just a biological computer. We can upload and download knowledge on our home computers. The aliens had found a way to upload and download information in the mind of a biological robot.

I thought about what would be possible if we found a way to upload and download information on the human mind. It would be possible to completely change a person's mind. Hell, it would be possible to download a person's mind from his or her body and have another person's mind put in its place. In short, people could change bodies. The whole idea still to this day fascinates me. Someday, someone will figure out how to do this. As with all new inventions, it has an upside and a downside. The downside is that an evil world leader could program an army of perfect soldiers, which is a scary thought. On the upside, it would be possible to completely change a person from being a criminal into being a respected and law-abiding citizen. You also would not need to go to college. A college education could just be downloaded into your mind. I just know that when it happens, I want to be there.

I had my driver take me and my boy back to my grandfather's palace. This was not the first time that one of my projects did not work out, and it won't be the last.

My boy and I slept well that night. When you had someone like my boy to cuddle up with at night, you really didn't need any extra blankets. He was a hot little body and he kept me warm at night.

The next day my boy gave me an hour-long massage. After a quick shower, I was ready for my next, and possibly my most important, meeting.

After a small breakfast of American-style waffles, I was ready to meet with a man who had been a bodyguard and helicopter pilot for a prince who was pretty much the main man in the child sex-slave community in Saudi Arabia. The man's name was Fahd Nassif. He had been trained by the US Army in security and later as a helicopter pilot. He was later hired by a Saudi Arabian prince who was very much involved in the kidnapping of children, up to the age of eighteen, to be used as sex slaves in the Middle East. He went along with the program because of the money. The prince paid his staff very well. But after about ten years, the pilot could not live with what he had done in the employment of the prince. The part of the job that finally got him to quit his well-paying job was the dumping of used-up child sex slaves in the desert.

I did not have to travel for this meeting—Mr. Nassif came to me. We started our discussion in my grandfather's den. Mr. Nassif had been briefed on the reason for my visit, and he was eager to help.

I told him of the young girl that I was looking for, and he gave me several names of princes that would be interested in such a young lady. I did not tell him that the girl in question had been chipped by her parents. If I could get within ten miles of her, I could get a fix on her location. The names he gave me would be a great help.

"Mr. Nassif, I have been told that you flew the helicopter a number of times that deposed of unwanted child sex slaves. Is that true?"

"Yes, General, I flew forty such night missions in my ten years of employment with the prince."

"How many slaves did you dump in the desert?"

"I would estimate about four hundred slaves. It is something that I am deeply ashamed of."

"Did you dump them just anywhere in the desert?"

"No, General, I always dumped at exactly the same location. I thought that I may someday need to prove to people that this sort of thing actually happens. The Saudi government has always denied such things happen in this country."

He now pushed a small piece of paper toward me. I looked it over. It was the location, in longitude and latitude, for what I would later call the child slaves graveyard.

Well, I now had names of some of the main players in the game. Then Mr. Nassif added something new to the mix. He must have been reading my mind.

"General, if you want to catch all these rats together at one time, it can be done. The society has a general meeting at the same time and location each year. At this meeting, they party, fuck their child slaves, and trade slaves. Over thirty players attend each year and will bring with them at least one hundred child slaves. I give you this information in case you want to hit them, General."

He then pushed a folded up piece of typing paper across the table. I looked into his eyes and said, "Mr. Nassif, do you want me to hit them?"

"It is the will of Allah that you do this, General."

The information checked out. The girl that I was looking for was still alive, and she was the prisoner of one of the men on the list. The big party once a year was confirmed a few days later. I owe a great deal of things to my grandfather and his connections. I could not have gotten such information without their help.

There was just one thing left to do before I flew to DC to have my orders clarified and to report to some very powerful people on my progress so far. I needed to find the desert graveyard.

My grandfather provided me with a helibus. A helibus is an aircraft the size of a standard city bus that is lifted off the ground by four props. The aircraft has two ringed props on each side of the aircraft. It is an advanced type of helicopter. My grandfather also provided me with four armed guards.

We flew out at night south toward the Rubal Khali desert in southern Saudi Arabia. This patch of sand was five thousand square miles of the most hellish desert on Earth. The local people just called it The Sand. No one went there. It was the perfect place to dump a body.

After flying for several hours, the aircraft slowed down and began to land. Landing lights suddenly went on and a few moments later we touched down. This was the location that I had been given by Mr. Nassif. It was an hour before daybreak and I could already feel the heat. Then the sun started to come up. I was not ready for what we saw.

The ground around the aircraft was littered with human bones.

Mr. Nassif was telling me the truth. I walked out over the sand dunes, sometimes stepping on bones and skulls. There must have been hundreds of them. Most of the remains were of small people not yet fully grown. I inspected several dozen skulls. Their dental work showed that these people were not locals. They had had good dental care, as you would expect in Europe or the United States.

I just shook my head. "So the stories are true. This is the way it ends for a kidnapped child slave. They are disposed of like garbage."

The two aides from the island that had flown in the last day of my stay started to photograph the remains before the sun made the desert too hot to stay. I would need the film to make my point at my meeting with the DC power brokers.

The flight to DC went smoothly. I and my boy arrived during the night, which gave me enough free time to get a decent night's sleep before the meeting. Room service fed the both of us, while I studied my report to the committee.

My car arrived about 10:00 a.m. The meeting at the Federal Security Building was scheduled for 11:00 a.m. Since I was going to be gone most of the day, I gave my boy several hundred dollars and told him to see a movie and to do a little shopping. Sometimes being my boy's master is a lot like being his dad. He smiled. My boy liked to watch current sci-fi and horror movies in 3D.

The meeting was in a large conference room. Almost twenty important and powerful people were already seated at the table when I was escorted to my seat. One man spoke to me briefly before the meeting got underway.

"General Andrews, I am Mr. Schulze, and I am eager to hear what you have to say today. I hope you have good news concerning my granddaughter."

The chairperson for this meeting turned out to be Mrs. Hollows.

Knowing that Mrs. Hollows was going to run the meeting relieved a great deal of stress. She owed me a favor and I may need some help with what I was going to propose. I also was thankful that the two Saudi princes that were part of this child slavery ring were not part of this panel.

Mrs. Hollows opened the meeting with an overview of the situation, and then she gave me the floor. "Gentlemen and ladies, the situation is simple and complex. I was given the assignment to find a young lady that had been kidnapped and to free her. Well, I am glad to report that I have found her and she is still alive."

Mr. Schulze showed a sign of relief. "But there are problems involved with freeing Mr. Schulze's granddaughter. You see, she was kidnapped by a Saudi Arabian prince and she has been forced to become a sex slave in his palace."

Mr. Schulze's face became beet red at this point and he said, "General, if you know where she is why can't you free her?"

"Mr. Schulze, it is a matter that is very complex. She is held in a foreign country under heavy guard. Yes, I can organize a team to free her, but with great risk attached to her and the members of the team. My orders are not clear on what type of response I can order to free your granddaughter—a small team effort or, as I would like to propose, a large effort that would not only free your granddaughter, but a hundred or more such sex slaves and possibly end the Saudi child sex-slave problem for good."

I was asked to explain what I wanted to do. By the end of the meeting, I had obtained the permission to go ahead with my plan. I was also given all the support that I would need. If I needed something, all I needed to do was ask and it would be provided. It felt good to have a blank check on this plan. This type of situation seldom happens in dealing with a government agency. Finally, I was going to destroy the evildoers, something that I had wanted to do since I was a ten-year-old kid.

I had two months before the princes had their annual desert

meeting. The needed military and paramilitary units, and the needed supplies and equipment, were assembled and sent to a US military base in Iraq. The diplomatic requirements I had to tend to myself.

I scheduled a meeting with the US ambassador to Saudi Arabia. The ambassador had already been informed of my top-level clearance. He was in DC for a conference. Our meeting was brief. I informed him that I would require diplomatic status on my next trip to Saudi Arabia and at a certain day and time I would need an appointment with the king of Saudi Arabia. If the ambassador needed extra help in such an effort, he could say that I was a grandson of a senior prince of the House of Saud and I would have a very important message to deliver to him. The ambassador said that he would provide the diplomatic status the next day and arrange the appointment when I needed it, but he would need two weeks or possibly a month to make the proper arrangements.

After doing the necessary groundwork to start the wheels rolling on my project, I and my boy left for Saudi Arabia and my grandfather's palace. My grandfather and his associates were already onboard to supply needed intelligence for the operation.

After settling in to a suite in my grandfather's palace, I started to organize what I called the strike team. The personnel were being assembled in Iraq. The early reports showed that everything was ahead of schedule. My man on the inside, a spy that my grandfather had arranged, kept track of Mr. Schulze's granddaughter. She was still alive and in good health. If events turned to the negative side in regard for our main target, our inside man was to inform us and then we would make plans to take her out of the prince's custody.

I only had one small problem: my slave had very little to do. My grandfather suggested that he be put to work as household staff. My boy actually seemed happy to help out. He got more to do and he got to talk to and work with the other house slaves,

Sabao and Muhammad. These three slaves seemed to have bonded and had become close friends.

During the weeks that followed, the project came together. My personal life was put on hold, except for fucking and sleeping with my boy. I kept in contact with Linda on the island and with Joan and my kids. It was good to take a break once in a while to talk to my two families.

I made several trips to Iraq on so-called diplomatic missions to inspect the progress of assembling the needed men, supplies, and equipment. On my last trip, I was surprised that I was able to get two RX 109s for the project. These aircraft were the new anti-gravity craft. Each one of the aircraft looked like a big, long, cigar-shaped aircraft with a flat bottom. They could each transport over one hundred people at a time. They were silent, extremely fast, and could not be detected by radar. Both were armed with new laser weapons and equipped with the knock-out device that I had requested.

The personnel were veterans. They were also well armed. If things got dirty, the men on this project were ready for hard combat. They were even armed with my favorite gun, the MR 105. This gun was not really a gun. It was handheld artillery. Hopefully, lethal force would not be necessary.

The plan was simple. The RX 109s would fly the strike teams into Saudi Arabia. The knock-out devices would be used to disable all personnel on the ground and in the target building. The teams would move in and rescue the sex slaves and put them on one of the RX 109s. The former slaves would then be flown to the US base in Iraq. The princes would get a warning. A letter in Arabic would be taped to each of their chests and simply state that we had taken their slaves and they would be freed. Lawsuits by parents of the children would be filed against the princes involved in the world court and their names would be become part of the public record. Yes, I would love to just dump the whole lot of them in the desert, but that would cause too many diplomatic problems. The letter would also state that if they continued to engage in such activities, next time we paid them a visit to rescue sex slaves they would disappear from the face of the Earth.

When I got word that the mission had succeeded, I was one half hour away from my scheduled meeting with the king of Saudi Arabia. I was to inform him of what had just taken place and ask him to support what had already happened.

When I and the US ambassador were ushered into the presence of King Fahd, I politely bowed and introduced myself. "Your majesty, my name is General Andrews. I am an officer in the American Federal Security System."

"Yes, General, my good friend, your grandfather has already introduced you to me. Your grandfather is an old and dear friend of mine. Let's all be seated."

"Your majesty, I am here to ask your support for something that has just happened in your country, without your government's approval."

The king acted startled.

"Your majesty, several military strike teams, with authorization from the highest level of the Order, have conducted a raid on a palace just south of Riyadh. They succeeded in freeing over one hundred child sex slaves that had been kidnapped from foreign countries, such as the United States. The news about this raid and the recovery of the remains of over four hundred child sex slaves from the middle of the Rubal Khali desert will be on the world news in just a few hours. To save face and honor, I would like to request that you say that you had approved the raid in advance as a way to stamp out this activity once and for all, rather than to issue a strong protest of the raid. My people will then say that you had approved the raid."

I then handed the king a list of the princes who were involved in the child sex-slave trade. The king looked at the list and then his aides. He remained silent for a few minutes, as if he were thinking. I doubt that he had ever been put in such a position.

"I do not know how to respond, General, at this time. I will have to consult with my people and get more facts before I can give you an answer."

Nothing more was said. I and the US ambassador were escorted out of the king's palace. Only time would tell how the king and his government were going to act. The king and his government had up to now always denied the existence of the child sex-slave trade.

On the ride back to American Embassy, the ambassador asked, "Why was I not informed of this, General?"

"We decided that only a few insiders needed to know. It was a matter of security, Mr. Ambassador."

"I know how things work, General. I don't like to be blindsided like that. It hurts my credibility as a diplomat."

"I understand, but it could not be helped."

Would the king endorse the raid and tell official lies in support, or would he be outraged and cause economic and diplomatic trouble? Doubtful, was my opinion, of the king causing trouble. Saudi Arabia was no longer the great economic threat that it once was. New technologies such as the GEET had greatly cut down the need for the US and Europe to import foreign oil. The GEET technology alone had double and tripled the gas mileage of the average car. The oil business was not the big money maker for the Saudis that it used to be.

I was betting that the king would support the raid. What choice did he have? But I had the usual thought in the back of my mind: what if? What ifs like this situation could mean the end of my career, or at least make me unwelcome in Saudi Arabia. I was the one who was responsible for organizing this raid. If the shit hit the fan, the brown stuff would all land on me.

After a pleasurable, Western-style meal, I and my grandfather started to watch the TV. The staff was told to watch other channels. The first report came from the BBC. The story was favorable and accurate. The US channels followed suit. The first news reports were followed by interviews with military officers and diplomats. Freed slaves were later given airtime to tell their stories. The story of the human remains of sex slaves, followed the next day. The world news was doing what it was supposed to do: broadcast the current news. The Saudis could not stop the story from airing.

Several hours later, I got a phone call from the US ambassador. He confirmed that the Saudis were onboard. The official lie had been approved. The king of Saudi Arabia was going to be a hero to most of the world, officially.

What about me? Well, I was the shadow figure who officially did not and could not exist. I got a promotion to major general and the thanks of the board members at Federal Security Agency, including a big thinks and hug from Mr. Schulze. His granddaughter was among the rescued child slaves. The two Saudi princes who were on the governing board of the Order lost their seats on the board. But officially I knew nothing about the whole affair.

CHAPTER 19: WILMINGTON

After all the fuss and stress, I decided to take a vacation. Go where, do what? I had no idea. Then my boy Jimmy said something. A story about Wilmington, North Carolina, was on the TV. It was a story about President Wilson. He had been raised in Wilmington. My boy seemed fascinated by the program. When the old pictures of Wilson's childhood in Wilmington were shown, tears appeared in Jimmy's eyes. When I asked what was wrong, he just said, "That is my hometown."

So the where to go part of my vacation was solved. I would take my boy to visit his hometown. Was I taking a risk? Of course I was. But I trusted my boy to remain loyal to me. Was I wrong? Well, I was going to find out.

I booked a large beach house in an area called Top Soil. We arrived in Wilmington in the early hours of the morning. It was still dark when we got to the beach house. We could smell the ocean. I awoke at about 9:00 a.m. Jimmy had already gotten up.

I found him on the back porch. He was looking at the ocean and smiling. "Sir, I used to walk along this beach when I was a kid."

"Well, kid, why don't we take a walk and you can give me a tour of your beach?"

It was a good way to relax and forget about the world's trouble. We both took a peaceful walk on the beach. It felt good to feel the wet sand between my toes and sometimes having to take a sudden run to avoid the incoming surf.

The car rental company delivered the car I had ordered, so I and my boy drove it in to Wilmington to see some of the town that Jimmy grew up in. Walking along the riverfront caused Jimmy's memory to clear up.

"Look, there is the old battleship." It was the Battleship North Carolina, a relic of World War II.

"Look, there is the ice cream stand that I and my friends used to get ice cream sandwiches from."

Then it happened.

"Jimmy Rose, is that you?"

Jimmy's face just lit up.

"Roger, Roger Wheeler."

They both hugged each other and started to talk a mile a minute.

"What happened to you, man?"

"Oh, after my parents died, I had to go live with my uncle for a while."

"You mean your Uncle Earl."

"Yes, but it did not work out very well."

"I heard that he committed suicide a few years after you went to live with him. People who knew him said that he was seriously depressed when he came back from the Middle East. They said that he kept saying that he had done something terrible. But he would not say what."

All I could think was, *Damn, now I won't get to kick his butt.*

Jimmy seemed in good spirits that rest of the day. He and Roger started off where they had left off. They were both fourteen years old again. It was an interesting day for me. For Jimmy it was a great day.

Jimmy and Roger filled in the gaps. Well, Roger did. Jimmy made up a lot of stuff. I was his employer, a rich government administrator, and he was a my valet and house manager. I guess that was the closest to the truth that he wanted to get. He knew enough about the so-called normal world that Roger could not begin to understand his life.

That night, as Jimmy cuddled up next to me in bed, he looked into my eyes and said, "Thank you, sir, for bringing me here. You are the best master in the world."

I felt relieved. He was still my boy.

The next few days we traveled around the Wilmington area. We took a tour of a real Southern plantation and a civil war dirt fort. We went by the house that Jimmy grew up in. We even met more people who were Jimmy's friends or friends of his parents. Jimmy seemed to greatly enjoy talking to these people from his childhood.

Our whole stay in Wilmington was relaxing and interesting except for one incident with another Federal Security Officer. His name was Captain Jerome Holt. We had the misfortune to run into him in a local seafood restaurant. I spotted him as a proud member of the Fascist Element just by watching his body language. Having a bully attitude and being very impolite are not common Southern characteristics.

The other people in the restaurant seemed to know him. They acted scared of him and people in the restaurant tried not to make eye contact with him or his aide. To me, they smelled like trouble. So, naturally I had to stare at them. I also contacted my uncle, who was now the general in command of the Federal Security Agency's paramilitary units. I had him listen to and watch the captain from my laptop as the scene unfolded.

My staring got their attention. The captain sent his aide over to have a talk with me.

"Hey, mister, why are you staring at two Federal Security Officers?"

"Oh, I'm doing a personal investigation of the local Federal Security personnel. You two are breaking quite a few rules of proper contact tonight."

The aide thought that I was a smart ass. "Mister, if you keep staring at us, I will arrest you."

I smiled and he left. At this moment, a lady sitting next to us whispered. "Don't bother them. They are bad news."

I just kept staring.

I then got up and announced, "Ladies and gentlemen, I am a Federal Security Officer and I am investigating the conduct of one Captain Jerome Holt, who is sitting at that table over there." I pointed at the captain. Rather than back down, as an intelligent man would, he just got madder.

"I will be here as long as necessary to listen to your complaints."

The captain walked over to my table and demanded my ID. I gave it to him. "No way, asshole, that a young man like you is a major general in the Federal Security System. Your ass is mine."

"Before you do something stupid again tonight, you may want to talk to your boss first."

"Major Colt is out of town. I am in charge of this town."

"No, I mean your real boss, General Andrews in the DC office."

I turned my laptop computer around. The screen had my uncle on it. The general said, "Captain, this is General Andrews in Washington, DC. I am relieving you of your command. Start to clean out your desk. You will receive your transfer papers in the morning. A review of your conduct will determine if you are to be demoted in rank. Do you have any questions, Captain?"

"No sir."

I have always found it amazing to watch a bully being cowed. They all act like little children who have been caught with their hands in the cookie jar. The people in the restaurant now started to clap. It seemed I was now a local hero. Well, for at least the next few days.

The next day, the captain and his aide were transferred to a remote part of Alaska. The captain was later demoted to the rank of sergeant and the Federal Security Agency sent a team down to restructure the Wilmington office. My uncle was restructuring the whole paramilitary part of the Order. He was flushing out the Fascist Element. I was happy I was back fighting the Fascists again.

Chapter 20: Back Home

After an interesting and stress-free week on the beach, we headed back to the island. Linda and Princess were overjoyed to see us again. I spent the next two days getting to know my girl again and again.

The fight against the Fascist Element in the Order was reaching a critical stage. My uncle and his supporters were weeding out the Fascist influence in the Order. The Fascists and their allies, the Lizards, were said to be plotting something military in nature. Communications from Caos confirmed that the Lizards were planning something big. The Lizards wanted to regain the power in the Order that had been lost. What were they planning and what targets would they hit? That was at the moment unknown. My uncle and the Nordics were working on the problem.

Meanwhile, on the island I had a pile of work to do. The latest auction had gone well. We were finding the young bodies that our clients had wanted. The fight with the Fascists had not changed the basic operations of my island. It was still earning its nickname of Slaughter Island. So far, about one thousand condemned prisoners had been executed.

The elite and powerful of The New World Order still came to the island for its blood sport. The only real difference was that most of our clients had switched sides in the power struggle that was taking place with the Fascist Element. They increasingly supported the side that I was on. The elite and powerful of the world like to be on the winning side.

Since a military option was about to be played by the Fascists, I had ordered my staff, especially the military units on the island, to prepare a proper defense. The work was nearing a stage of completion when I returned to command of the facility. The underground command and supply system was almost complete. The island had a vast natural cave system that covered almost the whole island. The caves had been altered for military uses. Storage rooms had been constructed and filled. Blast doors were installed at key points. A light rail system had been built so that heavy laser weapons could be moved from one end of the island to the other at a fast pace. We were getting ready for the worst possible situation. We even had a last option that could, if needed, destroy the island itself.

Why would the Lizards want to attack my island? There were three basic reasons. The first was that the island was also an intelligence-gathering center for The New World Order. That is the good guys' part of the Order. Second, the island was a storage area for gold and securities. The island at this moment had over three billion world dollars worth of gold in its underground vaults. The third and most important reason was me. The Lizards and their Fascist allies had found out about my secret talents and how I had engineered the big heist. The looting of the Fascist cash reserves had pretty well destroyed their push for control of the Order.

The Lizards wanted my ass, literally. I had been told by Caos that the Lizards, who liked to eat human flesh, wanted to execute me by eating me while I was still alive. The idea of being tied down and unable to move while a bunch of fucking Lizard aliens bit off large pieces of my biceps and triceps seriously shook me up. My job was stressful enough without thinking about ending my life in such a brutal manner. Killing me would stop me from using my talents to help the anti-Fascist cause. My psychic abilities had seriously hurt the Fascist cause, and the Fascists wanted me and my talents removed from the struggle. They wanted to regain lost power, and I was in their way.

The situation was getting more stressful and confusing every week. Caos kept me informed. I was ordered by my superiors not to leave the island. It had become unsafe for me to fly to any part of the world. I was being watched and tracked.

While the military on the island were preparing for a war that may or may not come, life went on as normal. With the latest auction over, the purchasers of condemned prisoners were starting to arrive. I saw many familiar faces among the crowd. Mr. Akito and his son Ichiro had purchased two more condemned men to test their sword skills on. Mr. Herbert Stone, the Texas billionaire with a great lack of class, had also shown up. This time he had purchased a muscular young man to use his bullwhip on. But the client that was to get my attention was a new client that sort of looked like my high school science teacher.

Mr. Oliver did not look dangerous in any way. He was an average-looking guy. One would say that he looked intelligent. He was about six feet tall and one hundred sixty pounds. Mr. Oliver did not look like the beast that he really was. But it has been said that evil has a very ordinary face. This strange man was a big supporter of the Fascist Element. I ordered my security people to keep an eye on his movements on the island.

Mr. Oliver was expecting to be very busy during his stay on the island. He had purchased four men and two women prisoners. After introducing myself as the island commander and getting past talking about the general social stuff, Mr. Oliver got down to the reasons he had bought so many prisoners.

"I want to see people suffer unbearable pain, as I have suffered in life."

Mr. Oliver was a sadist who got off on inflicting pain on other people. This was a need he had, but it was one that he couldn't follow up on in his personal life.

Mr. Oliver was a very wealthy high-tech businessman. He had achieved a lot in the business world. His name was one that almost all people involved in the high-tech business would recognize. But his business success did not give him the satisfaction that inflecting horrible amounts of pain did. He was a beast, and he was here to worship on the altar of pain. Was he a nut case? I could not say at this point in time.

Mr. Oliver invited me to witness his work firsthand the next day. I accepted the invitation, just to see what this strange man was really into. So while a war was brewing and I was confined to my island, I had decided to get my mind off the realities of world politics and watch a stone-cold sadist do his art.

The next morning I was to witness a master perform his art. His words, not mine. Mr. Oliver had rented a large torture room in the execution building. It had been outfitted to suit his particular tastes. I did not know what Mr. Oliver had in mind. He simply told me that I would be impressed.

The prisoner, a muscular, naked man in his early twenties at most, was led in by the guards. He was wearing a blindfold and his hands had been handcuffed behind his back.

Mr. Oliver put his right hand on the man's shoulder and said, "I am Mr. Oliver, your new master."

The man said, "Fuck you. I am no one's slave."

Mr. Oliver ordered him to step up on the platform. The prisoner started to resist. That is, he resisted until his new master gave him a little help with a cattle prod to his bare ass. Every muscle in the man's body tensed up and he screamed. He then obeyed his new master.

Now that the prisoner was standing on the round, two-foot-high platform, Mr. Oliver quickly put a hangman's noose over his head and around his neck.

"What the fuck are you doing, asshole?"

Mr. Oliver hit the man's upper back with the cattle prod. The man screamed and he nearly lost his footing; the rope around his neck stopped him from falling off the platform.

Mr. Oliver now walked around to stand in front of the prisoner. "Now slave, each time that you speak without my permission I will punish you. Do you understand, slave?"

"What the fuck is your problem?"

With that comment, Mr. Oliver grabbed the man's nuts and squeezed hard. The man screamed again and he nearly lost his balance. The noose saved him for a second time.

"Okay, okay."

Mr. Oliver was beginning to train his slave to follow his orders. I could only think that if this man knew what he was in for, he probably would have hanged himself.

The equipment bag held several surprises. The first things that Mr. Oliver took out of the bag were large fish hooks and fishing line. In just a few minutes, the man felt the first fishhook pierce his right nipple, followed by at least twenty more hooks on other parts of his naked body. The final two hooks went through his ball sack. Each time a fishhook pierced his skin, the prisoner's body would tense up and he grit his teeth, but he remained fairly quiet. When Mr. Oliver had the hooks in, he tied the fish lines to an overhead beam. Mr. Oliver now removed the noose around the man's neck.

When the box was kicked out from under the prisoner and his body dropped several inches, the man screamed and he started to cry. "Oh shiittt, why the fuckkk are you doing thiss to meee?"

Mr. Oliver did not answer. He just sat in a chair and smiled. The man twisted and squirmed on the fish lines as his body adjusted to the pain. Drops of blood started to run down the man's naked body.

I did not know that I was supposed to talk during this performance, but Mr. Oliver asked me, "What do you think, General, of the show so far?"

"Well, Mr. Oliver, I think that you have caught yourself a big one."

He laughed a little.

Mr. Oliver had more than one act to his show. The second act was an electric performance. He hooked up metal clamps to the prisoner's balls, nipple, earlobes, and toes. The last piece of equipment was an anal probe. All of the clamps and the probe were hooked up by electric wires to several big batteries. Mr. Oliver pushed a button and the prisoner's muscles contracted as he screamed at the top of his lungs. The pain must have been almost unbearable.

The man yelled, "Please stop, pleeeasse. I can't taaake this shittt!"

Such cries for relief did not help. Mr. Oliver just smiled. His eyes lit up and he kept switching the battery on and off until the man fainted and his body went limp.

Mr. Oliver woke up the prisoner by throwing a cup of water in his face. When the man revived, the torturing started again. After torturing the man for twenty minutes or so and listening to a flood of foul language from his victim, Mr. Oliver was ready for his final act. When the prisoner had revived again, Mr. Oliver smiled and said, "Well, dude, it is time for you to go now." The controls on the batteries were set to maximum output and the prisoner's body tensed up. Mr. Oliver did not turn off the machine until the prisoner's skin started to burn. The man was dead, and Mr. Oliver seemed pleased.

Mr. Oliver thought it had been a personal pleasure to have me witness what he called his art. But for me, it was my duty. I have never gotten off on torturing people.

I had a similar invitation from Mr. Akito and his Ichiro, but I declined. Even Mr. James, loudmouth billionaire from Texas, invited me witness his performance. I think Mr. Long Horn had taken a shine to me since I now had stars on my shoulders. The feeling was not mutual. I turned him down. I had more pressing matters to attend. My biggest concern at this point was the security of myself and my two families.

The first attempt by the Lizards to capture me took place a week later. Security on the island had been strengthened. The best state-of-the-art security technology had been installed. But with all such systems, there were problems. One problem almost cost me my life.

I had thought that my villa was well protected. It was secure according to the island military. The villa had armed guards and heavy steel security doors at key points. Phony people had been installed in my bedroom. These were dummies that gave off heat patterns like a real person.

I and Jimmy and Linda had our sleeping quarters moved into a recently finished bunker just off the basement of the villa, on the opposite end of the building from my bedroom. A back-up security system had been installed in the caves of the hill behind my villa. Laser cannon could be rolled out on train tracks in case of need. Twenty-four-hour security was in place.

Did I feel secure? Of course not. I knew that any security system could be compromised. My instincts, as usual, turned out to be correct.

I had just gotten through with entertaining about thirty very wealthy people at my villa. As usual, my boy had outdone himself. The meal was great and my guests were pleased. When the last guest departed, it was very late. I told my slaves to forget cleaning up for now. It was time to go to sleep in my villa's new security bunker, just off the basement.

I had been asleep for only about an hour when the security alarm and the lights in the bunker went on. I quickly got to the command phone and contacted security.

"This is General Andrews. What the hell is going on?"

The officer in charge of the graveyard shift answered. "General, your security guards are out cold and you have intruders in your home. Their ship is hovering right over your house. We are preparing to open fire with the laser cannon and security is on the way. Sir, you should get into the tunnel system."

Both of my slaves were now dressed, and we opened the back door to the bunker and started to walk into the tunnel system when I heard a loud electronic sound and a few seconds later something shook the ground. The electronic sound I knew was the laser cannon opening up on the intruder. The ground shaking was a puzzle for now.

When we got into the main security tunnel, a security captain handed me a communications device. It connected me to central command.

"Well, General, I have good and bad news. The good news is that we got the bastard. The bad news is that the alien ship lost power and it dropped straight down. Let me just say that you have a real big conversation piece sitting on your dining room table right now."

All I could say was, "Ahhh shittt! You mean that it fell onto my house, don't you?"

"Yes, sir, it took out your house."

The security troops captured only one live Lizard trooper. He, or it, was a member of the ship's crew. The Lizard troopers on the ground were crushed by their own ship. My villa was a total loss. I could do nothing except look for my dog Princess. She turned up unhurt. My boy was teary eyed when I brought her back to him.

The whole attack had made me feel a lot less secure. I contacted Caos and he agreed to take the members of my two families to a safe location. This task was accomplished in the next two days. Now I was living in a tunnel system unsure of what I should expect to happen next.

The next month showed no let-up in the Lizard assaults on key leaders of The New World Order and their allies. My own uncle was almost killed in one attempt. Two world leaders died and one disappeared. The enemy was hitting the command structure of our side of the Order. We in turn hit them. So far, we had more than evened the score. The important point was that they could not bleed as much as our side. They were losing the war.

The world press did not know much about the reality of what was going on. World governments had put a lid on any news about the war. The average person was not to be told of the war that was raging for control of the Order and the world.

My island has been on lockdown since the war started. The important people who were on our side and the former Fascists who joined us were moved into the tunnel system. The clients that were on the island before the attack, that were part of the Fascist Element, were executed. This was all-out-war and it was getting brutal. We had been told by Caos and my uncle that a full-scale Lizard assault against the island and me could come at any moment.

While we waited for the attack, I decided it was time to learn more about our enemy. I and several senior officers inspected the Lizard craft that had crashed into my villa. We entered the alien craft from a side door that had been half blown off. Our laser assault had done some serious damage to the craft. Several large holes had been blasted through the Lizard ship.

The inside of the alien ship was simple in design. The center of the ship was just a hangar-type structure, used for carrying troops and supplies. The rest of the ship was just a motor for anti-gravity and the control room. The craft did not seem to have any defensive weapons. It was just a personnel carrier. The smell of Lizard blood filled the air.

The defense of the island hung on three plans. The first was the laser cannon that had been placed in different caves around the island. In concept, we were defending the island the same way the Japanese did during World War II. The second line of defense was the large flash bombs that we had placed in center flat areas of the island, such as the airport. These areas would be landing sites for the alien troop ships. The last plan was the fail-safe plan. Under different parts of the island, large flash bombs had been buried. This plan was to be used in case of defeat. If the enemy had a strong foothold on the island and we were being overrun, the fail-safe system would be used. The system would destroy the island. Of course, no one wanted to get to that stage, but if it happened, almost all of us would be dead anyway. The idea was to destroy the alien forces on the island.

Could we expect help from the US Navy and some other nation? The answer was no. The United States had carrier task forces in the area, but they were not a match for the Lizard military force that we expected to appear on our shores. The US Navy's carriers were just too outdated to take on the heavy laser cannon and other weapons of a Lizard armada.

What about our space allies, the Nordics and the Grays? While they were helpful in many ways, as I had just witnessed when Caos took my two families to safety, they could not come to our aid. Neither of them had any heavy war fleets in the area. They would be helping us with intelligence and a few secret operations.

The United States was planning, with the help of other nations, to strike at three Lizard underground bases in different parts of the world. My uncle referred to this operation as the "packages."

He told me I would be informed as to the delivering of the packages. The packages were nuclear weapons.

The final defensive measures, the laser shields, had just been completed. The laser shields were reflective barriers that could be flipped up to protect the caves that housed our laser cannon. They could take several direct hits before they failed. It would be enough time for our cannon to disable several Lizard warships. But in the end, we knew that we would lose our laser cannons.

Chapter 21: The Attack

Their spacecraft appeared on our radar early in the day, just after sun up. The radar blips were both large and small. We were facing a space armada of thirty large warships and twenty small craft. The Lizard fleet consisted of troop carriers, fighter craft, and heavy warships. The enemy craft stood motionless in formations, about one thousand feet over the ocean, on three sides of the island, for about a half hour. Our electronics showed that they were trying to figure out their attack plan. They were collecting data on our defenses.

The alarm went off just after the alien armada was detected. Soldiers ran about the tunnel defense system manning their posts. Everyone knew that the first fifteen minutes of battle would decide who would win this fight. Every gunner had the same instructions: do as much damage as possible, as fast as you could.

The troop ships were our main targets. The warships were only there to escort the troop ships. The Lizard troops on the ground would decide the victor in this battle. The warships could pound us, but only the alien infantry could win this battle.

Stopping the alien infantry was our battle plan. In order to capture the intelligence center, which was in the tunnel system, and me, they had to use their infantry. The warships could only provide support for the ground troops. As in all wars, the poor bloody foot soldier would decide who won this battle.

I had under my command only two hundred soldiers and about one hundred armed civilians. Our estimates on Lizard ground numbers were upward of two thousand infantry. On paper, it looked bad, but we were dug in and well armed. Our situation was not hopeless, just doubtful.

After thirty-two minutes of silence, the alien armada opened fire. They would draw first blood. The first laser cannon shots targeted our laser weapons. The shields held. While the alien lasers were recharging, our laser artillery opened up on the alien troop transports.

In the first salvo, we knocked out or seriously damaged half of their transports. The remaining alien troop ships quickly moved out of range of our lasers. Now the alien warships would exchange highly accurate laser fire with us. We were now in a slugging match with the Lizard heavy warships, a battle that we could not win.

I ordered the remaining laser cannons to be moved back into the tunnel system to a safe location. Hopefully, I could still deploy the remaining laser cannon when the Lizard troop carriers came back into range when they had decided to land troops on the island.

After about an hour of pounding the island's defense system and receiving no laser fire in return, the aliens brought in their remaining troop carriers and escorts. I gave the order to bring forward the remaining laser weapons and to target the approaching alien troop carriers. Our second salvo hit many of the remaining troop carriers and some warships, one of which fell into the ocean. After that, we steadily lost our remaining laser guns, one by one.

It was time for me to move further down into the tunnel system to work the flash bomb system that we had set up. Moving past the cave opening of the tunnel system presented a bloody sight. We passed a laser gun crew, or what remained of them. Their laser cannon had taken a direct hit. The gun crew and their weapon were scattered all over the tunnel.

The trip down the tunnel system to the command center took about fifteen minutes. The captain in charge of the center said, "Sir, we have lost control of the airfield. Their transports are now landing."

"Captain, prepare to detonate the flash bombs under the airport."

"Yes, sir!"

I ordered the blast doors in the deeper part of the tunnel system to be closed. Our battle plan, at this point, called for preparing the tunnel system and its bunker system to withstand a nuclear attack. Once the Lizards lost their combat troops they could be expected to employ nuclear weapons. That's when it happened.

Suddenly there was a loud pounding sound and I passed out. When I awoke, I was no longer in the tunnel system. I was lying naked, on a bare mattress, in a jail cell. I got up and walked around the cell. I had been locked up in a cell in the prison that houses convicted criminals for the auction.

I quickly figured out that I had been captured and imprisoned in the same jail that I had once managed. All I could think was that the Lizards, once that they had gotten a heavy warship over the top of the island, must have used some sort of advanced knock-out device on us.

I looked through the window bars of my cell. The sight in front of me was extremely depressing. The cell looked out over the center courtyard of the prison. The prison yard had been converted into a mass execution center. It was packed, from end to end, with quickly constructed gallows. The dead bodies, over one hundred in number, were hanging from the gallows. The faces of the victims were hard to look at. They were twisted in expressions of acute pain. Most of the bodies had been half eaten by the Lizards. The ground around the gallows was covered in blood.

I recognized many of the victims. In the center of the courtyard hung the bodies of Mr. Akito and his son Ichiro, to the left of them hung the body of Mr. Herbert Stone. These people were former supporters of the Fascist Element who had changed over to our side in the last few months. I sat down on the mattress. What had I done? Should I have evacuated the island rather than chosen to fight? I had led good people to their deaths.

As I was going over and over in my mind what had happened to me and what I called my people, a man walked up to my cell.

"Well, nephew, how does it feel losing a battle?" I recognized the man's voice. I turned around to stand face to face with my Uncle Omar.

I said, "Well, I could have predicted that you had something to do with this whole affair."

My uncle smiled. "Yes, William, several powerful people and I have had our eyes on you for some time now. When you were a fourteen-year-old kid, I had a burning desire to get rid of you. At that time, I thought of you as a black mark on our family. If I had been head of our family at the time, I would have sold you to a slaver. Since you were a very pretty and hung teenage boy, I am sure I could have gotten a very good price for you."

My uncle smiled at this point. A slight feeling of fear shot through my body. Only because of my grandfather's love for me had I avoided the fate of standing naked on the block at a real-life Arab slave auction, waiting to be sold to some sadistic bastard. I had no doubt that because of my very self-centered attitude that my bones would now be littering the Saudi desert, if my Uncle Omar had had his way with me. I never would have been able to adjust to a slave's life as my slave Jimmy had. I would not have lasted long enough to see my eighteenth birthday.

But only because my grandfather was still alive and I was his favorite grandson was I able to avoid that terrible fate.

"Later, when you became a young man," Uncle Omar said, "I just wanted to discredit you in my father's eyes. I have to give you credit, nephew. You have a lot more talent than I had expected. But then I decided that you could be of use to our cause. At first, you were very helpful to us. That was, until you turned into a traitor."

"So you are the one of the men behind the curtain, Uncle. One of the shadow figures that has been testing me and guiding me in my Federal Security career?"

"Yes, you had such great potential. If you had remained loyal, you could have become one of the most powerful men in the world. It is sad for me to see what you have become. You have been reduced to a naked prisoner in a prison that you at one time commanded. It is ironic that the same system that you set up to execute condemned prisoners will now painfully kill you. Maybe it can be termed some form of justice.

"William, you will suffer the same fate of those people in the prison courtyard, the death of a traitor. Yes, William, the Lizards, as you call them, thought that, in view of your crimes, you deserved to die in a very painful manner. Since my employers like to eat live human flesh, you will be the main course at their victory ceremony tonight. You will be taken naked to the place of execution. Your hands will be handcuffed behind your back. A hangman's noose will be placed around your neck, with the knot behind your head. After the dinner, as guests are assembled, you will be hanged. Since the hangman's knot is behind your head, your neck will not break. It will take twenty to thirty minutes for you to die. Your tongue will swell up and your eyeballs will inflate and almost pop out of your head. While you slowly strangle at the end of the rope you will be eaten alive. I have been given the honor of watching your execution. I am looking forward to seeing how brave you act as the Lizards bite off your balls and rip off big hunks of your flesh." He smiled in a sick manner and left.

I was glad to see my evil-minded uncle leave. It was a real pain in the ass. His sickly smile was starting to get to me.

I sat naked on the bare mattress and reflected on my life. Well, this seemed to be the end of me. Maybe it was appropriate that I die in this manner. It is the same manner in which I have executed hundreds of condemned men and women. Maybe, this is some sort of justice. Or maybe, it's just that old Catholic guilt-trip crap that keeps popping up in my life.

I had pretty well accepted my fate when help came from an unlikely source. While I was looking out my cell window, Caos walked up to my cell.

"General, we must move fast. The guards have been knocked out and my ship is on the roof."

I didn't need any help in making a decision. I followed Caos out the cell door, through a corridor, and then up a narrow staircase to the roof of the prison.

I looked around and saw nothing. My heart sank.

"No, General, my ship is right here."

Caos pushed a button on a handheld control device and a door opened in the middle of nothing. Once inside the craft, I could see that it was the same scout craft that Caos usually flew. Caos handed me some clothes to wear and I quickly got dressed.

As Caos prepared to leave, I said, "Wait. Can you take me to the center control silo in the middle of the island?"

"General, why do you want to go there?"

"I want to see if I can set up the flash bomb system to destroy this island with the Lizards still on it."

"I see, General, but how do you know that the system is still operational?"

"I don't know. But it is worth a shot."

I showed Caos the location of the security silo on a computer map he had of the island. Caos agreed to my plan and his craft lifted off the roof of the prison. In a few seconds, it was right over the command silo.

I asked Caos to scan the underground bunker to see if any Lizards were inside and if the equipment was still operational. The scan only took two minutes. The bunker was still functional and no one was inside.

I know the codes for the system, so if it was still operational I could program it to detonate. I opened the hatch at the top of the silo and I started to quietly move down the ladder. When I got to the floor, I silently walked over to the door of the command center. I did not hear or see any Lizard troops. Either they had left, or they had not found this command center.

I punched in the code to enter the room. I was surprised. The computer was still on. It seemed that no Lizards had been in this room. I quickly sat down, booted up the computer, and started to enter the correct codes. All the systems came on line. The system was completely operational. I sat down and smiled. It was now payback time.

I set the detonation system to blow in ten minutes. When the program was locked in, I left as fast as I could get out of the room and up the ladder. The only problem that I ran into was finding Caos's ship. As luck would have it, I walked right into it. The craft was cloaked, or invisible, to human eyes. The door opened and Caos and I were soon off the island. Caos flew a zigzag course to avoid any laser weapons that might try to lock onto us.

When we were in orbit around the Earth, Caos focused his view screen on the island. It was not there. The island had evaporated and left only open ocean and mud in the water. My island was gone and with it the Lizard armada and, I assume, my Uncle Omar. I was the only survivor.

On a Nordic space station located beyond Earth's moon, I was reunited with my two families. My twin sons were overjoyed to see me and tell me what had happened to them. Josh ran up to me and said, "Dad, you wouldn't believe what happened. We flew in a real UFO, and we met aliens. It was so cool, Dad."

Yes, it must have been really cool.

My two slaves were teary eyed and happy to see that I was still alive. Because of the bad news that had been received about the battle for the island and its total destruction, they had expected the worst.

On the other hand, the different races of aliens onboard the Nordic space station seemed to be very interested in this new creature that my slaves and children had brought with them. It was called a dog. Princess and Corky were a big hit with the different alien races. My boy Jimmy and the twins seemed to enjoy showing them how to play with their pets. It seemed we were the only race that had these life forms.

After going over the current situation with Federal Security personnel and several groups of aliens, I came to realize that the conflict with the Lizards was not a settled affair. The whole war could go on for years and we could still lose. Meanwhile, I was a man without a country, or even a world, so to speak. It was not safe for me and my two families to live on Earth. I was in fact officially dead. I died on the island. It was best to let the Lizards believe that I was no longer a threat to them.

I was now to be some sort of secret weapon. I would live, with my two families, on an alien planet. The new job was intelligence work. I would not be able to return to Earth until the battle with the Lizards was over. My two families seemed excited about the prospect of space travel and finding a new home on one of the Nordic home planets.

But I am not certain of how I will adjust to my new role. Only time will tell. The only thing that I know for sure is that I still have what really matters to me: my health, my two strange families, and my work.

As for the price that I had paid to get to where I am in the power structure of The New World Order, was it worth it? Did I do the right thing in helping to save the lives of billions of innocent people, or was I wrong and the Fascists were right? I hope to live long enough to be able to answer those questions.